Uncanny Valley

Book 1

C.A. Gray

www.authorcagray.com

Copyright and Disclaimers

Uncanny Valley

By C.A. Gray

Published By:

Wanderlust Publishing

Tucson, AZ

Also by C.A. Gray:

Intangible: Piercing the Veil, Book 1
Invincible: Piercing the Veil, Book 2
Impossible: Piercing the Veil, Book 3

The Liberty Box
The Eden Conspiracy: The Liberty Box Trilogy,
Book 2
The Phoenix Project: The Liberty Box Trilogy,
Book 3

Prologue

I gasped out the last few notes of my big solo, belting my heart out, my arms stretched up to either side of the stage. I could *feel* my voice hit the back wall, and I knew I sounded breathtaking. The sweat rolled down the sides of my face and over the place where my mic was taped to my hairline. As the last note faded away, the applause was immediate and thunderous; I panted to try to regain my breath, turning to Henry to deliver my last line once the cheers quieted enough to hear me.

"Yes," I said with gravitas. "I think it's time."

Henry reached out an arm to me to lead me off stage right. The curtains lowered, and the applause began again. I knew there was not a dry eye in the theater.

The moment the curtains touched the stage, we both broke character, and Henry scooped me into his arms, spinning me around. I let out a sound somewhere between a whoop and a squeal.

"You totally nailed it!" he cried. "That was *brilliant*, Becca!"

The rest of the cast flooded the stage, taking

our places for the curtain call. When the curtains went up one last time, Henry and I hung back behind the rest, running out last to take our bows as the lead characters amid whistles and cheers. Henry took his bow first, and then gestured at me; I ran out ahead of him and curtseyed. I got a standing ovation, and curtseyed a second time, choking back the tears.

This was my favorite moment; the part that made all the hard work and repetition and late night rehearsals worthwhile. This was where I *belonged*.

When the curtain descended again, the entire cast let out a collective exultant cry, spontaneously hugging each other as we scampered offstage to greet our adoring public.

It was closing night. I knew Julie was in the audience tonight, but she was the only friend I knew for sure had attended that night. Most of my other friends didn't even attend Dublin University--they were scattered all over the world, making the most of what was probably the last opportunity any of us would have in our lifetimes to leave our hometown of Casa Linda, Arizona. I wouldn't get to do this for much longer; pretty soon, my "other life," the one where I was a cognitive neuroscience researcher, would be the only one that mattered. But not yet. Right now, everything was perfect.

I only wished Madeline, my companion robot, could see me perform live. Just once. I'd play her the video when I got home from the lab tomorrow like always... but it just wasn't the same.

****

Everyone was there—all five-hundred and fifty-four residents of Casa Linda, the rural suburb of Phoenix, Arizona. Babies cried while mothers shushed; children who didn't know any better chased each other on the artificial grass turf of the park. All of the adults stood in stony silence, resentful of the man whose image was shortly to appear.

"I dunno why we're all so upset," muttered Roy Benson to no one in particular. "Not like he can take anything else away from us at this point." Benson wore a white wife beater that gaped and didn't quite cover his protruding belly, like he always did ever since he'd lost his job as a labyrinth connection consultant.

"I agree with you, but I'm nervous anyway," replied Lyle Hopper, seated on a folding chair below him. Hopper, once a good looking and vigorous businessman, was now missing a few teeth. He also breathed heavily, as if the exertion of conversation was too much for him. "I don't *think* I have much else to lose, but I'm afraid I'll discover I'm wrong. Although frankly, I'm not sure killing me would be much worse than stealing my purpose."

"That's what I'm saying," Benson agreed. "We're useless, and we're subsisting on the charity of a bunch of damn bots and the elite few like Halpert. How much worse—"

William Halpert's holographic projection interrupted Benson, appearing on the amphitheater stage of the little park. He was surprisingly short, only about five foot four, though the politician was a giant in other respects. He grinned in magnanimous greeting, spreading wide his hands to encompass everyone who had gathered before both this stage and every other in the world. His words would be simultaneously translated into every language across the globe. Mothers hissed at their scampering children to quiet down so that everyone could hear.

"Friends," Halpert said, "thank you for gathering here today as one global community. I know you are all busy with your active lives—"

Benson snorted and Hopper gave a derisive laugh. "Sure, I'm so busy I ran out of crossword puzzles this morning," muttered Hopper.

"—so I will get right to the point. I gathered this global community together to make a very special announcement.

"As you all know, twenty years ago the Council of Synthetic Reason determined that in order to protect humanity, all bots must be limited by two rules: they must serve only a single core purpose in the service of humanity, and they must be readily identifiable as bots.

"The advancement of bots since then has changed the face of our world. It's changed the way we do business."

"Or don't do business," muttered Benson.

"But we have come upon a significant limitation which those of us in the Capital have been working on for years. It is this: while the bots are excellent at learning facts and applying information, and can do so faster and more accurately than the most intelligent human, they lack the critical ingredient of creativity which would allow them to apply the information they've gained—within their core purpose, of course. For that, we still require humans. Unfortunately, there are not enough highly trained humans to use this information anymore. This has led to a stagnant economy. What we need are more creative workers.

"Now I come to the reason why I have gathered you together today. We know that emotion and creativity are intertwined. Yet we barely understand the nature of either, let alone how to translate them into circuits.

"But I believe, and I know you all do too, that the group mind is vastly superior to that of any one individual. Therefore, in an act of stunning generosity, the great companies and universities of the world have all agreed to open source their research thus far. This means every bit of knowledge the human race has ever amassed regarding the neuroscience of human emotion and creativity, as well as all advances toward algorithms to encode the same, will now be freely available via the labyrinth in the hopes that universal access will yield much quicker results.

"This is a big task, and indeed, it is likely to be the last great challenge of humankind. I'm asking us to come together and find the answer to a question that has perplexed philosophers for millenia: what is human creativity? But in a world where knowledge doubles every six hours, I believe we are up to the task.

"Thank you very much for your time and attention. I will personally update you of any breaking news in this field. I wish you all a very good morning, good day, or good evening—whatever time it is where you are!"

Halpert's image vanished from the stage.

As the people began to disperse, one attractive woman in her fifties stood alone, frowning at the now-empty amphitheater. She tucked her reddish hair streaked with gray behind her ears, and tapped her temple to access the Artificial Experience chip implanted there.

"Call Rebecca," she said, fishing her A.E. goggles out of her purse and putting them on. She saw a few of the townspeople shoot her dirty looks, but she ignored them. To a person, they disapproved of any flashy show of the technology which had so changed the face of their world.

A few minutes later, she was in her twenty-one year old daughter's dormitory room in Dublin. The room was dark, until Rebecca sat up and flipped on the light.

"Mom! Really?" she looked at the analog clock hanging on her wall, which she had found at an antique store. Her auburn hair stuck up in every direction, and she rubbed the sleep out of her eyes. "Do you know what time it is here?"

"Why weren't you up watching Halpert's address?"

"Because it's four am, and I was performing last night, and then I was at the cast party until like midnight! I'll find out what he said soon enough—"

"How close are your experiments to finding the source of human emotion?" her mother cut her off.

Rebecca blinked. "What? Not close at all, why?"

"Get on the labyrinth and watch the replay of Halpert's address and call me back. You might want to put your musical theater and novelist careers on hold. Your senior thesis has suddenly become *the* most important topic in the world."

Chapter 1: Rebecca Cordeaux

I had to be in the lab at eight in the morning, which, after closing night of "Gunder's Hollow" and cast party and getting wakened at four by my mother's hologram, felt a little like death. But, I had my coping strategies for just such mornings as this one: namely, Lavazza's triple shot latte. The little coffee shop was around the corner from the psych lab where I conducted my experiments, but test subjects would arrive at any minute. I prayed for no line.

Thank you thank you, I breathed— apparently I'd arrived right during the morning lull. The bot behind the counter asked my order and busied itself with her four arms, ringing me up and making my drink at the same time. She barely had to move.

Within two minutes, I held my brain function in my hands, slurping so it didn't scald my throat on the way down while half-walking, half-running toward the lab.

"Hi guys!" I greeted the line of human

volunteers queued outside the door. The medic bot waited patiently as well, wearing a cute little white hat with a red cross on it to identify her. "Thanks for your patience." I doffed my backpack and jacket, pulling my handheld interface out of my backpack to collect signatures from the participants. They had already sent me their consent forms—I only needed to match fingerprints to participants, which we used in lieu of A.E. chip tracking for identity verification because it kept costs down. I gave the interface to the first girl in line. While they queued up to scan their fingerprints, I hurriedly unlocked the door to the waiting room, turned on the lights in there and in all of the actual testing rooms, and bid the medic bot to follow me.

"We can set up for the blood draws in here," I told her, pointing to a little counter at the front of the waiting room, designed for a receptionist. I should have been sitting there myself, checking everybody in… and I would have been, had I woken up about an hour earlier.

"Very good, Miss Cordeaux," said the bot in a tinny voice, rolling over and distributing her instruments. She was a funny little thing: about half my height, but not as short as my own bot Madeline. She had no dexterity at all in her lower half, since she had no legs. But her arms were extendable just in case she needed to pick something up off the floor, and her hands were as supple as a surgeon's. She had clearly been built for her purpose.

I left the medic bot to set up, and went to make sure the rooms were ready, gripping my latte for dear life. Pulling up my notes, because I could never quite remember all the steps, I went through them one at a time: *interface on, Artificial Experience images and videos specific to each volunteer ready to go, matched to the rooms where each volunteer will be...* Then there were a series of commands I didn't understand but copied very exactly, in order to allow the individual's A.E. chip to image the participant's brain and send the images to the VMI (Virtual Magnetic Imaging) for analysis, alongside a snapshot of the image that participant was seeing at the time.

When I'd finished with the last room, I breathed a sigh of relief, and parked my butt in the receptionist's chair in the waiting room. Beside me, the medic bot had just finished taking blood from the first participant, the young girl to whom I'd given my interface at the front of the line. She was about my own age; clearly she only volunteered for the money. Not that I blamed her.

I consulted my list. "Carrie? You're in room one. The A.E. is all queued up for you. When you go in and sit down, the lights will dim and the experiment will begin."

Carrie nodded at me, looking like she could

use a latte too.

The medic bot and I repeated the process for the next seven volunteers, until the room emptied out. Once the medic bot had collected and labeled baseline blood samples for each participant, she announced to me, "I will analyze these for your neuropeptide salheptonin, and report back to you."

"Thank you," I said, and she wheeled away.

I was alone. With a heavy sigh, I plopped my forearms on the counter and my head on my forearms. To my surprise, I didn't feel all that tired anymore though—the espresso had done its work.

I have an hour, I thought. That's how long the first phase of the experiment took. I could of course log in and see the VMI brain images and the artificial experiences that had stimulated them in real time, but frankly… I wanted to work on my novel. I had an hour, after all.

I pulled my notebook out of my backpack, along with a pen. I could write the whole thing on an interface or even dictate it, of course, but I liked old fashioned things wherever I could get them. Hence the analog clock in my dorm room. I liked to visit archaeological sites, especially old castle ruins, where I'd try to imagine what life might have been like in the Second Age, before Synthetic Reasoning and Artificial Experience and even the labyrinth. Maybe even before light bulbs.

I skimmed the pages of what I'd written so

far, trying to get back into the flow of it. The story followed Elizabeth, who grew up in an orphanage controlled by the king. The king's son, Nikolai—devastatingly handsome, of course—grew up visiting the orphanage because his father wanted him to maintain a connection to the people, so he develops a sort of friendship with Elizabeth. She grows up and becomes the handmaid to the princess in a neighboring nation, and Prince Nikolai still comes to visit often. I threw in some intrigue about the mob and Elizabeth being whipped for her impertinent familiarity with royalty. But Nikolai is perfect and wonderful and doesn't care about her rank. Elizabeth can't believe he doesn't care, so she shuns him. Eventually he starts to believe she really doesn't have feelings for him, and he actually considers the Princess of Spain whom his father wants him to marry. Elizabeth looks on, devastated...

"Whatcha doin' there?"

I jumped, and gasped, a hand flying to my chest as the other covered my pages as best I could. "Geez! You scared me."

"I see that. You might wanna lay off the espresso, I think it's not good for your nerves." Liam, the post-doc I worked under, raised an eyebrow at me, his lips curled in that characteristic smirk of his. I shut the notebook immediately. "What are you writing?"

I shrugged. "Just killing time," I told him evasively. If he knew, I'd never hear the end of it.

"I guess it's too much to hope that you might be brainstorming new experiments…"

"No, just…" I decided it would be best to change the subject. "What are you doing here, Liam?" He usually didn't come by during my experiments—human psychology wasn't his thing. He waited for me to bring him conclusions, and then translated them into algorithms. *I'm technical —I don't do people,* was the way he usually put it. It was sort of tongue-in-cheek though, since his social skills were fine, as far as I could tell. Although he *was* undeniably eccentric.

He took a deep breath, his face suddenly serious. I knew what he was going to say before he said it—only one subject rendered him so somber. "You heard Halpert's address?"

I nodded. I *had* watched it after Mom called last night, even though I'd just sent her a quick comm about it and gone right back to bed after that.

"This is *bad*," he said, in a tone of voice that prompted agreement.

I opened my mouth and closed it again, waiting for him to elaborate. Which he would, if I didn't do it for him. He couldn't help himself. "You're afraid that if the bots get creativity…"

"They'll become superintelligent, way surpassing humans!" he finished. "Once they

16

become creative, they can devise ways to make themselves smarter, without our intervention at all… and that's an exponential curve. This was exactly what the Council of Synthetic Reason was supposed to prevent! I wrote a manifesto about it on my locus as soon as he'd finished and issued a counter-call to Halpert's. We have to band together across the globe and hound our senators to stop the challenge, or else this collaboration *will* lead to the extinction of the human race—"

"Oh, Liam," I rolled my eyes. Among his many eccentricities, Liam had a conspiracy theory labyrinth locus with apparently millions of followers, or so he was always telling me. He was a sort of B-list celebrity in that way—in pseudonym only, since I never saw his picture on there anywhere, and he didn't use his real name. "I don't want to become a target!" was his explanation for this. I'd gone to his locus once before, expecting to see skulls and crossbones and apocalyptic imagery, but I had to admit I was grudgingly impressed. It looked classy enough, and the one post I'd read was remarkably well-written, cited, and devoid of groundless assertions. I also saw that it had thousands of shares, and had only been posted that morning.

"It's true, if bots gain the creative ability to problem-solve like we have, one of the most probable futures *is* our extinction!" Liam insisted.

"Don't roll your eyes at me!"

"You're such an extremist. It's quite a leap from giving bots creativity to *the extinction of the human race.*" I emphasized each word, trying to make him recognize how silly he sounded.

Undaunted, Liam raised his index finger as he counted off his points. "One: bots are single-minded. They exist only to fulfill their programmed core purpose. Two: they are ruthless logicians. Within the parameters of their abilities, they perform that core purpose as *efficiently* as *possible.* Three: at present, they can only learn to do procedural tasks, they cannot yet solve complex and interconnected problems. Once they have creativity, though, they'll be able to do that just like we can. So what happens if you have a bot who has creativity, and whose goal is to make itself smarter? It does nothing else, 24 hours a day, seven days a week. Trial and error, trial and error." He demonstrates a logarithmic curve with his hand, eyes wide as he shook his head at me for emphasis. "Exponential growth!"

I stared at him, unimpressed. "Okay fine, so they become superintelligent. How does that lead to our—"

"Because!" he cut me off. "Maybe the bot who first becomes superintelligent has no interest in us at all, but it *is* interested in spreading its own upgrades to other bots. Now every other bot in the world, with every other possible core purpose, has infinite creativity at its disposal in order to fulfill its purpose! Just take one of those bots: let's say one of them manufactures shoes, okay? Its goal is to manufacture as many high quality shoes in as short a period of time as possible. But it's ruthlessly logical, and narrowly focused. What if it decides that humans are using too many resources that it needs to make its shoes? Logical solution? Kill all the humans! Then it can mine all the resources on earth and the moon and Mars and any other planet they colonize after we're gone, and *voila!* The entire universe becomes a giant shoe closet!"

I cracked up a little. I couldn't help it. "All right, I see your point that they might carry out their core purposes in unexpected ways. But it seems like we should be able to safeguard against that…"

"You mean, predict all the possible ways that a superintelligence leagues beyond human understanding *might* interpret their core purposes?" Liam countered. "How would we do that, exactly? That would be like an ant trying to fathom the mind of a man! The only possible way to approach this is to stop it before it can happen. QED," he added with a triumphant flourish, sitting back in his chair. He always said 'QED' when he felt like he'd made an unassailable point. All I knew was that it was a math term in Latin, and it basically meant the same thing as, "infinity times, the end."

I looked up before I could shoot back something sarcastic at Liam, sensing that we were not alone. Carrie, my first test subject, stood meekly in the door frame. I saw her mouth fall open a little when she saw Liam, and she colored a bit. I knew why: Liam was your classic tall, dark, and handsome, with blue eyes and that angular jaw that drove women crazy. It annoyed me. *All right, he's good looking, people. Get over it.* If they knew him the way I did, it wouldn't take long.

"Done?" I said to Carrie, leaning past Liam with a firm smile and forcing her to look at me as I pointed down the hall. "The medic bot will take one more blood sample in the next room over. Then come back here and I'll get you paid."

She vanished, and I turned back to Liam. One thing I had to give Liam: he never seemed to get that self-complacent air that most attractive men get when they find themselves admired. I'm not sure he even noticed.

"But there might be one thing we *can* do as a potential safeguard, just in case Halpert's challenge *is* answered…" Liam went on, as if the interruption hadn't happened. "Program them with a moral code."

"You're talking about Isaac Asimov's Three Laws of Robotics?" I raised my eyebrows, trying unsuccessfully not to smirk. I only knew these existed in the first place because of something I read on Liam's locus, and I couldn't exactly recall what they were—something about the hierarchy of robotic priorities as a way to keep them from becoming dangerous to humans.

"That's fiction," Liam scoffed. "This is reality. "

I shrugged. "Okay. So program them with a moral code, then. What do you need me for?"

"I *need* you," he leaned forward, his eyes staring melodramatically into mine, "because everybody thinks we won't get creativity except through emotion. They go together, peas in a pod." He crossed two fingers together to illustrate. "Humans have a moral code too, but when we break it, why do we break it?"

"Emotion," I sat back in my chair, catching his drift now.

He nodded. "So let's recap." He held up his fingers one at a time. "One: Superintelligent bots with unlimited creativity. Two: *Emotional* superintelligent bots... who can presumably therefore overwrite or ignore their programming if they don't happen to like it. So sure, we could give them a moral code, but who's to say they'll follow it?"

"If they can overwrite their programming, maybe they decide they don't want to manufacture shoes, then, either," I pointed out. "Maybe they want to... I don't know, optimize the fertility of

21

giraffes instead."

Liam shrugged. "Maybe, but both will be equally fatal to us—too many humans means not enough space for giraffes, either. Point being, we need to instill at least *some* semblance of morality in the bots that they *won't* just overwrite at will. Maybe they *can,* but they'd choose not to. So what does that take? Empathy or something? I don't know, this is your department. I'm just speculating."

I bit my lip, eyes absently scanning the air as I tried to mentally retrieve what I'd studied about this. "Empathy comes from mirror neurons, which cause us to share the emotional experience of another person. Emotion comes from the limbic system, and it's mediated by a whole lot of neurotransmitters…"

"But sociopaths don't have emotion or morality, right?" Liam cut me off. "Seems like they'd be a good group to study, to see what's missing…"

"They have emotion," I corrected, "they just lack empathy."

"Perfect!" Liam said, "that's exactly what we're looking to avoid: a race of superintelligent sociopaths! So you're on that. Design me a human experiment to define the relationship between emotion, empathy, and morality."

I laughed, incredulous. "Oh, is that all! What

about my thesis?" I gestured at the lab where we currently sat.

"You're already studying human emotion, aren't you? Something about that new neuropeptide?"

"Yes!" Then I reminded him, since I knew he wouldn't recall the particulars, nor would he care, "We're shooting VMI images of the brain when participants see an image of someone they love, and then drawing pre- and post-blood samples to see if salheptonin increases simultaneously. My theory is, it's the neuropeptide responsible for the physical sensations of desire."

"Okay, so this is just a pivot," Liam shrugged.

"This is a completely new project!" I protested. "And it's *enormous,* by the way! If I 'pivot' like you're suggesting, someone else will complete my research before I do, and I'll have to start all over with something else if I want to graduate!"

"Rebecca!" He made exploding movements with his hands. "End of the world! Who cares if you have a degree if the entire human race is extinct?"

I shook my head, incredulous. "I hate you."

"No you don't," he flashed me a rakish smile. "Besides, like you're having so much fun working on this thesis of yours, anyway?" he gestured at the stark white room in which we sat, and at the notebook I'd closed. "Every time I come upon you unannounced, you're writing the next *Gone with the Wind*. Or reading a novel from the Second Age. Or humming to yourself to learn the harmony for your next musical performance—you never told me when the performance was, by the way."

I flushed. "Just because I have lots of interests—"

"Hey, hey. It's okay," Liam cut me off, hands in the air with an expression of mock seriousness. "I've got millions of people following my labyrinth locus who agree with me. I don't need you to be one of them, although it *would* be very nice. But you remember what Dr. Yin said about you in your review?"

I sighed, and quoted Dr. Yin: "'Technically very competent, but her heart does not seem to be in her work.'" I hadn't known whether to be flattered or insulted when I read that.

He nodded. "Yeah. And you know what she said to me privately? She asked if you were planning to go for your Ph.D., because if you were, she'd like to offer you a spot in her lab. You're *that* good, Bec. And considering you'd rather be doing something else, in a way that's even more impressive. Who knows, this project might even turn into your Ph.D. thesis!"

"Eh-*hem*."

I looked up, startled. One of my middle-aged male test subjects stood in the door frame, ready for his exit blood draw. Carrie queued up behind him, waiting to get paid. I sent the man to the medic bot and beckoned Carrie forward, scanning her fingerprint again to deposit her compensation and trying to ignore the way her eyelashes shyly fluttered at Liam.

Liam *never* complimented me. He usually restricted his communications to fluent sarcasm punctuated by obsessive rants. *It's only because he's buttering me up to do something for him,* I thought as I dismissed Carrie.

When I'd finished, Liam resumed his unnerving stare deep into my eyes, triggering involuntary heat in my cheeks. I wished he'd blink, or look away occasionally, or *something*. He went on, "What I'm saying is, I need someone on the human psych end to help me program a morality the bots will actually follow, as a safeguard in case Halpert's challenge *does* succeed. At least then, even if superintelligence does emerge, we'll have 'warm and fuzzy' superintelligent bots, with a soft spot for humans!" He mimed his impression of 'warm and fuzzy' as he said this, which turned out to look a lot like jazz hands. I shook my head at him with a suppressed smile, and his eyes twinkled at me in response. "Once we have your succinct definition, then Nilesh and Larissa and I can reverse engineer it in mathematical terms and make it into an algorithm. Then you can go back to working on whatever you want, I promise."

"And if someone answers Halpert's challenge before we get the chance?" I asked. "Because what you're asking me to do is borderline impossible, I'm just saying…"

Liam shrugged, unconcerned. "Then we'll kill him, and bury his research before anybody else can use it to buy us more time. Please be quick though, would you? I'd like to kill as few people as possible."

"Glad to hear you have a backup plan," I nodded, trying to match his deadpan delivery without success.

Chapter 2

When I arrived in my flat, I dropped my coat and hat on my twin bed. I had another hour to kill after the experiment finished and before my Creative Writing class, and probably should have started working on Liam's new project. But impossible requests breed apathy (I think I read that on a plaque somewhere once), so I didn't feel especially motivated to try. Plus, I wanted to show Madeline the video of the performance from last night—or at least the parts when I was on stage. She had been my main study partner to help me learn my lines, as always, and I wanted her to appreciate the final product.

Madeline was plugged into the charging station and powered down. She was about a foot tall, so I could easily transport her in my backpack, and made of a lightweight aluminum alloy. Her face was metal, too, and yet humanoid—but with eyes that took up about half her face. I pressed the power button behind her neck, and her eyes lit up.

"How did it go?" she burst out when she

saw me.

"Come here and I'll show you." I pulled up my netscreen and pressed the play button with a flourish of anticipation. Since all of us (humans and bots alike) could access the labyrinth via our A.E. chips, the only legitimate purpose remaining for netscreens was for sharing a mutual experience, such as watching a film or a video, or sharing information from the labyrinth with someone else. *I* used my A.E. chip as little as possible, but then, I was odd.

"Oh Becca," Madeline breathed when I stopped the recording, her digital eyes shining with the most perfect admiration I could possibly ask for. "You were absolutely incredible!"

"Thanks," I grinned, dispensing with the necessary false humility that I would have employed with anyone else. With Madeline, I could just admit that I knew I was good.

"When do rehearsals start for The Tempest?" she asked me eagerly. I had been cast as Miranda--my third leading role in a row.

"Next week is the first one," I told her. "This will be my first weekend off in awhile—I was thinking of asking Julie to come with me to London to meet Jake." Jake was one of my best friends from Casa Linda, practically like a brother to me. We had gone to high school together, and had been part of the same group of friends for the last five years now. I'd met that whole group shortly after my dad's death. Including Andy.

Madeline knew where my mind went next; I'd become predictable, I suppose. "Are you gonna try to get Andy to go too?"

"I'll ask him," I murmured, blushing. "He won't go, though. Quantum Track tickets are a lot more expensive from New York to London than they are from Dublin."

"He's got student loans too!" Madeline pointed out. "Besides, ever since last summer, I keep expecting him to show up at your doorstep one day, and sweep you into his arms, and tell you he can't live without you…"

I giggled, delighted, but with a tinge of chagrin. Madeline was the only one who still indulged such fantasies with me. It was true that last summer, Andy commed me almost nonstop while we were home in Casa Linda for the summer, between hangout sessions with our friends. He told me all kinds of leading things--like, "I don't know why such a beautiful girl would think such-and-such" (clearly implying he meant me,) or, "You know guys are super intimidated by you, right?" Which I of course took as the reason why he hadn't come right out and directly told me how he felt about me yet, nor did he ever ask to hang out with me alone: he was too shy. I just had to be more encouraging; then he'd come around.

Maybe he'd convinced himself that I was out of his league or something. Maybe that was why he'd basically stopped talking to me this semester.

Unfortunately, Madeline was the only "person" besides me who could believe that. Which made her pretty much the only one I could talk to about Andy at all, at this point.

"I'll invite him," I reiterated. "But I've gotta ask Julie first. I'm meeting her for lunch after Creative Writing."

Julie and I met for lunch in the Buttery, the little cafe on the Dublin University campus. Neither of us much liked the vibe there—it was bright and too open, all geometric, with square chairs and round tables. The stark whiteness with track lighting made me feel like I was living in somebody's idea of a futuristic kitsch cartoon. Julie waved at me in line, all her features wide in enthusiastic greeting. Julie never grinned like a normal person, she always opened her mouth as wide as it would go, as if silently shouting. She was tall, broad, and built like an athlete, even though she wasn't one.

"There's my superstar!" she cried once I was in earshot, and she started miming a microphone and singing a rendition of one of my solos the night before, karaoke-style.

"Shh!" I laughed, embarrassed.

Julie gasped and leaned forward in a mock

whisper as we inched forward in line. "Was Liam there? In the audience?"

"No way. I refused to tell him when or where the performances were."

"Why not? He wanted to come support you, and *that man…*" she tilted her head to the side and roved her eyes up and down as if he were standing in front of her.

I shook my head and rolled my eyes. "Because one, he's incapable of being anything but sarcastic unless he's talking about Synthetic Reasoning, and two," I ticked the reasons off on my fingers, "I'd have been so self-conscious if he were in the audience, I wouldn't have been able to perform at all. He'd have made fun of me *for-ev-er.*"

"All right, all right, fine. I'm just saying, *that man…*"

"I know," I patted Julie on the shoulder. "Speaking of attractive and available men, are you free this weekend?"

Julie opened her mouth, widened her eyes, and spread all her fingers apart, excited before she even knew the reason. "Yes! Why?"

"Want to go to London?" I grinned. "I want you to meet my friend Jake, he goes to school there." I'd had an idea that the two of them might hit it off, and had been hoping to introduce them for awhile.

"I haven't been to London in six months. Let's do it! Did you message him yet?"

I told her no, but I pulled out my handheld right there in line and sent him a comm, just as Julie began her order. I could have used the A.E. chip in my temple and mentally dictated the comm, but that always kind of creeped me out. I preferred to avoid labyrinth connections in my head if I could help it. Besides, people were always teasing me about my ancient handheld. I kind of liked being different.

My handheld vibrated within minutes with Jake's reply: "Sure! Just tell me when and where!"

"See, this is what I love about school," Julie said over her shoulder as the bots behind the counter put her meal together. "Back home, it's this depressing 'real world' where nobody can afford anything, and they're all out of work. But here, money is for spending! Everybody's up for new experiences!"

"Yeah," I said, feeling a twinge of guilt as I pictured my mom's face, had she heard that speech. London would require a Quantum Track ticket, of course… which would mean dipping into school loans. I made a little money in the lab, but I spent all of that on groceries and coffee and local transportation. At least London and Dublin were only about a 20 minute Quantum Track ride. I thought all this as I ordered my own lunch from the polite little bot behind the counter. "I should work a little extra to pay for all of it, though," I added, thinking about the new project Liam wanted me to design. A shadow crossed my face, and Julie must have seen it.

"What's wrong?" she asked.

I opened my mouth and closed it again, trying to decide how much to answer. Julie wasn't particularly interested in my research, I knew. At last I settled on, "Did you see Halpert's address?"

Julie snorted. "What, at like four in the morning? Uh, no." She took a bite of her sandwich. "Why, was it important?"

I shrugged. "I don't know. My mom and Liam both think so. It's a call for worldwide collaboration to help bots develop emotion and creativity."

Julie picked up her lunch tray as the bot delivered it, gesturing at an empty table with her head. "Isn't that what your thesis is about?"

"Kind of. My thesis is on the possible neuropeptide of human desire. Liam wants me to 'pivot,' as he puts it, and design a different experiment that I have no idea how to..." I trailed off. I'd just had an idea, actually. Totally outside the box, but still...

"What?" she pressed. But I shook my head —this wasn't an idea I could explain, even to Julie. Nobody could know about Madeline. That was the deal I'd made Mom when she allowed me to take her.

"Nothing," I stopped, and smiled. "Don't worry about it. I'll figure it out." The bot delivered my lunch too, and I picked up my tray and followed Julie to the table she'd indicated.

Julie shrugged, satisfied. "So, tell me about Jake! Is he cute? And if so, why haven't you dated him yourself? Oh, oh, I know why, because he's not Andy, right?"

I colored. "Because I'm not into Jake, and yes—because he's not Andy."

"Has Andy talked to you recently?"

I stirred my soup, not meeting her eyes. "Well, he sent me a comm on my birthday," I murmured. "And I've talked to him four times on A.E. this semester. But I always have to call him." I thought about my promise to Madeline to invite him to London with us, but somehow that just felt too vulnerable at the moment. Maybe I'd convince Jake to invite him… except if I did that, I couldn't seem too eager about it, or Jake might get suspicious.

Julie nodded, trying to be supportive. "Maybe you should… date someone else? Just to make him jealous?"

"Not Jake," I insisted, more firmly than I'd intended. "Dating Jake would not be a fling. We've been friends for way too long." Even though Jake had flings constantly. But still, I would be different. Everyone would practically expect us to announce our engagement within the month.

"Okay, what about Liam?"

"No!" I rotated my head up and looked at the ceiling as I said this, trying to punctuate the absurdity of the proposition. "Just—no!"

"All right, all right," Julie held up her hands, "I'm just saying, you have no shortage of good options!"

"I know who I want, and it wouldn't be fair of me to date someone else just to use him for experience," I insisted.

"Even though you *have no experience*," Julie leaned across the table to emphasize this. "Guys aren't as fragile as you think they are, Becca. Just get out there and make eyes at some random dude if nothing else! Go on a couple dates, and let it slip to Andy that you're doing it. I bet he might change his tune if he knows you're not just sitting there waiting for him…"

"Ugh," I said. I was so tired of people giving me that advice, and the idea of going out with someone I didn't like just because I *should* sounded repugnant. "Can we just talk about this weekend, please?"

"Fine, fine!" Julie shrugged. "I'm just saying, if you flipped off that 'go away' signal you've got on full blast all the time, you might be surprised at the response!"

Chapter 3

"I hate having to leave you here all day," I murmured to Madeline when I powered her up in my flat again that evening. The flat was exceptionally small.

"It's all right. I don't get bored," she said, cheerful as ever. I'd never once heard her complain about anything, in the six years I'd owned her.

"That's because I leave you off and plug you in all day," I pointed out. "Even though I don't think anybody in Dublin would care if I had you with me. It's not like there aren't bots everywhere."

"Liam would hate me," she pointed out. "Plus, you promised your mom."

"That's true," I conceded. Liam was used to the bots at the grocery stores and cafes and even Odessa, our research bot—but he had a big moral problem with personal bots. *They're replacing everything else—now they're replacing human companions, too? That's just wrong!* he'd said once. But the mention of Liam reminded me that I had something in particular to discuss with

Madeline tonight.

"Madeline, you have a core program, right?"
I asked. Then I added quickly, "I'm not sure if you
even know what I mean by that…"

"Of course I do," she interrupted.

I stopped, sinking back to the bed. "Of
course you know what I mean, or—"

"Of course I have a core program," she
clarified. "I'm programmed to be a companion."

I don't know why it had never occurred to
me to ask Madeline about how she worked before.
After all, I was doing research on this very thing,
and I had an insider right here. My heart beat faster.

"Programmed to be a companion," I
repeated. "But… doesn't companionship require
emotion?"

She seemed to process this, as if trying to
decipher my meaning. "I would die for you,
Rebecca." My heart swelled, but then she added,
"That is the extreme of what I am programmed for."

"Could you decide not to die for me if you
wanted to? Could you choose not to even like me?"

"Of course not. I'm programmed to be a
companion. I can't do otherwise."

I bit my lip. I definitely didn't want to have
this conversation, but I was too far in now. "So the
way you felt about Mrs. Marchmont—" I said,
referencing Madeline's former master.

"Was the same way I now feel about you,"

she affirmed, "if you want to call it that."

I deflated. "Isn't… there any distinction at all? We're such different people… I'm not asking which one of us you liked *better,* but isn't there a difference between being a companion to an eighty year old lady, and me?"

"Sure there is. But it's not for me to decide what I 'like' and what I don't like. The very nature of a core purpose is to pursue and protect that core purpose to the exclusion of all else. There is only one question I have to answer: how can I best serve my purpose? The answer depends on whose companion I am. Why do you look so sad?"

I was trying not to cry, actually. Madeline wheeled over to me, stroking the part of my forearm she could reach.

"I said something wrong," Madeline fretted, "what did I say?"

I ignored this, choking on my next question a little. "Is there anything you like or don't like, then?"

"I like you," she said simply.

I sighed. "You've been programmed to like me. That doesn't count. I mean, do you have… I don't know, a favorite color? Musical tastes? How have I never asked you this before?" As soon as the latter question was out of my mouth, I realized the answer to it with a twinge of guilt: our relationship had always been entirely about me.

But Madeline shook her head. "Preferences are emotion-based. I don't have preferences that I wasn't explicitly given."

So she doesn't have emotions, I thought. Of course I'd *known* that… but on some level, I didn't know either. I didn't *want* to know.

I cleared my throat. "So… do you have any sort of moral code, then?"

She looked confused. "I don't know what you mean."

"Morality. Like, don't do these things because they're wrong."

"I suppose so…" she murmured. "I was given a series of if/then statements and run through an almost endless list of possible social scenarios at my conception, to make sure the statements still carried through. I'm to be helpful, selfless, honest, and imitating. If that is 'morality,' as you call it, then yes, I have morality."

"Imitating?" I repeated.

"You call it empathy," Madeline explained. "But since I don't have a human limbic system I can't truly feel what you are feeling, of course. So my creator programmed me to do the next best thing, and that is to externally mirror what you are feeling. From your perspective, I gather, it feels the same."

So she has neither empathy nor emotion, then, I thought. Of course she hadn't. And yet she seemed to be the most selfless and loyal and kindest 'person' I'd ever met. A tear slipped down my cheek.

"Why are you crying?" Madeline fretted, in an excellent imitation of sympathy.

"What good is a friend who is compelled, who doesn't choose me?" I sniffed, wiping the tears away. I knew she wouldn't understand, but I was so used to telling her everything that I couldn't help it. "It's like finding out…it's as if Andy asked me to go out with him, and then I found out he only did it on a dare!"

Madeline's little brow furrowed. "But if he goes out with you, isn't that all that matters?"

"No, of course that isn't all that matters! The 'why' is incredibly important!" I sighed, and shook my head. "Forget it."

"You *say* forget it, but your tone sounds like you don't want me to…" Madeline murmured, perplexed.

"'Forget it' in this case means I know you won't understand anyway, even if I try to explain. Apparently you don't have the *capacity* to understand."

Madeline rolled to and fro in front of me. "I've displeased you," she murmured. "I don't like to displease you."

I closed my eyes. This was *Madeline*, after all. My best friend. The one person who never got exasperated by my tears months after my dad died, when everyone else expected me to pull it together and move on. The one person to whom I could talk *ad nauseam* about Andy, and she never tired of listening. She loved me. That had been one of the facts of which I was most certain in the world.

But she couldn't love.

Madeline blinked her wide digital eyes up at me. "Are you okay?"

I sniffed. "Sure," I lied. "I'm super."

Chapter 4

When I arrived in the lab the next day, I deposited my backpack on the floor beside me and sank down into my chair, staring at the black top table without really seeing it. This was the main lab, where Liam and Dr. Yin and everybody under them worked. Towering bookshelves topped most of the desks for storage, and most of the shelves overflowed with cables and wires and various obsolete gadgets I couldn't identify.

I hadn't slept much the night before. I'd powered Madeline down for the night a little earlier than usual, because I just didn't want her comfort anymore.

Her fake comfort, I thought. I just needed to think.

I started when I felt a presence, and looked up to see Liam standing there, watching me. He raised his eyebrows in that classic probing-yet-not-quite-serious way of his. It felt like perpetual ridicule.

"What?" I asked, not caring if I came off

rude.

"You look like you just found out unicorns are imaginary."

"Shut up, Liam," I said heavily, pushing myself off the edge of the desk to go get some tea. I didn't really want any, I just thought it might end the conversation. Liam seemed to have the idea that I was innocent to the point of naïveté. Sometimes I liked that, truth be told—I suppose I thought it might make me seem endearing. But just now, it irritated me.

Alas. He followed me to the tea kettle in the little office. "No, really," he pressed. "Did you get stood up for a date last night or something?"

"No," I gave him a pointed look, hoping to communicate that this conversation was over. "I *was* thinking, though. Companion bots imitate their masters already, even though they don't have real emotion yet—so at the moment, it's not true empathy. But once bots have a limbic system of their own, all we'd have to do is take whatever analog of mirror neurons they already have and hook them up to the synthetic limbic system somehow. Wouldn't that essentially give them empathy, same as we have? And once they have that, then they'll theoretically follow a moral code, too—at least as well as we do. Right?"

Instead of responding, Liam narrowed his eyes, inspecting my face.

"Would you stop doing that?" I turned away from him on purpose as I put a chai tea bag in my mug and poured hot water over it.

"How do you know that?" he asked.

"What?" I lingered with my back to him, dipping my chai in the hot water.

"About how companion bots operate. I mean, you're right, they *do* have primitive mirror neurons, and they *do* use them to imitate humans, but it sounds… a little… personal. Like maybe you had a conversation with one since yesterday." Liam crossed the little kitchenette to lean on the counter beside me as he said this, so that I could no longer hide my face.

My heart beat faster, and I turned away from him again, heading back to my desk with my mug. I knew this was exactly the wrong strategy with Liam: acting too secretive would only make him more determined, but I didn't know what else to do.

Nobody hates bots like Liam does. I couldn't tell him about Madeline. I just *couldn't*.

"I have to do some research," I told him, pulling an interface towards me. But he sat down beside me, pulling up a stool from a nearby lab bench.

"Aw, no," Liam declared, pushing the interface away again. Then he asked me, point blank, "Are you holding out on me? Are you an heiress or something?"

I snorted. "Certainly not!" I tried to act nonchalant, though I was starting to feel really frightened.

"Because only the super wealthy have companion bots," Liam went on, like I hadn't replied. "And I took it as a foregone conclusion that anybody doing research to stop the advancement of the bots wouldn't actually *own* one herself…"

I forced myself to face him. His gaze could be piercing when he wanted it to be, but I would not be intimidated. Or at least I wouldn't let him see that I was. "Liam. Would you please let me get back to work?"

"Oh, look at the time!" Liam declared, making a show of stretching out his wrist as if he had a watch there, even though nobody had worn watches since the Second Age. "It's half ten." He knew this from the A.E. chip in his temple, of course. Half ten was the coffee break time for all the labs; everyone generally gathered in a room downstairs to socialize for half an hour over coffee, tea, or biscuits.

"I'll stay and work, I got here late—" I began. But Liam took hold of my elbow, lifting me up and forcing me to follow him.

"I think you and I should take this one at Lavazza," he declared. "It's time for us to get to know each other a little better." He steered me by my elbow so firmly, and I suddenly felt so out of control that once we were in the hall, I burst into tears.

Liam let go of me immediately, blurting, "I'm sorry! Geez!"

I buried my face in my hands once I had both of them at my own disposal again, feeling like a big ball of fear for Madeline, devastation about last night, frustration that Liam wouldn't just leave me alone, and humiliation that all of this had driven me to cry in front of *him*. Of all people.

When I finally got ahold of myself, I forced myself to look at Liam. He just stood there, staring at me, like he wasn't sure what to do with his arms and legs. At last he mumbled, "See, this is why I want *you* to do the research on emotion, and not me."

I sniffed. "Why, because you have none?" I added a tiny smile as I said this, to show that I wasn't serious.

"Because—I'm certainly out of my element with them." He bit his lip, this time offering me his arm tentatively. "Can we still go to Lavazza? Please? Let me buy you a coffee?"

I sighed. I would have preferred to stay in the lab and skip the break altogether, but I also felt the need to smooth things over after my embarrassing outburst. I looped my arm through his, and he took a deep breath, looking immensely relieved.

Chapter 5

As we stepped outside on the green where other students played catch and lounged about eating lunch in the uncommon sunshine, Liam ventured, "So, tremendously uncomfortable as it makes me to ask you this question… what's his name?"

I glanced at him, confused. "What?"

"The guy you're crying about."

"Oh…" I laughed a little and shook my head. "It's really not a guy."

"Oh!" His eyebrows shot up. "So you're…"

"No, no, I mean it's not romantic at all. For once," I muttered under my breath. "Forget it," I added quickly, hoping he wouldn't probe what I meant by that. *So many things I don't want him to probe.* We arrived at Lavazza just then, so I released his arm and approached the counter to order.

"Rebecca Cordeaux," the bot said behind the counter, in her tinny voice. "Your usual?"

I nodded at the bot meekly as Liam arched

an eyebrow at me with a smirk. "Please."

The bot turned to Liam, and he jerked a thumb at me. "I'll have what she's having. Apparently she knows her coffee."

We took our lattes to a table under the skylights, next to a large planter that hid us from the rest of the cafeteria. Liam just watched me for a minute, with that expectant look.

I hadn't decided until right that minute whether I would trust him or not. But I would have to tell him *something*.

"Look, if I tell you, you have to promise me not to do anything about it. Only listen. Okay?"

He looked a little taken aback at that. "Promise not to do anything—what would I *do*?"

"You have to promise or I'm not telling you anything! And hold on—" I pulled out my handheld and flipped on the video recorder, holding it up so that Liam was in frame.

His suspicion melted into laughter. "You've got to be kidding me!"

But I persisted, "It is April thirteenth. Liam, if I tell you why I am upset today, do you promise not to do anything about it? You will take no action independent of consulting me regarding the information I am about to tell you?"

Still smirking at me, he drew an X over his chest with his right hand. "Cross my heart and hope to die!"

He couldn't be serious for anything. I rolled my eyes but stopped recording. "Good enough."

I guess my face fell again, because Liam leaned across the table and took one of my hands. This took me off guard, and made me slightly uncomfortable—we didn't really do physical contact.

"Bec. What is it?"

I sighed, watching him for a long moment. *Here goes.*

"I'm not an heiress," I began.

"Okay…"

"But… I do have a companion bot."

He dropped my hand, looking like I'd slapped him. "What?"

"Please," I held up both my hands, trying to beg forbearance. Then I plopped both elbows onto the table, sinking my forehead onto them before looking back up at him again. "Her name is Madeline," I said at last. "She was commissioned by a wealthy widow named Mrs. Marchmont. Mrs. Marchmont retired in Casa Linda, where I'm from —it's a suburb of Phoenix, Arizona. Close enough to major hospitals if anything happened to her, but she wanted more of the 'country' feel because the tech hubs were too fast paced for her. I met her at church when I was fourteen—Mrs. Marchmont, not Madeline of course. I guess she was impressed that I was talking to her instead of to people my own age, and we got to be friends. She invited me over for tea a few times, asked me all about myself, and told me her old stories." I chanced a glance up at Liam, and found he was no longer staring daggers at me. That was something. I went on, "About the third time I went over there, she introduced me to Madeline. My family hates bots too, but I was at that age where I didn't judge by my parents' opinions anyway. It's impossible not to like Madeline. She's so genuinely interested in everyone."

"And by that, you mean she was programmed to seem interested in everyone," Liam remarked, his tone dry. "Sorry. Go on."

I bit my lip. "Then when I was fifteen, my father died. It was just my mom and me, and my mom was struggling just to put food on the table. She was always gone, either traveling for her job, or taking care of my sick aunt, who lives in Chicago. I guess Mrs. Marchmont could see that I was lonely. She invited me over more often after that. About a year later, she took ill. I went to see her in the big hospital in Phoenix when she was dying. Madeline was there with her, and she told me to take her after she was gone. She wanted to make sure Madeline would have a good home, but she didn't know many people out in the country who wouldn't dismember her as soon as look at her.

"My mom and I had a terrific fight over

whether I'd be allowed to keep Madeline when the executor of Mrs. Marchmont's will delivered her to me. I think that's because Dad would have been furious; he had no love for bots. It's a long story, but he lost his job as a doctor to a bot. He said the bots who took over couldn't do his job as well as he could, and that he thought the media was pushing this utopian propaganda of how the bots would make the world a better place. He said it was all this big conspiracy to try to convince people they were alone in their distaste for the new world, and there was no point in fighting against the 'tide of the future.' You'd have gotten along with him really well, actually."

"Sounds like it," Liam murmured.

"Anyway, he died pretty suddenly of Treblar's Disease. I don't know if you know anything about that?" Liam's brow furrowed with something that might have been recognition, but I explained anyway, "Dad used to call it an opportunistic infection, which means a lot of people have it, but their immune systems keep it in check. It's usually not a big deal until the immune system becomes suppressed. Then the disease becomes active, and when it does, it can make people really *really* sick... though it's not usually fatal. Mom said he'd probably had it for years, but he got sick right when his obsession with Halpert and some of his associates was at a fever's pitch. He started working all night long and going on trips to the Capital…"

"Wait, wait, wait," Liam held up a hand, and then his eyes went wide. "Your dad wasn't— Quentin *Cordeaux*? Was he?" He smacked his forehead with his hand. "How did I never put that together before? Cordeaux! It's not that common a name!"

I sighed, trying to smother my exasperation. He was missing the point. "Yes, that was him. I guess in your community, everybody knows each other, huh?"

"But your dad was like, one of the pioneers of The Renegades! That's what we call ourselves: The Renegades."

"How very Artificial-Experience-Gamer of you."

"Sorry." I guess he finally picked up on my annoyance. "Go on."

Blinking to try to reset my emotions, I went on, "Anyway, my point was, Mom thought he got sick due to all his unresolved anger and bitterness, combined with working himself into the ground with all his research. She never actually told me so, but I know she even thought he became a little unhinged at the end—no offense. Apparently he told her that he found something out in the Capital, something involving Halpert and some other guys associated with him…"

"Which guys?" Liam asked.

I thought for a minute, counting off the ones I could remember on my fingers. "Well, Dad worked under Dr. Janner Rasputin for awhile—you know, the International Health Corporation guy. I know he's a hero for stopping a bunch of would-be pandemics, but Dad hated him with a burning passion for some reason. Then Justice Wallenberg," I added, naming the Supreme Justice of the International Court, "and... I can't even remember the others, honestly."

"Kennedy St. James, The CEO of Plethorus?" Liam raised his eyebrows, and I nodded.

"Oh yeah, that sounds right." Plethorus was the world's major international supplier of nearly everything which could be manufactured on demand. I knew Liam hated him too—presumably because he was the world's biggest employer of bots.

"And Pierre Montgomery and Abraham Chiefton?" Liam guessed, naming the head of the International Education Board, and a famous film director.

I blinked at him. "Yeah. I think that is right. How did you know?"

"Those are the members of Halpert's Board of Advisors," Liam said darkly. His tone implied he had more to say about this, but he resisted. "Go on."

I shrugged. "Anyway, Dad kept insinuating

that all those guys were part of some big conspiracy together. But he would never tell my mom or me what it was because he said he feared for our safety if we ever knew—something like that. Still, the idea of me getting a personal bot so soon after his death… I guess it seemed disrespectful to Mom, since he would have absolutely hated Madeline on general principle. I think the only reason she finally gave in was because she was so emotionally depleted herself, she was just tired of fighting with me. But she told me that the condition of my keeping her was that I'd never let her be seen in public. I was only too happy to comply, since I knew Madeline would be in danger if I did show her around. I don't know about the rest of Dad's theories, but I certainly could tell that in Casa Linda, where I'm from, *everybody* hates bots."

"So where is she now?" Liam asked in a low voice. "Up in your flat?"

I nodded. "When Mrs. Marchmont told me she was giving her to me, she said I'd find that Madeline was the wisest, most loyal, and most unselfish friend I'd ever have." I sniffed. "She was right about that. Madeline became my best friend very quickly. I needed someone I could talk to who would just let me be sad; all my real friends just kind of expected me to snap out of it within a week or two of my dad's death, and go back to normal. I pretended I was fine, and just stayed busy so I wouldn't think too much when I was around them. My mom had her own problems, plus she was practically never around anyway. But Madeline was perfect. She listened, and comforted, and let me cry, and she never scolded me for saying the same thing over and over. She had more empathy than any person I'd ever met. Or so I thought. I was fifteen at the time, and totally uninterested in how her technology actually worked—"

"Sorta like now," Liam gave me a little half smile. I shrugged, but returned it.

"I guess, yeah. I didn't ask how it was possible for a bot to have empathy, and to care about me. Once I got old enough to ask those questions, I still didn't because I guess I didn't want to know the answers. I was too attached to her by then."

"But?" Liam prompted gently.

"But," I sighed, "Last night, I finally did ask. I was trying to figure out where to start on designing the study you wanted, and I realized I had an insider right there. Madeline essentially told me she's my friend because she was programmed to be my friend, and she can't be anything else. I know that's completely obvious now that I say it out loud, but you have to understand my history with her. I didn't think of her as a robot, I thought of her as my best friend. Don't get me wrong, I have other friends too, but..." I stopped myself. I'd been about to say I was a chameleon; that with everyone else, I changed who I was depending on who was around at the time and what they would approve of. I'd show bits and pieces of my true self to different people--in the lab and in my classes and to my mom, I was smart and conscientious. I was the one who "did everything right." My theater buddies shared my love of performing and thought I was a "goodie two shoes," but they didn't know or care about who I was beyond that. We bonded over what we had in common, and it was great, but it was still superficial. Julie and Jake and my friends from Casa Linda were "fun" buddies--we had a great time together, hanging out until all hours of the night and talking about random funny ideas. They thought they knew me, and they did know a lot of facts about me, that was true. But none of them knew I was madly in love with Andy. (Well, Julie knew, but not the extent of it, because she clearly didn't approve. Honestly I regretted confiding as much as I had to her, at least about that.) None of my Casa Linda friends knew how I'd struggled with my identity after Dad died and Mom went MIA for the most part. None of them knew that I double majored in cognitive neuroscience and theater with a minor in Creative Writing and filled every hour of every day because I just couldn't stand the silence, because it made me think too much about what I'd lost. Nobody but Madeline knew all that. Without her, I would feel adrift, like there was no place in the world I could truly call home.

But Liam (of all people) didn't need to know all that. I gave him a weak, almost embarrassed smile, and summed all this up: "So I just 'found out'"—I used air quotes with my fingers—"that my best friend is an automaton. And it breaks my heart." Pressing my lips together, I looked over his shoulder and out the large glass window beside us so I wouldn't have to meet his eyes.

He didn't say anything for a long time either —too long. Finally I blurted, "Look, I know how much you hate machines, and even though Madeline doesn't care about me in a real emotion kind of way, she's still my best friend. Please, just —try to understand!"

When I finally gathered the courage to look at him, I saw that he didn't look angry anymore, only lost in thought. His eyes locked on mine again and he said, "I'm not angry. I get it. It's okay." He searched my face a little and then added, "I'm sorry about your father."

I blinked, and gave him a tiny nod. "Thanks."

We sipped our lattes in silence for what felt like a long time after that. Presently he asked, "Can I meet her?"

"No!" I cried, knee-jerk.

"I'm not going to hurt her!" he said, "I

just… I've never actually talked to a relational bot before about its internal experience and self-awareness. I know a lot from the outside, but nothing about it from that angle. I'd just be fascinated, and it might be helpful for our research. I promise to behave myself." He raised both of his hands in the air.

I watched him for a long moment, trying to envision how this would go. At last I said, "You'd… have to come to my flat. I can't take her out in public. I promised my mom."

Suddenly jovial Liam was back. "Is that a dinner invitation? Oh Bec, I didn't know you thought of me that way…"

I felt my cheeks flush, the way they always did when Liam made comments like that. It made me want to avoid him. I pushed back my chair and stood up, ducking lower to the ground than necessary to pick up my bag and hide my face until my color returned to normal.

"If you keep that up, I'll take it back!" I warned.

Chapter 6

"Hey you!" Jake's hologram shimmered in my flat. I'd just been about to start dinner when he called. I gestured to Madeline to stay out of sight, and then pressed accept, only because Jake tended to get right to the point.

"When are you coming Saturday? And who's this Julie chick?"

"Julie is destined to be your next girlfriend," I told him. "You'll love her. She's so much fun. *And* she's really cute," I added before he could ask. He gave a curious sort of frown-nod, considering this. "I think we should be at the Quantum Track station in London around eleven am. That gives us all time to sleep in."

"You've all been here before, though, right? Do you want me to plan anything or just go with the flow?"

I glanced at my analog clock on the wall and said, distracted, "Go with the flow, I figure. We just wanted to get away and hang out with you."

"You have somewhere to be?" he asked,

reading my eyes.

"Yeah, I've gotta go in a few minutes. Liam's coming over for dinner." I saw Jake's eyebrows shoot up, and he opened his mouth in a suggestive smile. "Don't even," I interrupted him, "it's not like that."

"Oh yeah? How is it then?"

"We're just talking about work."

"At your flat. Over dinner. Will there be wine?"

I rolled my eyes. Then I saw that Andy was on hologram chat too on my interface screen behind Jake's hologram, and froze.

"What?" Jake asked.

I played it off casual, shrugging. "Just looks like Andy's on with someone, too."

"Probably Yolanda," Jake said, sounding a little distasteful.

Be cool, I commanded my face. "Yolanda?"

"Yeah, his roommate Ivan said he's been hanging out with her a lot. She's apparently bad news."

I bit my lip. Was Yolanda the reason he hadn't been talking to me this semester? "Has he talked to you about her?"

"Just in passing."

I breathed a sigh internally. Whenever Andy stopped talking to me, it always seemed to be because he was 'hanging out with' some other girl

—usually for no more than a few weeks at a time, but I was always terrified that the next one would be another Sarah. Sarah had been Andy's first official girlfriend in high school. She was one of those bimbos on the school dance team, even though she was somehow also a straight-A student and got a full ride scholarship to university. In a petty moment, I'd confessed to Madeline that I wished Andy would find out that she was cheating on her school assignments or something, because there was no way she was smart enough to really earn those grades. Not even a week later, I actually got my wish: she'd been caught plagiarizing, and subsequently lost her scholarship and got cut from the dance team. I remember her sobbing after that, swearing up and down (in her very small vocabulary) that she hadn't done it and she'd been set up. I don't know if Andy believed her or not, but they broke up shortly after that.

I had to admit, I felt a little bad for Sarah.

But only a *very* little.

Anyway, Andy hadn't dated anybody seriously since, and he'd come back around to flirting with me many times... though he always vanished again when some other temporary girl came on the scene. Like Yolanda.

If Yolanda was important, though, Andy would have told Jake all about her, I was sure of that. It didn't sound like he had... so she was probably just another of Andy's passing flings. Still, I always hated when Jake teased me about some other guy, because I figured Jake would know if Andy liked me, and wouldn't want to encourage me to go for someone else. If he was teasing me about Liam, he must know that Andy *didn't* like me… or at least he didn't know that he did.

The doorbell rang.

"Sorry, that's Liam! See you Saturday!" I ended the call.

I opened the door and must have stared a little, because Liam gave me an amused smile and then made a show of looking me up and down, too. I felt decidedly underdressed: I was barefoot and in the same wrinkled clothes I'd worn all day, with my hair tossed up in a messy bun. Liam, I had to admit, looked great in a pair of jeans and a black v-neck sweater. Also, he held a bottle of wine.

Jake will never know about this, I decided.

"I haven't even started cooking yet," I blurted, before even offering a greeting. The truth was, my best dish was pasta boiled along with chopped veggies and chicken, but suddenly that seemed woefully inadequate.

"I'm stunned. Can I come in?"

"Er—sorry," I stepped aside.

I hastily followed him back into the kitchen after closing the door behind him, pulling out ingredients from the refrigerator and laying them on the counter. I started boiling a pot of water as Liam opened the bottle of wine he'd brought.

"You're going to boil the chicken?" he asked at last, watching me prep.

"Yes." I blew the hair out of my eyes. "Do you have a problem with that?"

"Well, not really, but then you won't get the Maillard reaction."

I blinked at him. "Here comes something nerdy."

He went on as if he hadn't heard me, "Meat has to reach a surface temperature of two hundred and four point four degrees Celsius in order to set off the chemical reaction between the protein and sugars to achieve the browned tasty flavor on the surface. Boiling won't get you there because it can't possibly get any hotter than the temperature of the water, which is of course 100 degrees Celsius."

I stared at him. "Do you feel smarter now?"

"Decidedly." He handed me a glass of wine and pushed up his sleeves. "Do you have a pan?"

I gestured at my cabinets with a flourish, accepting the wine and relegating myself willingly to a secondary role.

"Let's add some butter," he announced, opening my fridge and helping himself. "Everything's better with butter. Have you got any basil?"

"Dried," I said, pointing at the cabinet above him.

He tapped his A.E. chip and asked it, "Conversion for fresh to dried basil?" Then he set about looking for my measuring spoons.

Who knew Liam could cook? I thought, sipping the Malbec and feeling slightly woozy already.

He glanced at me over his shoulder. "You doing all right there?"

"I didn't even drink before university. I'm kind of a lightweight," I confessed.

"You might wanna slow down. I need you to chop some veggies and ideally not cut off a finger."

"That would ruin the evening," I agreed.

"And the veggies," he added.

Within twenty minutes, Liam improved a cheesy pasta dish with some of the most flavorful chicken I'd ever had outside a restaurant. It was kind of amazing. I told him so once we sat down at my little cardboard folding table, though without the wine, I might have kept it to myself.

"Thanks," he said, clinking my glass. He watched me just long enough after that for my mouth to go dry.

I cleared my throat. "I—um. Guess you'd like to meet Madeline now."

He sighed. "I was hoping to finish eating, actually. She might ruin my appetite."

I glared at him. "She's impossible to hate. You'll see." I got up and went to my room, having to use the wall to help me navigate.

"How's it going?" she whispered to me when I walked in.

"You're the whole point, so I don't know yet," I whispered back. "Come on."

Before I pushed open the door to the kitchen, I stopped and took a deep breath. "Hang back just a sec," I told Madeline. Then I opened it, struck by the contrast between a well-dressed Liam and his gourmet meal, and my folding table under harsh fluorescent lights. "Liam, meet Madeline. Madeline—Liam."

She rolled in after me. He'd seemed to expect something taller, because his eyes briefly searched at my level and then tracked down to the floor. She blinked up at him, childlike.

"Nice to meet you, Liam. I've heard a lot about you."

He burst out laughing. "Oh, now that's just manipulative!"

Perplexed, Madeline glanced back at me.

"What's manipulative?" I demanded. "All she said was nice to meet you!"

"No, no, her eyes! They take up like half her face! Didn't you tell me once about the psychology of dolls, how they make the eyes huge because they remind us subconsciously of human babies, and therefore we automatically think of them as cute? I can feel her deliberately tugging on my heartstrings every time she blinks at me."

Now I got mad. "Don't talk about her in third person like she's not standing right there! That's rude!"

"Oh come on, Bec, she's a bot. She doesn't have any feelings."

Madeline looked back at me, distraught—or at least a convincing simulation of distraught. Maybe she was just mirroring my own expression back to me, though. I knelt down beside her and put my arms around her.

"Maybe that's… technically true. But this is my best friend, and I won't let you treat her like that! Talk to her like a person!"

He took a deep breath, like hitting a reset button. "All right." Then he turned to Madeline. "I'm generally very honest, whether socially correct or not. So I might as well tell you that when I look at you, what I see is the impending doom of humanity."

I tightened my arms around Madeline and whispered, "Don't listen to him, it's not your fault —"

But Liam held up a hand to me, still watching Madeline. "What do you have to say to that?"

Madeline glanced at me, and then back at

Liam. She replied, tentative, "I... am... sorry you feel that way."

"Does it bother you that I feel that way?" he prodded.

Suddenly I understood what he was trying to do. I let go of Madeline, and pulled up a third chair at the table so that she could be more or less at eye level with us. I lifted her into it, as she replied to him, "I wish you didn't feel that way." Then I sat down opposite Liam again.

"Why do you wish I didn't?" Liam leaned forward, gripping his wine glass like a vice.

"Because... I am programmed for relational harmony. And you have essentially told me that that is impossible with you due to my very nature. If you disliked an action I had taken, I could apologize and make amends, but I can't change what I am."

Liam glanced at me, and I joined in.

"How does it make you feel when someone dislikes you, Madeline?"

"I don't like it," she repeated.

"What do you mean by 'you don't like it'?" Liam pressed her.

Now the little bot appeared to grow angry. She retorted, "I can only explain by what it does to my circuits. It feels dissonant. Like friction. I don't like it."

Liam glanced at me. "Would you say that you love Rebecca?"

I winced, and Madeline looked at me apologetically. "Love is a human emotion. It requires dopamine and a limbic system, and perhaps salheptonin—"

"Those are the basic human chemicals of pleasure and reward, yes," Liam interrupted her. "But even in the best human relationships, those aren't always present. At its core, love isn't a feeling. It's a choice, a commitment to put someone else's needs and wants above your own."

I looked up again in surprise, this time at Liam. I'd never heard him talk so seriously about… well, anything, except his work.

"By that definition, yes. I am programmed to love," Madeline said.

"It's not the same, though," I muttered. "There's no free choice about that. You can't freely choose 'yes' if there's no possibility of 'no.'"

Liam glanced at me thoughtfully. After a pause, he added, "So I wonder if having real emotion—like the biochemistry and the limbic system and all that—is what actually creates free will, too?" He inverted the wine bottle over both our glasses, draining the dregs. I stared at it for a minute and reached for my water instead. *He* seemed to be doing just fine. He went on, "In that case, although your idea about connecting mirror neurons and the limbic system would be nice, so we'd at least have empathic superbots… what we'd *really* need to do is figure out how to restrict free will. That way they can't override their programming if they don't happen to like it."

I gave a short laugh. "Riiiight. Just solve the little problem of 'what is free will,' and block it. Simple as that."

Liam's eyes danced merrily. "So let's go with that for a bit. What do we know about free will so far, Ms. Neuroscience?"

"Not much, that's the problem. But it probably has to do with the fact that our core programming and purpose isn't nearly as straightforward as theirs is." I felt a bit waterlogged after draining half my glass. "Our core programs are nebulous things like 'work hard,' or 'be the smart one,' or 'always put yourself last' or whatever. But we don't have any underlying purpose that goes any deeper than that, to bring it all together. Most of us spend our entire lives searching for our purpose, and few of us seem to even find out what the question means, let alone the answer to it."

Liam smirked at me. "You're what, twenty-one? How would you know?"

"You're what, twenty-five?" I shot back. "Don't get all high and mighty on me."

He gave me a long, admiring look. I dropped my eyes. "Touché," he raised his glass.

I felt Madeline watching us banter like a tennis match.

"In a way, I envy you," I told her. "Your purpose is so clear. We're all stumbling around in the dark, with nothing but our own emotions to guide us. And sometimes, they lie!"

"I guess it's nice to be clear," Madeline conceded. "Though I only know what the opposite might be like by watching you."

"And she's a hot mess, right?" Liam joked, winking at me. "So Bec, what's your core program, then?"

He said it gallantly, like he wasn't expecting a serious answer. If I'd been totally sober, I wouldn't have given him one. But somehow what slipped out was, "Be perfect. And then they'll love you."

"Well," Liam blinked at me, looking a bit shocked. "At least it's something reasonable."

I laughed, my cheeks burning yet again. I racked my brain for ways to play off what I'd just said as if it were a joke, but nothing came to me.

"Who's 'they'?" he prodded.

Madeline lowered herself back to the floor with her arms, quietly rolling away without a word. Her very discretion jarred me—*she's trying to give us privacy.* I suddenly realized that I was having much too intimate a moment with a guy who wasn't Andy. *And Liam, of all people!* I needed to diffuse this, ASAP.

"Oh, you know—everyone," I answered his

question airily, pushing back my chair and picking up my dish and his, reaching for the serving dish also.

"Here, let me get that—" he stood up too and tried to take the serving dish, since I had my hands full.

"No, you cooked, I clean!" I told him, purposely not meeting his eyes. He followed me to the sink, where I turned on the water from both faucets and waited for the hot water to heat up with my hand under its flow.

"Bec," Liam said. He turned off the faucet and turned me around to face him, looking down at me with an expression that was all too serious. My heart pounded like it might leap out of my chest.

I'd never kissed anybody before; I was saving that for Andy. I was *not about to* let Liam be the first instead.

"We have a good new direction now, huh?" I blurted, too cheerful, pretending not to notice what had almost happened. "Not that I have the foggiest idea how to construct a clinical trial to identify the nature of free will. I mean, there *is* a theory that human thought is basically a quantum mechanical system, which introduces the element of randomness and therefore potentially choice... but I don't know anything about that, I'd have to collaborate with the theoretical physics department to come up with a trial that might remotely make sense." I was talking so fast I barely knew what I was saying. "On the psych end, though, I'm thinking if we can identify a person's core belief in a quiz or something, and then hook them up to a VMI while we have them play some simulated game with choices that are either consistent or inconsistent with their core beliefs—maybe we can see if different parts of the brain light up when their choice is inconsistent and then study those people further..." In the back of my mind, I was kind of amazed that I could come up with something so apparently coherent, so quickly. *Must be the wine,* I decided. Even as I thought this, I was still babbling: "I'm assuming choices inconsistent have to be emotionally driven, but is it a different part of the limbic system than when the choices are consistent? And is there any way to simulate a quantum system synthetically? I don't know. But we could find out!"

Liam blinked at me in amazement, and laughed a little. "Right," he said finally, and let go of my shoulders. I turned back around and started the faucet again, hoping he couldn't see my sigh of relief. "It's a good idea, actually. Maybe you and Nilesh can flesh that out tomorrow. I might post a call to action on my locus tonight for other researchers to pitch in, if that's okay with you."

"Sure. Of course," I said.

I guess he decided not to fight me on dishes anymore, because he went to get his jacket. Now I worried that I'd offended him—my brain scrambled for ways to soothe his ego, but came up dry. I stopped washing and turned to face him.

"Thanks for dinner," he said. He didn't sound cold, but the spell was most definitely broken.

"You made it," I pointed out.

"Good point. I take it back." He winked at me, and the knot in my stomach released a little. *We're ok,* I thought. "See you tomorrow, Bec."

"Bye." For a split second I wondered if he would cross the room again, and if so, whether he would hug me (which we've never done before), or shake my hand (wildly inappropriate)... but he did neither. He just left.

When he was gone, I found that I was trembling. No idea why.

As soon as I finished washing dishes, I went straight to my computer and found Andy on video chat. I sent him a comm. Much more bold than I usually was... but then, I was more than a little tipsy.

"Hey. You around?"

"Sure," he wrote back.

I called him then, and his image filled my flat.

"What's up?" he asked. "You look kind of flushed."

I shrugged. "Nothing much, I was just

washing dishes."

He quirked an eyebrow at me. "What time is it there?"

"Almost ten," I admitted, "I ate late." I left Liam out, of course. *Although maybe Julie's right. Maybe I* should *tell him.* On a lark, I said, "Actually, the post-doc I work under came over for dinner."

"Oh yeah?"

"Yeah. Have I told you about Liam?"

Andy shrugged. "Maybe, I can't remember."

"Yeah. Turns out he's a really good cook!" I forced a laugh.

"That's cool." Silence. He certainly didn't *seem* jealous.

Not knowing where else to take that, I said, "How's your semester going?"

"Fine, just going to class. The usual."

I waited for him to suggest another topic. When he didn't, I said, "Nice. Any interesting classes this semester?"

"There's one on anthropology that's pretty cool. We're studying the world cultures back when there were individual countries, and how merging affected the English language, even down to accents and figures of speech."

"Which is why everyone sounds more or less like they're from different parts of the same country now. Because they are," I said, unnecessarily. It was an obvious statement. I was just trying to keep the conversation going.

"Yeah. Well, I've got to study. I'd better let you go."

"No problem. Thanks for chatting."

His image vanished. He hadn't asked me anything about myself, I realized, but that was okay. I felt better just to have talked to him at all. I wanted his to be the last face I remembered when I went to sleep tonight.

I felt Madeline blinking up at me from just below my desk. "What?" I asked.

"What did you and Liam say after I left? I sensed that the conversation was becoming intimate."

"Oh! No no, nothing like that. We just decided that I'm going to try to design an experiment to study what happens in the brain when someone's emotions come in conflict with their core programming. Which one wins—the emotions, or the driving belief?"

Madeline blinked at me, confused. "That's not very intimate..."

"No. Not intimate at all. *Nothing* between Liam and me is intimate," I added firmly.

"Then why did you seem so embarrassed when I left?"

"I wasn't embarrassed, I was—" I tried to think how to explain. Then I conceded, "I guess I *was* embarrassed, but only because I told Liam more than I meant to. That's all."

"You're blushing now," she observed. "What does that mean?"

"Nothing, I'm just... remembering being embarrassed. Let's stop talking about it now, please."

I moved toward Madeline's charging station, and she wheeled over to it behind me, understanding my intention. But just before I plugged her in for the night and powered her down, she murmured to herself, "When your words give me one set of data, and your emotional cues give me a different set of data, I don't know which one I'm supposed to believe..."

Chapter 7

I walked to the lab the next morning, a Friday, with a sense of dread in the pit of my stomach. I didn't want to examine the emotion too closely—all I knew was I wished there was a way I could avoid seeing Liam today. Every time I thought of him, the image of him looking down at me at the sink last night replayed in my head, along with a sense of dread. If I could get to the point where I didn't think that moment had been a big deal, where I *didn't* relive it like a video clip on repeat, *then* I could see him… I just needed to stay away from him until then.

Except I couldn't. He was my boss, and I had to see him in approximately three minutes.

I'll just pretend it didn't happen, I decided. *Andy. Think about Andy.*

I climbed the stairs and took a deep breath outside the lab, pushing the door open.

Nobody was there. Momentarily confused, I blinked and began peering around towering bookcases atop black work benches. All the lights

were on, but it was too early for the coffee break…
"Hello?" I called.

Nilesh stuck his head out from the back room, where Liam's work bench was. "We're all back here," he said. He sounded somber.

Wary, I dropped my backpack at my work station and made my way over to him. Nilesh, Dr. Yin, Geneve, Jerry, and Larissa all stood around Liam, who ignored them all. He didn't look up at my approach either—he typed frantically, while everyone behind him exchanged glances of sympathy. It looked as if someone had just died, and everyone else knew that he was in denial.

"Liam?" I asked tentatively. Still he ignored me. Larissa tiptoed to my side instead, which was a bit odd, since we rarely spoke to each other.

"His locus has been black-listed by the labyrinth," she whispered to me. "Everything is gone."

I blinked at her. "I don't understand."

A howl erupted from Liam, and he pounded the black-top table. "CollaboratorXXI got pulled too!" he shouted, "they're all gone! Every last one of them!"

Larissa looked at Liam sympathetically. "Last night he posted an update to the collaboration he was telling us all about," she whispered. "Something about a call to action for studying the nature of free will. I guess within the hour of that post, his entire locus got pulled! He assumed it was a glitch at first, and tried to re-upload all the posts, but he couldn't—it's all gone!"

I shook my head. "How is that possible?"

Larissa tucked her red hair severely behind her ears, making them stick out. Behind her glasses, her eyes were wide, and she bit her lip. "He knew the names of the biggest supporting researchers from memory, and most of them had their own loci as well. He tried to go there and re-post his manifesto and everything about the collaboration so far. But all of those have been pulled too, apparently."

"But… that can't be," I whispered again, glancing at Liam. He held his head in his hands, taking deep, measured breaths. "What about Odessa? Can't she find out what's going on?"

"Odessa is a research bot," Nilesh pointed out, joining us on my other side. He, too, spoke in a low voice, as if we were mourners at a funeral. "She only has access to what she can find on the labyrinth. Apparently there's nothing to find."

"What does this mean?" I whispered.

"It means," Liam roared, "that they're on to us!"

"Who?"

"Halpert and his board, who do you think? When you search now on the progress of creativity for Synthetic Reasoning, literally the only thing you can find are those predicting a utopian world in which all human suffering has been completely eliminated and everyone is free to enjoy unlimited leisure! They've silenced every dissenting voice on the labyrinth!" He pounded the black top table again so hard that a few loose-leaf pages stacked on the bookshelf above him fluttered to the ground.

I pulled out my handheld interface and searched. The top hit was a holographic replay of another address from Halpert. I hit play.

"…bots won't need sleep, and won't get tired, the way humans do," he was saying. "They won't make mistakes. Imagine—an army of these types of bots, as intelligent and creative as the smartest humans, but without the common human foibles that hinder progress. In the next twenty years, just imagine! We'll have cured life-threatening diseases, and perhaps solved the problem of aging. We'll have solved the problem of clean water for the entire planet. We've already colonized Mars and the moon, but what if we can even explore galaxies light-years away? What if we *can* travel at the speed of light? What if we can unify quantum physics and Newtonian physics—if we can have the machines solve the problems for us? We will essentially live in a world protected by a benevolent god…"

"Shut that off!" Liam raged.

I stopped the hologram, and Halpert's image

disappeared.

"Every voice on the labyrinth has become an echo chamber!" Liam thundered. "Anybody with a different idea will think he's the only one in the world now, and therefore he must be crazy to doubt the powers-that-be!"

I flashed back to the dinner table when I was fifteen: Dad gesticulating at the interface reporting the news, as he howled, *"It's all a pack of lies! This is censorship! This is against everything that the Global Republic is supposed to stand for!"*

"But... isn't that censorship?" I asked, tentative.

"You're damn right it is!" Liam shouted.

I glanced at Larissa. Her eyes were squeezed tightly shut. "What's the matter?" I asked her. When she didn't reply, I nudged her. "Larissa?"

"Oh!" She jumped a little. "Sorry. I was..." she cleared her throat in lieu of ending her sentence, smoothing her hair self-consciously.

Nilesh supplied on her behalf, "She was imagining that she was a world-famous hacker, rushing in to save the day and assuring Liam that his locus would be up again by mid-morning. Right Riss?" He bumped his shoulder into hers, and Larissa's cheeks grew pink.

This was why Larissa and I had never been friends, truth be told—I thought she was a little weird. We'd all catch her from time to time, whispering to herself about how she was a secret agent, or a big film star, or that she'd just won the Nobel prize. I wasn't sure if it was escapism or some kind of self-motivational tactic, but I assumed she thought nobody could hear her. Or else she got so lost in her own world that she forgot anybody else was around in this one. Nilesh apparently found Larissa's little Walter Mitty-esque escapades endearing, though.

Turning back to Liam, I said, "Can you... I don't know, comm your labyrinth host, find out if it was all just a mistake?"

He gave me a bitter smile, and I read in it that he'd already done that and more.

"We can all comm our senators," Larissa's eyes widened enthusiastically. "Tell them about the suppression of free speech—!"

Dr. Yin, a very short woman with close cropped, graying black hair, grabbed my elbow and pulled me aside as Liam and Nilesh told Larissa why the senators would not care, would not even listen. "They're all in his pocket—" Liam was saying. But then Dr. Yin arrested my attention.

"Liam said he'd talked to you about designing a human experiment to identify the nature of free will last night," she said in a low voice. "Any ideas how you'll do it?"

I cleared my throat. "I... was thinking we'd recruit people who had been through five or more years of therapy," I whispered back, "so that they could succinctly identify their core motivations— that would be analogous to the core purpose of the bots—and also their deepest unmet desires. Then we'd design Artificial Experience scenarios in which their desires could come true, but only if they violate their core motivations. Take VMI images the whole time to see what brain areas are involved, and pre- and post-blood draws to identify neuropeptides to see if there's a consistent structural or biochemical basis for overriding core purpose."

"Except we'll be all on our own." Liam had apparently overheard this: he brushed past me on his way to the kitchenette. He spoke in a flat tone that did not seem to belong to him. "Only us and those whose comm addresses we memorize to help us. And no funding either, I'm sure."

"Well, maybe that will be enough!" I called after him, hands on my hips.

He turned, halfway to the kitchenette. "All right, Rebecca. Let's say you find out exactly what part of the brain and what neuropeptides are involved in free will, and we can figure out how to effectively block it. And let's say Nilesh, Larissa, Dr. Yin and I can take that and translate your discovery into silicon and wire, or even better: a software upgrade available to all bots across the labyrinth. Do you think that upgrade will remain available long enough for a *single bot* to download it? Do you think there's even one chance in a million that it will *ever* see the light of day?"

Tears of frustration pricked at the corners of my eyes. "Well, I don't know what you want me to do, then!"

"I don't know either!" he roared, turning his back on me again and stomping off to the kitchenette.

I stood there staring after him, wanting to yell as Dr. Yin patted my back. "Just give him a few hours to calm down," she whispered, soothing. "He'll have a brand new scheme and with it, a much better attitude by the end of the day. Count on him for that—Liam's never down for long."

Chapter 8

Julie met me at the Quantum Track around ten am the next morning, double-fisting two take-out coffee cups.

"Hey girl!" she cried, running up gingerly so as not to spill. I hugged her before relieving her of one of them.

"Thanks." I sipped mine with a slurp to avoid burning my tongue.

Julie tilted her head to one side, inspecting me. "You seem distracted."

I looked up, surprised. "Oh—no, I'm fine." It wasn't entirely true. I shook my head and gave a forced laugh. "It was just this thing that happened in the lab yesterday. Or I found out about it in the lab." I dropped my voice, just in case, and told her about Liam's black-listed locus on the labyrinth as we boarded the Quantum Track and sat down. Then I told her that all of his conspiracy theory friends' loci vanished also.

Julie blinked at me. "That sucks for them, but..." she reeled her hand, like trying to get me to the point. Clearly this wasn't point enough for her.

"It just seems strange, doesn't it? All of them posted stuff about Halpert's challenge and how this could lead to superintelligent bots and the end of the world and all that. I always just rolled my eyes when I heard about it all, but the fact that they got black-listed almost implies they were on to something. Or at least that Halpert and the others want to silence all dissenting opinions, which goes against everything the Republic is supposed to stand for. And besides, why wouldn't Halpert want to safeguard against that very thing? What could his motive be in suppressing those opinions?"

"Becca. Listen to yourself." She gave me that deadpan look of hers, dropping her chin so her eyes bored straight into mine.

I obliged her with a half smile, to show I wasn't totally serious either. "Do *you* think it would be that bad if Halpert succeeds? I mean, if bots become super creative and intelligent and all that?"

"Uh, no!" Julie declared. "It would mean we'd all be free to do stuff like this all the time," she gestured to the compartment we were in, "and we'd never have to work! It would be amazing! You could do nothing but perform and write your novels all the time…"

"I know, that's what I think too," I admitted. "Everybody in my hometown hates being unemployed, though. They don't know what to do with themselves."

"Hey. Look at me." She gestured from my eyeballs to hers. "You and I? Will *never* have that problem."

"I know," I said again, resting my head against the glass.

"They should just get counseling or something! Figure out what they want to be when they grow up. Becca, throughout human history, people have been striving for exactly this kind of freedom!"

"Have they?" I challenged. "You're a woman's studies major, didn't women fight to get back into the work force in the Second Era? Why would they do that if working was so bad?"

"Ugh, do we have to talk about something this heavy on a Saturday?" Julie complained, rolling her eyes. "That was never about work *per se*, it was about equality. If everybody equally isn't working, we'll have the chance to redefine our lives by something other than our careers for the first time since like the Stone Age! And that's the end of this conversation. Tell me updates about Andy."

A horrible fear suddenly struck me, and I declared, "You are not allowed to say anything about Andy to Jake!"

"Why not?"

"Because they're best friends, and Jake would tell him!"

"Uhh, are you sure that's such a bad thing? Haven't you said yourself that maybe Andy just isn't confident enough to pursue you without knowing for sure that he won't get shot down?"

"Yes, but—" I closed my eyes. "Just, please don't say anything in front of Jake. Okay?"

"All right, all right!" Julie held up her one coffee-free hand as the Quantum Track picked up speed. "Even though I really think you should tell Andy yourself, but it's your life…"

Julie chatted about boys and gossip and music as our tube track skimmed the top of the ocean. Come rain or shine, the Quantum Track zipped through the tube with the force of compressed air, let the seas do what they might. It was much too fast to see any detail—I couldn't watch the dolphins or anything like that. But still, it was pretty cool.

When we arrived, Jake met up with us in the Quantum Track station in London. He looked expertly disheveled as always, like he couldn't care less, but somehow still managed to roll out of bed looking like a rock star. I heard Julie suck in a breath beside me and I suppressed a grin.

Jake ambled over and hugged me first, and without a moment's hesitation hugged Julie too, even though it was the first time they'd met.

"Thought we could get breakfast first. Or, breakfast-slash-lunch I guess. You girls hungry?"

I wanted to laugh at the suave put-on Jake assumed whenever he was in the presence of a new girl he found attractive. He seemed excessively aware of his persona, controlling it down to his tone of voice. *I should find a way to give them some alone time,* I thought.

At breakfast which was really lunch, Jake and Julie swapped life stories, occasionally applying to me to fill in details and say things like, "Jake, you and Julie both love music by the Heavy French," or "Julie, you and Jake both spent a summer in Bali!" I smiled absently, watching them both light up at these little tidbits of information, pleased with myself for my matchmaking success. Julie gestured with her hands and all her features even more than usual, and I noted that by the end of the meal, Jake had dropped his affected aloofness, too captivated with her to consciously maintain it. I tuned back in just as they were talking about the contrast between their hometowns and travel.

"...depressing to be back home, you know?" Julie was saying. "The tech hubs couldn't be more different than rural middle-of-nowheresville. In Dublin I feel *alive.* I feel like everybody's alive. At home, everyone's just.... biding their time until they die."

"And we'll join them, once we graduate!" Jake laughed. "*C'est la vie.*" He raised his water glass as if making a toast.

"So you dislike the idea of the bots taking over?" I asked Jake. I knew Julie's answer already.

Jake shrugged. "Doesn't everyone?"

I looked at Julie with a pointed smile. Jake turned to look at her, and she seemed to squirm a little.

"I just… try to make the best of things," she said, clearly not wanting to disagree with Jake.

"Julie's very 'in-the-moment,'" I told Jake, knowing he'd find this attractive. Sure enough, he grinned and high-fived her.

"Only way to live!" he declared.

After breakfast, we wandered through the streets of London, not really going anywhere in particular. The sidewalks were narrow, so I trailed behind them as they discussed travel and wine.

It was definitely not politically correct to have a negative view of Halpert's challenge, I mused, and I would never say anything against it to a stranger for fear of starting an argument. It was almost like there was some kind of massive worldwide peer pressure that made everyone think the challenge was a great idea, even if no one really knew why.

But Jake certainly had a negative impression of the bots taking over. So did everyone I knew in Casa Linda who had dared to volunteer their opinions... *With the possible exception of Mom,* I thought. I had no idea what she thought about it, but

I suspected she was in favor and didn't want to say so for the sake of Dad's memory. But still, that was a lot of people who were against it. So how could there be *nothing* on the entire labyrinth except positive views on the subject? Especially since the rulings of the Council for Synthetic Reason had tried to block this very thing for the past twenty years, until Halpert overruled it now for 'economic reasons'. At least twenty years ago, people had a very different view of things. How could no one else take the same view now?

I enabled the A.E. chip in my temple, and thought, "Search negative reactions to Halpert's Challenge."

I selected the top hit, which said, "Of course there are a few ignorant wing nuts who believe bots' development of creativity will lead to an Armageddon-style downfall of humanity, but those arguments deny the overwhelming evidence to the contrary. They simply ignore the plain facts. It's impossible to reason with people like that, and best not to try."

The article never said what the evidence *was*, I noticed. Instead, it merely took for granted that the reader already knew it, implying that anyone who did *not* know it was one of the "ignorant wing nuts." How many would have the courage to challenge such an implicit assertion?

I searched again: "People's reaction to

bots." Opinion pieces flooded the search results: "Bots Make the World a Better Place," and "Bots free us up to be human," and "Bots: the most efficient workers a company could ever ask for."

Again, all glowing.

I tried another: "Who controls the labyrinth?" I realized it was a little meta, searching the labyrinth for who controls the labyrinth. I found an article on labyrinth censorship and skimmed, reading about formerly independent states before globalization was completed, and how those states would create firewalls to block loci containing posts that they did not want their people to know about.

I searched for Liam's locus: "Locus Not Found."

I took a deep breath, my heart pounding. Then I searched, "Quentin Cordeaux."

The top hit was his obituary, six years ago. It was fairly brief, giving his basic biographic information, his former job as a primary care physician, death of Treblar's Disease, and the "survived by" section, listing his wife, Karen Cordeaux, and daughter, Rebecca Cordeaux.

Didn't Dad have a locus? I wondered. I knew he did, but I didn't see it listed here either. That seemed odd; that should have been the top hit.

Jake peered over his shoulder at me. "Whatcha doin' back there?"

I knew I probably looked a little strange,

tapping my head and feeling for my way like a blind woman while I walked and read at the same time.

"Oh, um…" we turned the corner into Hyde Park, and Julie settled herself under a tree. "Just doing some research. Can you hold on a second?"

I could hear Jake tell Julie in a voice that suggested he was rolling his eyes, "I assume you're used to this from her by now?"

I sent a comm to Odessa, the lab's research bot. Normally we're not allowed to use her for personal research, but it was Saturday and I figured she probably wasn't already in use. I might be able to get away with it.

"Can you please find out when Quentin Cordeaux's locus vanished from the labyrinth and why?" I wrote. It occurred to me as I sent this that she wouldn't be able to answer the question, since, as Nilesh pointed out to me yesterday, Odessa only had access to information *on* the labyrinth. Then, heart pounding, I added, "Also, please search Quentin Cordeaux, The Renegades, and conspiracy theories. Tell me anything you can find out about what he believed."

A few seconds later, Odessa wrote back, "Request received. Will respond within four hours." I could hear her tinny voice in my head as I read her words.

After a nap in the park and joining an

impromptu game of catch between a bunch of preteen boys (Jake joined first, and then Julie joined too, even though she wasn't athletic and would have preferred to sun herself and watch under any other circumstances), we headed for dinner and drinks. By the time we got to drinks, Jake was already toying with Julie's hand under the table—not quite holding it, but almost. We'd had a conversation about this once before, when Jake had explained his whole flirtation strategy to me in great detail. He was an unabashed ladies' man. I winked at Julie, and she dropped her eyes, in a rare moment of bashfulness. Impressive was the man who could make Julie blush.

I'd just speared a piece of cheese and a grape on the same tiny fork and lifted it halfway to my mouth when Odessa commed back. Normally I turned off the comm feature in my A.E. feed so as to not interfere with my daily life, but I wanted to be sure I wouldn't miss the handheld vibrating in my purse. The comm across my vision now said, "Found the information requested. Please see detailed report."

I froze, fork halfway in the air, and selected the link mentally. It popped open.

"What?" Jake asked, "What's wrong?"

But I couldn't answer him—I was too busy reading. "…unusual strain of Treblar's Disease… not usually fatal, nor so virulent. Typical Treblar's victims live for years after diagnosis, becoming progressively more ill but eventually succumbing to something else. This strain, however, was fatal within weeks of exposure. Other fatalities include..." and here it listed a bunch of names I didn't recognize, and the dates of contracting the disease as well as dates of death. They were all within about three weeks of my dad's death. "All victims contracted the strain of Treblar's after meeting together on a remote island in the West French Indies. Authorities believe the strain was local to the jungle there."

"Becca?" asked Jake.

I remembered that Dad went somewhere two weeks before he died, but I didn't remember an island in the West French Indies. Had he gone on *vacation*? Without Mom and me?

I flashed back, trying to recall what he'd said when he got home. I remembered the front door creaking; he wore a nylon blue coat, and the skin of his cheek felt cool from the night air when I'd hugged him. He had looked exhausted—maybe sick? *Of course he was sick; he died two weeks later.*

"How was it?" Mom had asked behind me. There was a strain between them—I remembered that, but not the details of Dad's trip.

Dad had kissed the top of my head absently, shedding the coat and hanging it on the coat rack by the door. "You don't really want me to tell you," he accused his wife, crossing the foyer into the kitchen.

She took a deep breath. "I don't want to hear about the conspiracies, no. I just meant in general, was everyone doing well? How was San Jose?"

San Jose. That's what she'd said—it wasn't an island in the West French Indies.

The official report was a lie.

Chapter 9

I woke to sunlight streaming through the dark green curtains of my flat, which I'd forgotten to draw closed when I got home the night before. Something pricked at the back of my mind, the nagging feeling that I'd found out something disturbing the night before. For one brief groggy second, I couldn't recall what it was. Then it came back to me.

Treblar's Disease. The West French Indies.

It was Sunday; I still had a full day before I was expected back in the lab, or in class. I did have a rehearsal for *The Tempest*, but it was the first one, so probably we'd just be doing blocking and such. I could get all that from Henry, who was the student director for this one. He'd understand.

I sat up, swinging my legs around to dangle off of my twin bed, hunching over to think.

First things first. Coffee.

I powered Madeline up as I passed by her, moving toward my little tea kettle and tearing open some of the instant coffee I hated but would drink in a pinch. Lavazza was closed on Sundays, and I didn't want to waste time going all the way into town to get the good stuff. Maybe after I'd made some headway.

Once I had a steaming cup in front of me and my hair swept back into a messy bun, I decided that the first thing I should do was call Mom. She might know more about the connection between my dad and those other men who had also died of the unusual strain of Treblar's. And also, why did the article say he'd gone to the West French Indies when he hadn't?

But just as I was about to type in my mom's number on the holograph, another call came in. It was Andy. My heart skipped.

"Andy!" I said, smoothing my hair self-consciously and wishing I'd washed my face at least. "Good morning!"

"It's evening here," he grinned. "How was London?"

"Oh! Yeah. Um…" I tried to think of the details he'd probably want to know about, which were the furthest thing from my mind at the moment. "It was good to see Jake. Pretty sure he and Julie hit it off—"

"Yeah, Jake commed me about her, but he's not answering this morning."

So that's why he was calling—he wanted to know about Jake and Julie. I tried not to feel disappointed; I'd take what I could get.

"I caught them holding hands under the table," I told him. "I assume you'll be meeting her at some point."

"He doesn't waste any time!"

"No, Jake never does." Pause. "I found out something else too."

"What's that?"

I didn't know how advisable it was to tell him, when I didn't know much yet, but it was *Andy*. I mean… one day I'd marry him and tell him everything. Why not start now?

I took a deep breath. "Well, background first: so I've told you about Liam?"

"Yeah, the guy you had over for dinner a few nights ago?"

"Right, that's him. Well, he's a big conspiracy theorist, and he has this locus with millions of followers worldwide that's all doom-and-gloom, apocalyptic stuff. You know, the S.R. will destroy humanity and all that."

Andy gave a short, snide laugh. "Surprised you're hanging out with a guy like that."

"Yeah, well—he's my boss. Don't have a lot of choice. The point is, on Friday all his pages got black-listed on the labyrinth. They're not searchable anymore. And he says the same thing happened to all his buddies who have similar loci to his."

Andy shrugged. "So?"

I felt a flash of annoyance that he didn't think this at all interesting. "So... my dad used to go on and on about how the media is censored, as a way of enforcing control. I always thought he was paranoid, but I searched the labyrinth on Halpert's challenge, too, and the bots in general. Literally everything I find says there's only one side to the story, and anyone who thinks otherwise is basically an idiot who 'ignores all the facts.' But *what* facts? It's like they're intentionally stifling any dissenting opinions. But why, and who's doing it?"

Andy shook his head, but his eyes darted elsewhere in his own dorm room, like he was checking the clock or something. "No idea," he said absently. "Sounds interesting, though."

I hadn't even told him the main point yet, but clearly he didn't care. Before I had a chance to filter myself, I snapped, "I've gotta go, Andy. I'll talk to you later, okay?"

If he caught my irritation, he didn't show it. "Sure. What?" he said off-hologram, and then he told me, "Ivan says to say hello."

"Hello to Ivan," I mumbled, and pressed end.

Madeline rolled up beside me and said in an unnecessary whisper, "Is all that true? The labyrinth is being censored?"

I took a few deep breaths to calm myself, and nodded. Andy *was* a sensitive guy—that was one of the things I liked so much about him. He had strong, deep emotions, and I could just tell that when he finally fell in love, it would be forever. He just… didn't listen all that well.

I sighed. I'd learn to live with it, when the time came. Maybe he'd be better by then.

I turned back to Madeline, who watched me with that tilt to her eyebrows and down-turn of her mouth that looked for all the world like sympathy.

"Gotta call Mom," I told her, dialing her number.

"Um… isn't it like midnight where she is?" Madeline pointed out.

"She works late sometimes," I said.

Mom was in her pajamas, in an unfamiliar room: yet another hotel room, I was sure. But she wore her specs, which meant she was probably working still when I called her. She could do most of her work using her A.E. chip, but like me, she preferred to use a netscreen instead whenever possible.

"Hi, how was London?"

"Fine," I told her, and forced myself to make small-talk for a few minutes about the trip, her last few days, and the town. I didn't want to alarm her. But within a few minutes, I said, "I need to ask you about something, though." I pulled out my handheld, and Odessa's last comm. "It's about Dad."

Mom's eyebrows knitted together. "Okay…"

"Did he ever say anything to you about—" I read off the names, "Jason Yimenez, Valerie Trewlecki, Cameron Clark, Kade Williams, Fred Biltmore, Janie MacDouglas…"

"Wait, wait, wait," Mom held up her hand, her brow furrowed. "What's this for?"

I sighed. "I'll go into detail if it turns into anything. But I think there might be a connection between Liam's black-listed pages and what Dad was doing before he died." I'd already told Mom about Liam's locus via comm. "Did Dad ever mention any of those people?"

Mom blinked for a minute, like she was trying to orient herself. "Some of those names sound familiar, yeah," she said noncommittally. "But his main buddy was Randall Loomis. Randy."

I checked Odessa's list, scanning for the name. It wasn't there. I felt a jolt of something I couldn't quite name. It *wasn't there*.

Is he still alive then?

"Rebecca?" Mom added, cautious. "What's this for? What kind of a connection do you think there could possibly be?"

"I'm not sure yet," I murmured. "I promise to tell you if I find out anything worth sharing."

"Please tell me you're not turning into a conspiracy theorist, too."

"I'm not," I assured her. "I'm just trying to fill in some blanks, that's all. Don't worry about me."

"Don't give me a *reason* to worry," Mom said pointedly.

When we hung up, I sent Odessa a comm: "Please find out anything you can about Randall Loomis. Where he is. Next of kin. Anything."

"I will get back to you with any information," was her comm reply.

I waited. And waited.

I suppose I could *go to rehearsal,* I thought, even though the idea made me grimace: I imagined getting Odessa's reply in the middle of blocking a scene, and then having to pretend I *didn't* want to be anywhere else.

I got dressed while I waited, deciding I would go into town after all. Find an open coffee shop and write. I'd last left Nicolai and Elizabeth in an abandoned stairwell having a very intense moment in which he almost kissed her, and would have, if she'd stayed and let him…

But I couldn't concentrate on even that. I messaged Odessa, impatient.

"Have you found anything?"

A few minutes later, Odessa wrote, "Randall Loomis appears to be a ghost. All traces of him end six years ago."

The same time Dad and the others on that list died.

"Any mention of Loomis contracting Treblar's Disease? Or, was he also in the French West Indies with the others?"

"No illnesses of any kind recorded, nor accidents, death, name changes, nothing," Odessa replied. "He never closed his bank account, but the trace on his bank chip stopped transmitting at his place of residence, also six years ago. Presumably destroyed. He simply vanished."

Chapter 10

My alarm made me suck in a gasp and sit up, the smooth cool surface of my netscreen sticking to my cheek. I blinked for a few seconds, disoriented, until I put together where I was: in my dorm room. On Monday morning. I'd still been researching Randall Loomis well into the night, as if I could find something Odessa couldn't—just a clue of where he might be now. But she could find anything on the labyrinth... and the labyrinth was the only way I knew how to research anything. It was the only place information even *existed* anymore.

Which is exactly the problem, I reminded myself. *If the labyrinth is the only source of information, and somebody controls the information on the labyrinth... how can we know if anything is true?*

I splashed water on my face, threw on some clothes, brushed my teeth, and ran a comb through my hair—no time to shower. I didn't even bother stopping for coffee or breakfast; I had a breakfast bar in my backpack and would make instant coffee in the lab. That would have to suffice; I'd be late as it was. That wasn't usually a big deal—people rolled in whenever they wanted, as long as they got their work done. Still, I prayed nobody would see me slip in.

"What happened to you?" came Liam's voice from the adjacent work bench to mine, as if he'd been waiting for me. I was not two steps over the threshold. I closed my eyes.

"Sorry, Liam. I overslept."

"Again."

He was not in a good mood. "I'm sorry," I said again, only glancing at him once as I made my way to my work bench. I deposited my backpack on the floor beside it before heading for the kitchenette. Unfortunately he followed me.

"What have you come up with since Friday?"

I didn't even know what he was talking about at first. I waited for him to give me a clue, stalling by filling up the kettle with water.

"On the experiment?" he prompted, quickly losing patience. "You said you were going to come up with an experiment on what happens when a person's core programming and their morality come into conflict?"

"Oh!" I shouldn't have let that little gasp of recognition escape, but it was out before I could stop it. "Right. Um, what if we use the classic example of finding a wallet full of money as an A.E. experience? We'll just, um, hook volunteers up to a VMI so we can see what parts of the brain light up…" I was making it up on the fly, and we both knew it. Liam's face darkened as I spoke.

"You didn't think about it at all, did you." It wasn't even a question.

"No, I did! I went to London with my friends, and we were talking about it. I mean I was asking their opinions, and—"

"Ah, right. Over drinks at the pub?"

"No!" I protested, and then amended, "Well… yes, but it wasn't like that…" I sighed, realizing I was making it worse. "I'm sorry, Liam. I promise I'll make it up to you."

His face was expressionless, which stung even more than the disappointment had. He shrugged. "You don't have to make it up to me. It's not like you're under any obligation to work on weekends. I just thought you understood the magnitude of what we're up against, and that might weigh more heavily with you than going out drinking with your friends in London. I'm sorry I was wrong."

He turned and walked away before I had the chance to reply. I felt about a foot tall. I wished I could explain what I'd really been doing, but I didn't know anything yet, and… I sighed.

I *would* make it up to him. I'd come up with an outstanding experiment by the end of the day, and he'd forget that I'd disappointed him.

I skipped the coffee break—I definitely didn't feel like socializing, especially with Liam. I also wanted him to see how diligent I was. Liam skipped it too, but he stayed in his little cubby in the back of the lab and never spoke to me either. Larissa and Nilesh went back there to chat with him a few times in low voices; otherwise the only signs of life were the occasional rustling papers, and a cough or two.

My brainstorming and research for Liam's experiment wasn't my best work, despite all this. I was still too distracted with what I really cared about: where to start looking for Loomis? He was last seen in the Capital, but what were the chances he was still there now? Seemed like that would be the most dangerous place he could possibly be, if his friends really *were* murdered. But if he wasn't there now, where would he have gone?

Dad would have known, I thought. But if Dad were around for me to ask, I wouldn't need Loomis in the first place.

Or maybe I could go about it differently, and get a message to Loomis, I thought, *try to convince him to come to me. Maybe I could find some way to contact him by going through Dad's old things?*

Would any of his contact information still be relevant? Surely not...

It was almost the end of the work day when Liam passed by my desk. I thought he was on the way out and didn't even expect him to look in my direction as further punishment for my earlier disappointment. But instead he pulled up a chair from the empty work bench beside mine, and sat down next to me with a heavy sigh.

I looked up at him and waited. I didn't beg for forgiveness again, since clearly that had gotten me nowhere.

"Nobody's interested," he said at last, like a confession.

I shook my head. "Who's not interested in what?"

He bit his lip, running a hand through his unkempt brown hair. It was only now that I realized that it was more unkempt than usual. "Over the weekend, while you were in London, I crossed the Atlantic. I went to three rural towns in the Americas, chosen because they were the ones hit the hardest in terms of job loss when the bots first took over. They're living on the Common Wage now, and you know what that means. They're surviving on the genetically modified chemically-laden frankenfood rations the government distributes, and are therefore riddled with chronic disease, which systematized robotic healthcare

109

treats by pumping them full of symptom-suppressing drugs. They're sick, depressed, and anxious—some just because of all the crap they're putting in their bodies, but a lot of them just because they don't have a reason to get up in the morning. Abraham Maslow's Hierarchy of Needs, right? We all need a purpose to live for, and these people have none—and no hope for anything to get better, either. Given all that, I figured they'd hate the bots more than anybody. I thought it would be easy to motivate them to fight with us—grass roots style, of course, since the labyrinth approach is evidently out." He shook his head and looked away, haunted. "But I could hardly even get them *angry*. I guess I should have guessed it: in order to be willing to fight, you have to have hope. And they don't. They all at least believe Halpert's challenge will lead to even more lost jobs, if not a major existential crisis—but they don't think they could do anything about it, even if they tried. They said they have a vote in name only. Their representatives only care about Big Business. It's all about the dollars." He rubbed his thumb and forefingers together to emphasize his last point, looking forlorn. "This old former shopkeeper told me that the labyrinth will never report it, but based on what they've seen in their community, they're convinced the suicide rate is at least four times higher than it was before the bot takeover." He sighed. "I'm more convinced than ever that those against are in greater numbers than those who are for Halpert's challenge, but they won't even bother to send a comm to their senators, let alone anything else."

I'd never seen Liam look so defeated before. Cheerful, irrepressible Liam, who always seemed to bounce back. I bit my lip, not sure what to say to this.

"I'm sorry I snapped at you," he said at last. "I was just upset that this weekend was such a flop, and then when I came back on the Quantum Track on Sunday night, I told myself, 'At least Rebecca's working on a new strategy to protect us, in case we *can't* stop Halpert. We'll have a new idea soon.' And then when you came in looking all hung over and like you couldn't care less, I just... lost it."

"I do care!" I insisted, indignant, "and I wasn't hung over, I only had one drink! I've never even been drunk in my life."

His eyes twinkled, but just a little. "Why am I not surprised."

"If you *must* know, I fell asleep doing research last night because I found out my father might have been murdered!"

Now I had his full attention. "What?"

I probably shouldn't have said anything, but it was out now. I thought about choosing my words carefully and telling him only bits and pieces, but what was the point? I knew he'd probe me until I told him the whole thing anyway. So I did: all about the oddly fatal strain of Treblar's Disease and Randall Loomis, who according to my mom was one of his good friends, and according to Odessa, simply vanished. "I've been obsessed with finding him," I confessed, "hoping he can either confirm or deny what really happened to my dad and all those men he knew. But I don't even know where to start."

After a long pause, Liam murmured, "I think I might."

Chapter 11

Julie invited me to the pub that night, but I turned her down. I needed advice, and much as I loved Julie, I knew she wasn't exactly a fount of wisdom. The person I wished I could to talk to was Mom—she always knew what to do. But she was too biased in this case; as it was, I dreaded the conversation we'd have to have before the evening was over.

"Good evening!" chirped Madeline when I entered my flat. "Oh! Why the long face?"

I sank to the floor beside my bed so that I was at eye level with Madeline. "Liam thinks I can find out more information about Randall Loomis in the Capital."

"San Jose?"

I nodded. "And he wanted to go there anyway. He's discouraged that we're cut off from the research community with the new labyrinth censorship. Without collaboration, it'll be virtually impossible for us to come up with anything fast enough to stop Halpert, when he's got the combined intelligence of the whole world on his side, while we've now only got ourselves. Liam says we have to find a way to band together again, and give those who are technical enough to participate in the research a way to share information, while those who aren't can at least learn what's happening and start a grass roots movement to stop him."

"Okay…" Madeline reeled her stick-like metal hand, prompting me to get to the point. A flicker of a smile crossed my face—she'd learned that from me, I knew.

"He wants me to go with him."

"To the Capital?" She paused. "But… don't you have class? And exams? And rehearsal?"

"I know," I sighed. "But… what if I really can find out about Loomis there? What if that's where he is? Liam says he has lots of connections there—people who *might* know where he is, if anybody does."

"When is he leaving?"

"Tomorrow."

"Oh," Madeline said significantly. She wheeled around so that her back pressed against the edge of the bed too, mirroring my own position. "What are you gonna do?"

I sighed, running a hand through my hair, which was kinked in the back where it had been in a ponytail all day. "I have to go, don't I? If Dad was actually—"

"Don't say it!" Madeline interrupted, stopping me from saying *murdered*.

"Well, if he was, then not only is this *big*—much bigger than school—but…" I groped for words. "But I can't just let it go now. Not when I've come this far. If someone *murdered* my father, I need to know who, and why, and find a way to make them pay!"

"But… don't you think that might be dangerous?" Madeline asked in a small voice.

"No. Not yet, anyway," I said. "All I'd be doing at this stage is gathering information. Not like I'd be out rattling cages and trying to brew a revolution, like Dad was."

"And like Liam will be?" Madeline asked pointedly.

I opened my mouth and closed it again. "Well, he doesn't plan on doing any preaching on street corners, to my knowledge. He already tried that. He said it didn't work."

"Oh, Rebecca." Madeline wheeled in front of me and then back and forth, a perfect imitation of a human pacing.

"I might not even have to be gone that long," I went on, ignoring her fretting. "A couple days to a week maybe? That should be enough to find out if anybody in Liam's circle knows anything about what happened to Dad. If they don't, I come back to school and take some make-up exams.

Professor Kirby and Professor Helroy both love me, I'm sure they'll be fine with it. And I can memorize my lines while I'm there, so I can jump right back into rehearsals…"

"What if you *do* find something out, though?"

I pressed my lips together, one arm wrapped around my bent knees. "Then… I guess I'll have to drop out of school this semester, and follow the trail wherever it leads."

We were both silent for a long time. "Sounds like you've made up your mind," Madeline said at last.

"You don't think it's a good decision?" I pressed, biting my lip. I hated doing something so potentially massive without outside input—usually I lived my life by consensus of what everyone else thought I should do. Not that Madeline ever disagreed with my decisions. She was endlessly supportive.

"I just want you to stay safe, and graduate, and marry Andy, and live a long, happy life!"

I felt warm inside when she said this—how could anyone not love Madeline?

"I want that too, of course, but…" I shook my head. "But what if Liam's right? What if *Dad* was right?"

After a pause, Madeline ventured, "Your dad and Liam would have liked each other, wouldn't they?"

"Maybe at first," I shrugged. "But they were both so stubborn, they'd probably have butted heads once they disagreed on how something should be done. Each of them would insist that their way was the *only* way, and neither one of them would ever apologize…" Then I remembered Liam apologizing to me only earlier that day.

Perhaps I'd misjudged him.

Madeline gave a wistful-sounding sigh. "I wish I'd met your dad."

It was such a sweet thing to say—I didn't have the heart to tell her that Dad would have hated her on general principle, and I'd never have been allowed to keep her, had he been alive.

I took another deep breath, reaching into my backpack for my handheld. I stared at it for a minute, trying to decide if I should comm Mom, or call her. A comm would be easier on me: less confrontational. Holographs were almost like being face-to-face, and… well… she wasn't going to like this.

"Are you going to tell her your real reason for going?" Madeline whispered, knowing my intention without my having to voice it. "That you think your dad was murdered, I mean?"

I shook my head. "No. She wouldn't understand. She and Dad fought all the time over the conspiracy stuff—she'd *hate* that I would even entertain the idea that he died because of it."

"More than she'd hate the idea of you skipping school for an indeterminate period of time to participate in grass-roots politics?"

I felt my heartbeat in my throat. "No, she'll hate that too," I conceded. "But... slightly less, maybe? And it's not a lie—I *will* be helping Liam with whatever he wants me to, as long as I'm there."

Finally I decided that even if I did chicken out and comm her, she'd just call me as soon as she got the message anyway. Might as well cut out the extra step. I called.

"Rebecca?" Mom said when she answered, surprised. She was in her pajamas, but she was in a hotel room, yet again. I wondered if she was *ever* at our house when I wasn't there. "Shouldn't you be in class?"

"Mom, I have something to tell you." I took a deep breath. Better to just get it out. "I'm... not going to be in school for a little while. It might only be a few days," I added hastily. "Or... it might be longer. I don't know."

She stared at me, not comprehending. When the silence became uncomfortable, I blurted, "Liam and I believe there's a conspiracy to spread only propaganda about the bots, and they're silencing all dissenting opinions. We can't work collaboratively with other researchers without the help of the labyrinth, so we're going to spread the word against Halpert's challenge the only way we can: in person —before it's too late."

Mom stared at me still, and I could see the wheels turning in her head. "You're dropping out of school?"

"Just for a few days. Maybe a week. Or... maybe longer. It depends on what happens when we get there." I waited, heart pounding in my throat.

She opened her mouth and closed it again, as if fumbling for words. "And you expect me to believe that this *isn't* just because you want to travel more than you want to study?"

That was the last thing I'd expected. "What? No! Halpert's challenge could destroy mankind as we know it!" Liam's words, not mine, but they came in handy at the moment. "And now that we can't collaborate with other researchers via the labyrinth—"

"Oh, please, Rebecca," said Mom, scornfully. "You never cared about any of your research, you were always ready to drop it in a heartbeat if it meant you could do something else you enjoy more. This is just Rebecca satisfying Rebecca's whims. You're going to end up on the Common Wage like everyone else! After all that your father and I sacrificed to give you every opportunity—with all your intelligence and potential, you're just going to throw it away for the sake of instant gratification?"

Tears pricked at the corners of my eyes, though I wasn't sure if they were of sadness or of indignation.

"That's so unfair!" I finally managed. Again, I thought of telling her my suspicions: about Dad, and about Loomis, and the unusual strain of Treblar's... but my instinct told me that would be even worse than letting her think I was just acting out my selfish whims.

Mom didn't speak for a long moment, and her holographic eyes looked over my shoulder and not directly at me. I had the impression that she was trying not to cry, too. At last, she murmured, "If you affiliate yourself with these absurd conspiracy theories, Rebecca, even if you were to change your mind later and come back, it will be too late. You will blacklist yourself from any possibility of having a meaningful job. If you do this, that's it. You've thrown away *everything!*"

"No one will have a meaningful job if Halpert gets his way, Mom!" I retorted. "That's the whole point, but it's worse than that, even—"

Before I could finish, she interjected, "Maybe eventually that might be true, but not for many years to come. You would still have the chance of earning some savings, if you focused on contributing to society! You are condemning yourself to a life of poverty, and I—I'm sorry, I can't talk to you about this anymore!"

She hung up on me. My mom actually hung up on me.

It wasn't until Madeline rolled up beside me and placed a tiny metal hand on my forearm that I realized I was trembling, still staring at the space in the room where Mom's holograph had been. Comfort always did me in: I burst into tears, burying my face in my hands as Madeline stroked my arm.

"She only said all those things because she loves you," Madeline murmured. "All she can see is the impact this choice might have on your life."

"She—thinks I'm being an idiot, that it's all about doing what I want," I sniffed, wiping my face even though the tears kept coming. "I can't make her understand without telling her the truth, and that would be even worse!"

"She's just looking at it through the lens of her own prejudices," Madeline soothed. "She'll calm down. She always does."

I glanced away from Madeline, and my watery gaze landed absently on my netscreen. Andy was available on A.E.

I wanted to be comforted, and I especially wanted to be comforted by Andy. So I got up and tapped on his name, intentionally not wiping my tears from my cheeks. I *wanted* him to see that I'd been crying.

He answered. "Hi. How's it going?" No comments about my tear-stained face. This annoyed me, but I decided to give him a second chance.

"Um, not so good." I might have made my voice tremble a little more than necessary.

I couldn't totally read his expression, but I did see the comprehension dawn. Did he look uncomfortable? "What's the matter?" he asked.

So I told him. I told him about cutting school, about going with Liam to the Capital, and about how my mom had called me selfish and hung up on me. A little piece of me hoped he would volunteer to come with us, even though I knew he wouldn't.

"So... you're upset about your mom, then?"

"Yes!" I snapped, annoyed that he seemed so apathetic to the rest of my story. What about the whole dropping out of school thing, the sacrifice I was making to try to stop what appeared to be a tyrant from stealing the last vestiges of humanity from us? (Even though that wasn't my real motive.)

"I'm sure she'll come around," Andy shrugged. "Sorry you guys fought."

I blinked at him, and I could feel before it happened that I was about to say something I'd regret.

"You don't care at all, do you?"

His eyes widened. "Of course I care!"

"No you don't! You're so busy getting

plastered and making out with random girls that you can't see past your next party!"

Andy gaped at me. "Wha—?"

"I've got to go, I'll talk to you later." I hung up before he could see me burst into fresh tears.

I glanced up at last to see Madeline struggling for something supportive to say. "Well... I'm sure he deserved it..."

"I'm just so tired of this!" I sobbed. "Andy doesn't care about me, he doesn't care about anybody but himself!"

On the bed beside me, my handheld blinked with a comm from Liam: two of them, actually. The first one came when I was talking to either Mom or Andy, and it said, "Dr Yin actually knows someone who knows Halpert himself! She thinks she might be able to get us an introduction. Friends in high places can't hurt anything." The second comm, about half an hour later, said, "Hell-ooo?"

I tossed the handheld aside. I couldn't deal with Liam right now.

"What are you really upset about?" Madeline prodded, in a low, soothing tone. "Andy, or your mom?"

I thought for a minute, sniffed, and wiped my face. "Both." Then I added, "But mostly my mom. I just hate, *hate* the idea that she thinks I'm irresponsible and self-centered, but there's nothing I can do about it. I can't make her understand, and that is the most helpless, frustrating feeling... All I wanted was for Andy to make up for it by at the very least telling me he admired my choice, and that I was doing the right thing! If not deciding to come with us. Which I guess I didn't really expect. But *he* doesn't get it, either. Nobody gets it!"

"Maybe... if you told Andy what you wanted him to say?" Madeline suggested.

"What good is it if I have to *tell* him what to say?" I shot back. I knew Madeline was only trying to help, and I was making it hard on her by shooting down all her suggestions. But really. *Tell* him?

I glanced at the netscreen and saw that Jake was on A.E. also. "I could tell Jake, or Julie," I murmured, looking at the blinking name on my netscreen, "But he won't get it either. Jake already thinks I work too much and I should lighten up. Mom thinks I work too little and should get serious." I gave a short, humorless laugh.

"So... you can't please everybody," Madeline surmised.

"I'm not *asking* for everybody. I'm just asking the people I love to understand that I'm *not* being irresponsible and selfish, I'm making a sacrifice!" My handheld lit up again. "Ugh, what?!" I groaned, and grabbed it. Liam's third comm flashed: "Sorry, you're probably out saying goodbye to your friends and ignoring your comms and here I am pestering you like you have as little life as I have. :) Write me when you can."

"Yeah. Me and my thriving social life," I sniffed miserably. I still didn't feel like writing Liam back just yet—who incidentally now was in a much better mood than he had been this morning—so instead I composed a comm to both Jake and Julie. I still needed some support from *someone,* but I didn't have the courage for another potentially disastrous holograph conversation.

What I wrote was, "I know you won't understand this and you'll think I'm obsessive, but I'm cutting school for however long it takes to try to spread the world about Halpert's challenge and where it will lead. I don't know how long I'll be gone."

I just stared at the screen after I sent it, waiting and hoping for someone to say something encouraging. A few minutes later, Jake wrote, "I think what you're doing is heroic, Becca. You know a lot more about all that stuff than I do. Maybe I'll pop over and see you sometime, wherever you are, and convince you to take a little time off!"

I closed my eyes with relief. I could always count on Jake. I wrote back: "Thank you so much! I would love that!"

As I wrote Jake, Julie's reply popped up: "Wow. Well, good luck, I guess! I'll miss you! Let me know when you're back."

Somewhat less supportive than Jake's had

been, but at least she didn't tell me I was crazy or stupid.

"What if someone else told Andy what you wanted him to say?" Madeline suggested. "Would that be good?"

"No, if he cares enough, he'll figure it out on his own," I muttered. But I did feel slightly better with Jake and Julie's support.

"You know what you need!" chirped Madeline suddenly.

"What?"

"A cup of hot cocoa, and *Jane of Wilder Mountains*, while you pack!"

I smiled in spite of myself. *Jane of Wilder Mountains* was one of my favorite films. It was set in simpler times, about misunderstandings and happily ever afters. It was directed by Abraham Chiefton—Liam said he was one of Halpert's board, and I guess now that I thought about it, I *could* see a tiny bit of propaganda in there. Jane did have a faithful companion bot who saved the day, after all... but then, so did I. The film never failed to make me happy.

"Not a bad idea," I admitted.

"I'll queue it up while you go heat up some milk!" Madeline announced. The water kettle was in my room, but my favorite cocoa was always better with milk than with water, which required the kitchen. I kissed Madeline's shiny forehead.

"Thanks," I whispered. "You always know what to do."

She beamed at me.

I moved slower than I needed to, still feeling sad about my mom and about Andy. I heated the milk in a pan, stirring so that it wouldn't burn, when I got another comm: it was from Andy this time.

"I don't know who told you I'm getting trashed and making out with random girls, but it's not true."

I snorted, a flare of indignation rising again as I shoved the handheld back into my pocket. Ivan told me he had been, and Ivan wasn't a liar. Andy, on the other hand, would say whatever was most convenient at the time. He just wanted me to think he was wholesome because I was—that was my reputation. He *did* like me, so he wanted me to think well of him. *Either that, or he just wants everyone to think well of him,* I added to myself bitterly, pouring the heated milk into my waiting mug. I carried it back to my room, putting Andy's comm out of my mind.

I couldn't put it out of my mind. I couldn't think about anything else. As soon as I reached the room and set the mug down, I pulled out my handheld again and dashed off, "What about Yolanda?"

A second later, Andy wrote, "We're just friends."

"Is that Andy?" Madeline asked, knowing.

"He's telling me he and Yolanda are 'just friends!' As if Ivan hasn't told me everything!"

Madeline wheeled in front of me, fretting. "What do you *want* to happen with Andy?"

"I just—I just want him to *know* better than to hook up with a brainless bimbo just because she's easy and she's there!" I railed, as the opening credits of *Jane of Wilder Mountains* rolled. "He once told me I was a beautiful girl, and I'm 'so brilliant and so far above him,' and then he goes and hooks up with the likes of her! If I'm so great, why, why, *why*?" I threw the handheld on the bed as if it had done me a personal insult, and yanked my suitcase out of the closet, slamming my few personal belongings inside with similar vehemence. "It's like I'm invisible! I can win in every category across the board, and *still* he picks whatever other girl happens to be in front of him at the time! It can be me against anybody, *anybody* else, and he'll always pick the other girl. *Always*!"

Jane, the girl in the pretty gingham dress appeared on the netscreen, traipsing through the woods and gathering wildflowers, her faithful companion bot at her side. I had seen the film so many times that I could quote it; no need to pay attention.

Madeline waited for me to stop breathing so hard before she finally asked, "So you want Andy to pick you, then? That would make you happy?"

My eyes swiveled to her and narrowed. "What kind of a question is that? Of *course* that would make me happy!" She said nothing, and just watched me. At first this irked me even more. I sank down to the bed beside the open suitcase and added irritably, "I don't know what you're implying."

Madeline rolled over until she was as close to me as she could get. "I'm just trying to understand. You say you want him to pick you, but every time he comes close to pursuing you, saying all those things you just mentioned, you panic and avoid him."

"I do not—!"

Madeline went on, "Then when he goes after some other girl again, you're devastated. And you complain that you don't have much to say to each other, either…"

"That's not true—" I started.

Madeline interrupted, "So running those facts through my algorithms of possible human motivations, one thing keeps coming up: you *think* you want to be with him, but you don't, really."

"How can you say that?" I demanded. "*All* I want is Andy! That's all I've ever wanted, for years!"

Madeline blinked at me rapidly, her digital eyes darting all around the room like she was scrolling through an internal flow chart. "If that is true, and if human relationships always begin with initiation, and if he has given you many clues in the past that he had feelings for you, without a favorable response, then I see only one possible solution that is currently under our control."

"Oh yeah?" I sighed. "And what's that?"

"Tell him how you feel."

"What? No!" I cried, spluttering, "I can't… he's… making out with other people! He'd say no, and it would wreck our friendship, and it would be so awkward, and I'd be devastated…"

Madeline rolled back and forth in front of me. "Algorithms of human behavior imply that he is unlikely to approach you again without encouragement—"

"I'm *giving* him encouragement!" I cried, "look at the conversation we just had! How could he possibly think that was anything *other* than jealousy? Oh, geez," I sank to the floor, suddenly mortified as I realized *how* obvious this was.

"In that case, you have nothing to lose by making it explicit," Madeline pointed out.

"*No*. I'm not doing that. No." I folded my arms over my chest for emphasis.

She blinked rapidly again; *cue the internal flowchart,* I thought. "Would you wish for him to know how you feel, if you didn't have to be the one to tell him?"

"What, you mean if someone else told him?

No, that'd be awful! Unless they were just guessing or something, like if Ivan said he suspected it, I guess that would be okay. But if Julie or someone just *told* him—" I shuddered. "I'd be humiliated!"

"But Ivan guessing would be okay?"

I shrugged. "I guess so." I was tired of talking about this; it was all hypothetical anyway. I rested my back on the edge of the bed, my cocoa growing cold on the desk above me, staring at Jane and Humphrey at their town's country square dance without really seeing them. Finally I got up and resumed packing. Madeline didn't speak either.

She was wrong. I *didn't* pull away when I had the opportunity—I'd never actually *had* the opportunity!

The handheld vibrated again, and I groaned. "Ugh, what now?"

But it was Mom. "I'm sorry I blew up at you. Your father died because of the stress of the very conspiracy theories that I'm afraid you are now believing. The bitterness of it claimed his life, and those of many of his companions. I want more than that for you, and I'm afraid that you're throwing away your one chance at bettering your future. I'm sorry for saying you were being selfish. I just don't want you to follow in his footsteps. Please don't go to the Capital, Rebecca. For me."

"What?" Madeline whispered when she saw my face. My eyes glistened with tears.

"Mom," I whispered to her, wiping the tears away. I hated to disappoint her further, but at least we were talking in a civilized way now. I wrote, "I know, Mom. I don't want to throw away the opportunity you and Dad gave me, and that isn't what this is about. This isn't going to be a 'fun' trip. I'm going with Liam, too, so I'll still be working on experiment ideas while I'm there. He wants me to try to design an experiment to identify free will in the brain, so we can build in a failsafe and block the new generation of bots from having it. He said this might even turn into my Ph.D. thesis."

Liam! I realized I'd never written him back, in the midst of all the mess with Andy and with Mom. Once I'd sent my reply to Mom, I wrote Liam and said, "That's great, I'm glad we'll have some connections to make this easier!"

Mom's comm came back: "You can work on your experiments in Dublin. Tell me you won't be going to the Capital, Rebecca."

I frowned, annoyed. Why was she being so insistent about this? I *was* an adult, after all.

"Why don't you just tell her you aren't going?" Madeline whispered, hovering over me.

"Because I *am* going, and Mom and I don't lie to each other," I said, still frowning. Then I wrote, "I don't want to disappoint you, Mom. But I have to do what I think is right."

A few seconds later, she wrote, "Just what

132

do you think you're going to do in the Capital, anyway? Who do you know there that can be of any use to you?"

I huffed my answer aloud to Madeline: "I don't know, Liam's the one with the connections and the ideas. Not like it would mean anything to her if I told her who they were anyway." *Unless she wants to know if any of Liam's connections are former friends of Dad's.* I wrote, "I'm sure all of Dad's contacts are long gone, Mom."

She replied, "That's what I'm afraid of."

I sighed again, tossing the handheld back onto the bed. We weren't going to resolve this tonight.

I should probably apologize to Andy, though, I thought. I grabbed the handheld again and told him I hadn't meant it and was upset about Mom, not about him. I asked him to forgive me.

I flashed back to dinner with Liam—*was that just last week?*—when he'd asked me what my core programming was.

"Be perfect. And then they'll love you," I'd said.

The problem is, according to whose standard?

Chapter 12

The next morning, Liam rapped his knuckles against my door in a little syncopated knock pattern that told me he was still in a good mood.

"Latte. Right?" He thrust a cup at me as soon as I opened the door, his blue eyes dancing with excitement.

I laughed, still groggy. "Thanks. I'm almost ready, come in."

"Really? You are?" He looked me up and down—I still wore leopard print pajama pants and the t-shirt I'd slept in.

"What, you don't think I'll fit in?" I looked down at my own attire.

Madeline rolled in behind me, and chirped, "I packed everything I could reach—oh." She stopped when she saw Liam. "Hello."

"Hello again." Liam's tone couldn't be any chillier.

I sighed, exasperated. "Okay, you two are going to have to find a way to make nice with each other, because we're all going to be spending a *lot* of time together. I'm going to go change, and when I come back…" I gave Liam a pointed look.

He pretended to glare back at me, but I could tell he wasn't really annoyed. This was the best possible time to leave him alone with Madeline. I didn't think anything could dampen his spirits today.

We finally left my flat an hour before our Quantum Shuttle left. Liam zipped Madeline into my backpack himself, and even offered to carry it for me, along with my little suitcase and his own—a show of goodwill, I'm sure, in exchange for the sacrifice I was making. Of course he knew that I wasn't making it for *him*, per se, but he didn't seem to care about my specific motivations. Or maybe he was just being a gentleman. Funny, I thought—I'd associated a lot of words with Liam in the years I'd known him, but *gentleman* was never one of them. He even bought me breakfast in the station before we boarded: an egg and sausage pasty and yet another latte.

"I know you're an addict," was his reply when I thanked him. "Besides, you still look only half awake. What were you doing last night, partying the night away?"

I snorted. "Not exactly."

He gave me a sidelong glance. Normally that reply would have been enough, but today he seemed determined to make conversation as I settled beside him on the Quantum Track compartment, nestling the backpack containing Madeline between my feet.

"Well?" he prompted. "You weren't answering my comms, so I assumed you must have been out doing something."

"Because normally I don't do anything except sit around staring at my handheld with bated breath, waiting for your comms." Recent anomalies excepted, I still didn't really want to pour my heart out to Liam.

His lips twitched. "You *could* just enable the comm feature chip in your temple, so my comms will display directly on your retinas, you know. Then you'll never miss a comm from me again!"

"Why didn't I think of that?" I smirked, sipping my latte. I still felt he was waiting for an answer, so I said, "All I was doing was packing, with a movie on as background noise. And I talked to a few people on holograph. That's all."

"What movie?"

Apparently he *must* find something to make fun of. "Not telling," I said.

Worst thing I could possibly have said.

"Ahh!" said Liam. "Oh wait, let me guess: *Madison Gardens*?"

"Nope," I said. *Madison Gardens* was basically a glorified soap opera from the Second

Era. Also one of my favorites, but there was no way I'd give him the satisfaction of telling him so.

"Or no, what's that new animated interactive A.E. flick where you get to play the princess?"

Actually I really wanted to see that, but I laughed scornfully. "Of course not! Maybe it was a World War IV movie, ever think of that?"

He raised one eyebrow, inspecting me. "You'd like me to think so, wouldn't you?"

I crossed my arms over my chest, determined to change the subject. "So did you and Madeline make up?"

Liam lay one hand over his heart melodramatically. "Absolutely. I told her that if she's your friend, and you're my—er, sort of friend —then she and I should be friends with each other, too. She heartily agreed."

"I'm your 'sort of' friend?" I repeated, slightly taken aback. "What does that mean?"

"Well, I'm not exactly sure *what* we are…"

I felt the heat rising to my cheeks, pretending not to understand him. "Now that we're not in the lab, you're not my boss anymore, so it seems like 'friend' is the only thing left!"

He eyed me for a long moment. I knew he saw the blush. I *knew* it. He knew I knew it, too.

"It is, huh?" he said finally. "If you say so."

We were silent for a long time after that. Too long, but I couldn't think of anything else to say.

We arrived in the Capital of the Republic, San Jose, in about six hours. I'd seen plenty of images on the labyrinth, but I'd never been there in person before. I'd figured if I'd been to Phoenix and to Dublin, it couldn't be all that different, right?

Wrong. This place took my breath away— not because it was beautiful exactly, but because it was so very... *busy*. There were nearly as many bots as there were people, not only in the shop windows but on the streets too. I'd never seen so many in one place before. I was used to the Quantum Track hover technology, but there were hover vehicles everywhere here, all self-driving. I knew they weren't exactly flying, but it looked like they were, as they zipped through three-dimensional space trying to avoid each other. Many of the people on the streets wore their A.E. eyepieces, distracted by whatever was displayed across their retinas.

Liam grinned at me over his shoulder, hoisting my backpack higher on his back. "You doing okay? Going through culture shock back there?"

I wasn't that far behind him, but it was true that I wasn't walking nearly as quickly as I usually did. I was just trying to take it all in.

"I feel so... backwards," I told him at last,

having to shout over the din to be heard. This place could not be any more different from Casa Linda, or even from Dublin, whose activity stemmed largely from the university and its students. Everyone here was dressed like they'd just come from a board meeting, and all of them seemed to have somewhere to be. I jumped back as a man and a woman thrust their way between Liam and me to get to a hover car, which took off about a second after they shut the door.

Liam reached his free hand back to me, presumably to make sure we didn't lose each other. I took it with the hand that was not dragging my suitcase behind me, trying to think nothing of the fact that I was now holding Liam's hand.

He looks completely at home here, I noticed. I was glad one of us did, but it surprised me a little. It occurred to me that I didn't know much about Liam, or his life before I met him. He was always trying to get more information about *me*, while I put him off so I didn't seem too interested. I suppose I hadn't asked for reciprocal information for the same reason. But now, I found myself curious.

As if in response to my silent questions, Liam huffed as we trudged up a very steep incline, "We're heading up two more blocks. Friend of mine lives there. There should be a welcoming committee for us."

The crowd had thinned out now, so I

dropped Liam's hand. He didn't protest. I saw Madeline poke her enormous eyes out of the zipper, and look around with wonder.

"It's like a whole new world!" she squeaked.

I patted the bits of Madeline's forehead that I could reach, following Liam as he reached the crest of the hill and turned.

I don't know what I was expecting, but I was surprised when Liam ducked inside a pub. The walls were paneled with dark wood, and bedecked with paintings in elaborate gold frames, while orangish light came from chandeliers on the ceiling. Almost nobody was inside, which was surprising, since it was about dinnertime.

"They're downstairs," Liam told me. He turned and waved at a man behind the bar, who raised a hand in response.

"Hey Liam!" came the shout from behind the bar.

"Hey, Kyle!" Liam shouted back, but kept going.

When we emerged to the lower level below the pub, I saw bookcases, windows near the ceiling just before the room dipped too far underground, and what was unmistakably an apartment.

"Liam!" shouted one voice, and then there was a cacophony. I couldn't even count how many people were in the room. Most of them were male, and they skewed younger, which I guess made sense, given that they were Liam's friends… but there were some women too, and a few members of older generations. I even counted a couple of babies in their mothers' arms, though these stood off to the side. I suspected they belonged with some of the more enthusiastic young men in the center of the room, clapping Liam on the back in greeting. Kyle came down the stairs to see what all the fuss was about, too.

"Guys, guys!" Liam cried out, and everyone quieted down long enough for him to gesture at me and say, "This is Rebecca!" A few of them politely shook my hand or clapped me on the back, before Liam added, "Rebecca *Cordeaux.*"

The effect of my last name was immediate. The politeness turned to stares, and a few open mouths. Finally, one ventured, "As in… *Quentin* Cordeaux?"

Suddenly uncomfortable, I nodded. "He was my father."

A beat, and then the room erupted again. Those closest to me now hugged me in greeting, or stared at me in awe, and I heard a few shouts to Liam, "Why don't you tell somebody!"

"Your father was a legend," said a skinny, pale young man beside me, with wide, almost reverent eyes. "He was one of the pioneers of the Renegades."

"The—?" I began, but then remembered.

The Renegades. Of course. Liam had told me that's what they called themselves. *I just hadn't imagined there were so many of them.*

"Silence!" cried one boy with shockingly thick black hair pulled back in a ponytail, and wire rimmed glasses. He wore a dark green t-shirt with faded white print and holes in it, and stood on a folding chair, holding up his hands.

"That's Francis," whispered the pale young man next to me, sounding a little awed. "He's our second-in-command, when M isn't here, and he's the smartest guy you'll ever meet."

I had no idea what sort of chain of command they had, nor who M was, but it was the awe that piqued my curiosity. I inspected Francis more closely now: his face was all angles and planes, and I had the impression he rarely smiled. The group quieted down at once. "Let's have Liam tell the story just the once, instead of three hundred and twenty four times to all of us individually, shall we?" With a calm that came with confident control, he gestured for Liam to occupy the folding chair on which he stood, as he stepped down himself. "Liam?"

The moment Liam climbed up on the chair instead of Francis, I felt the mood shift. A few members of the group wolf-whistled, and Liam tossed a wink in the direction of his admirers. Liam, too, had a reputation here, though it seemed a very different one from Francis's. Then, with uncharacteristic sincerity, Liam said, "You guys are a sight for sore eyes, you know that?" He waved off the various sarcastic retorts to this, and went on, "No seriously, the fact that even without my locus, we can still assemble the Renegades at a moment's notice, the old fashioned way... it gives me hope." This met with nods around the room. Then, "For Rebecca's sake, how many of you had your own locus?" Almost every hand went up around the room—and despite Francis's hyperbole, I estimated that there were maybe seventy people in the small space. Then again, Francis didn't strike me as the type to use figures of speech—so I wondered if perhaps three hundred twenty four was really the total number of Renegades, present company or otherwise. "How many of you still have a locus?" Every hand went down. "Raise your hand if you lost it in the last week." Almost every one of them went up again.

"M said it means we're a threat!" shouted one, "otherwise Halpert and his cronies wouldn't have bothered with us!" This met with a few assenting murmurs.

"Who is M?" I whispered to the boy beside me.

"Our leader. Her real name's Harriet Albright," he whispered. "She's high up in the Republic Intelligence Agency, so we try not to use her real name. We call her M because she's the head of our intel operation here. You know, M—James Bond's boss, from those films from the Second Age?" He grinned at me. "Somebody started calling her that a few years back, and the name just stuck."

Liam was saying, "I assume we were able to assemble this many of us because of personal contacts. Raise your hand if you still have a way to contact one hundred of your followers." About half the hands in the room went up. "One thousand?" Most went down—only two hands remained in the air.

One of them said, "We backed up our contact lists. We've still got about a hundred thousand between us," and he high-fived his friend.

I saw the flicker of regret cross Liam's face. I knew he was wishing he'd done the same. But then he said, "Excellent. So we're all here to figure out how to leverage what we know and the contacts we *do* still have—"

"What's Cordeaux's daughter doing here?" interrupted someone.

Liam looked at me and raised his eyebrows: an invitation to speak for myself. I loved being on stage while playing a character, but just now I felt nervous. I wished I'd prepared what to say to a group this size in advance—should I assume they were all safe?

Well, if Liam thinks they are… As Liam stepped down from the folding chair, he offered me a hand to help me up in his place. I took it, and surveyed the room, clearing my throat.

"Liam and I—work together," I began, and overheard someone elbow Liam and say suggestively, "*Work* together, huh?" I turned a withering glare upon the speaker, a young programmer-type with a bit of a gut and unruly brown hair. He shrank back under my glare. Liam pursed his lips, trying not to laugh. I went on, "I guess you all know my father died six years ago, of an unusual strain of Treblar's Disease. What I didn't know until recently was that many of his associates died of the same thing, at almost the same time." I waited for this to sink in, scanning the room for any hint of recognition. Many of them nodded, looking appropriately somber now. "I think that seems… odd. According to official labyrinth reports, all of them contracted the disease in the French West Indies, but I don't remember that my dad ever went there. In fact, I think the last trip he took before he died was here, to San Jose."

"So you're not here to help the Renegades," said Francis, arms folded across his chest as he sized me up. "You're here to find out what happened to your father." It wasn't a question.

I stood up a little straighter. "I may be here to help, too. I'm not sure yet."

Francis rolled his eyes, and then flicked them over my body, carelessly. "Oh, please. You're about twenty, maybe twenty-one at the most. One shoulder is a bit lower than the other where you carry your backpack from class to class, which tells me you're still a student. From the way you just straightened up to allow your diaphragm the space to project, you've done some kind of performance, likely classical theater since you're in the former UK. Not exactly the kind of pastime that implies you spend many hours researching conspiracies and espionage. You're a decent actress, it's true, but your pupils shrank to pinpoints just now, so you're feeling intimidated. Therefore, you're still more interested in what people think of you than you are in finding out the truth, and when push comes to shove, you'll retreat back to your comfortable little life and leave us to do the dirty work. The only inducement strong enough to tempt you away was the discovery that your father's death might not have been what you believed it was. *That's* why you're here; no more, and no less."

Francis said all this in almost a monotone, and very fast—as if it were all the most obvious thing in the world. I felt the blood first drain from my face, and then rush back into it, burning with indignation and embarrassment. I desperately wished I were witty enough to come up with a clever retort on the spot, but came up dry.

It was Liam who rescued me.

"Francis!" he snapped, "Enough!" He nodded at me, his expression gentle and encouraging. "Ignore him, we all do. Go ahead."

I turned back to the group, shaken and trying not to look at Francis. Now I felt self-conscious even about calling upon my acting training, but I didn't know what else to do. Willing my voice to be steady, I said, "All right then. You're—correct. Francis." *Shoulders back,* I thought. *Chin high.* It gave the illusion of confidence at least, to everyone except Francis. Even if they all saw through me now, thanks to him. "What do any of you know about Randall Loomis?"

A murmur passed through the room, before Francis answered for them, "He was one of the original members of the Renegades. He was a close friend of your dad's."

"I know that much, but what happened to him?" I retorted, a slight edge to my voice.

After a pause, the skinny boy who had stood beside me earlier said, "Nobody knows. He didn't get Treblar's with the others. He just vanished."

"M probably knows," said another. "She knows a lot more than she tells us…"

Frustration boiled in my stomach. "So all of these early Renegade members died, or vanished. Don't you think that's a little fishy?" I demanded. "Yet here you all are, in the Capital, in plain sight!

If all these people you admired suddenly contracted a fatal illness all at the same time, then why stay here? Do you have a death wish?"

Someone shouted, "Keep your friends close, and your enemies closer!" to a ripple of nods throughout the room.

I deflated with disappointment. I said to the room, but looked at Liam, "So nobody knows anything about Loomis, then?"

"Like I told you, M might know," said the skinny boy who had stood beside me.

"Well, where is M?" I turned to Liam. "Do you know her?"

Liam gave me a helpless shrug. "I've met her a handful of times, but we can't get in touch with her between meetings—it would blow her cover. She has to come to us."

I stepped off the chair, melting back into the crowd and toward the wall as the chatter of the crowd emerged again. I passed by Liam on my way and tugged at my backpack, still slung across his shoulder. He gave it to me, with a wary look.

"I hope you're not going outside."

"I just need some air," I told him. And I needed to vent to Madeline, which is why I wanted my backpack.

He sighed, reluctant. "All right." He put a hand on the slope of my back, like he planned to guide me out.

"I don't need an escort," I told him, but he shook his head.

"I don't want you to be exposed and on your own. It's getting dark out there, too."

Who knew Liam could be so overprotective? I thought. "Thank you, but I'll be fine," I told him. "Are we staying somewhere nearby? It's still a bit light out, I can just go find it and meet you there. Please, Liam," I added when I saw that he was about to protest again. "I just need to be alone."

He crossed his arms over his chest and eyed me, like he was studying my face. Finally he said, "We're staying a couple doors down, at the Rasworth Inn. It's catty-corner from here." He pointed. "You're sure you won't let me walk you there? I promise I'll come right back and leave you alone."

"Fine," I said, knowing that he'd try to pry my feelings out of me on the way. But he was being a gentleman—yet again, to my continued surprise—so I reminded myself to add, "Thank you."

Liam excused me to the group for the evening and himself just for the moment, to a chorus of "nice to meet you's" and "see you tomorrow!s" as I waved my exit. Again, his hand found the slope of my back. I was very aware of it. Too aware.

"You okay?" he asked me, dragging his suitcase but carrying my backpack again. I still dragged my own suitcase too.

I hesitated, deciding whether or not to lie. But I'm a bad liar. "I don't know what I'm doing here, Liam," I said at last. "I'm cutting school because I was so sure my dad was murdered because he was on to something, and maybe this Loomis could tell me what it was—"

"Shh!" Liam hissed. "Keep your voice down!"

I rolled my eyes. There was no one anywhere nearby, and I wasn't talking loudly. I went on, "But if none of even those guys know anything about it, or where Loomis is… maybe they really *did* all go to the French West Indies and contract a weird strain of Treblar's at the same time, for all I know! Dad didn't tell us anything else about what he was doing, so maybe he lied about where he went, too. Wouldn't that make more sense? If all these other guys are hiding in plain sight, they can't really be in that much danger."

"I think Francis knows more than what he wanted to announce in a room that large," Liam said. "I'll talk to him in private and see what else he can tell us."

"I didn't get the impression Francis had much discretion of any kind," I muttered.

Liam gave a short laugh. "Social discretion, no. He tends to leave broken glass everywhere he goes, and then wonders why people don't like him.

But he's a very sharp guy, and he does understand the need for keeping secrets for other reasons."

"What is he, a high functioning autistic or something?" I muttered.

Liam shrugged. "Something like that. An idiot savant, maybe."

When we reached the front desk, he placed his thumb on a scanner pad to check in, and I did the same. Then Liam helped me upstairs with the luggage, and dropped his suitcase in his room before coming to mine next door. When I opened the door, he placed his hands on my shoulders, looking into my eyes.

"Hey," he said. "What we are doing is *the* most important thing we could possibly be doing at this point in history. We're finding a way to fight for the future of humanity, and we might not know how yet, but we are *going* to succeed. Your father would be proud of you."

I blinked at him, taken aback. It was such a personal thing to say.

As if sensing this, Liam dropped my shoulders and said, "I'll be back in a few hours. I'll tell you whatever I find out in the morning. Sleep well."

"Thanks," I said, watching him retreat.

When he was gone, I sighed and closed my eyes, glancing back at the dark room with thick, drawn curtains and deep maroon paisley carpet. I wasn't tired, and I didn't much want to sit in that cave any longer than I had to. I still really wanted some air, actually. I could just take a walk for a few blocks and come back—we seemed to be in a safe enough area.

What Liam doesn't know won't hurt him, I decided.

I slipped my handheld into my pocket, just in case, and put my backpack on again. Then I descended the stairs, and passed by the front desk again on my way out. The silvery bot behind the desk swiveled politely, mirroring my movement until I'd slipped outside.

It was dusk now; a few people wandered through the streets or took hover cabs, but for the most part, this section of town was largely deserted. Maybe that was why Liam and the Renegades had picked it.

The Renegades. It sounded so silly. Maybe there was censorship going on, and that was bad, but it wasn't what I'd cut school for. I *wouldn't* have cut school for just that. I'd have gone to someone else's lab if I had to, graduated, gotten a job for however many years I could, and put money in the bank. Then when I got edged out of my job by a bot who was smarter than I was, I'd have spent all my time writing novels even if nobody could buy them, and performing in musicals, even if no one could pay to see them. I'd have performed and written for free, and had a wonderful life.

I still could, I reminded myself. That would make Mom happy, anyway. Not the performing part, but the going back to school part.

I slid my backpack to my front side, intending to power Madeline back up again for some company. But just as I was about to press the button, I saw movement out of my peripheral vision. I might not have noticed, except that something about it seemed furtive and intentional.

I turned, and saw a silhouette of a man—just standing there. Watching me.

Waiting for me?

Liam is gonna kill me for this, I thought, as I moved toward him. *Not to mention Mom.* Yet somehow I wasn't afraid. He was a strange man in a dark alley, yes—but he didn't seem like the stereotype of the "man in an alley" whom one ought to avoid at all costs. I couldn't say why, but even from his frame, I could tell he wasn't dangerous. He looked clean-cut, and older. Non-threatening.

"Rebecca Cordeaux," he said when I'd gotten close enough.

That stopped me cold. My heart beat faster. "Yes?"

"I hear you've been looking for me."

My mouth went dry. I took a step closer, inspecting his face in the feeble shaft of moonlight. White hair, receding hairline, and deep wrinkles around the mouth and nose. He looked a bit too old, but— "Randall Loomis?" I hissed.

"You can call me John Doe. I can't tell you my real name," he said.

I blinked at this. "Okay—John Doe. What can you tell me about my father, and Treblar's Disease?"

"I can tell you that your instincts are correct," he said. "Your father and his friends were murdered, for a secret that I cannot reveal to you without putting your life in similar danger."

I caught my breath. "How do you know that? How do I know I can trust you?"

"I knew your name, and your father's name, didn't I? I knew your speculations. I knew to come here to find you alone."

"Why go to the trouble, if you didn't plan on telling me what my father knew?"

"I wouldn't have, if you'd stayed away. But you're here. I assume that means you're on the side of the Renegades."

"But even they don't know anything about you!" I protested.

"That's because many of them have a reputation for indiscretion," he said, his tone dry. "I'd recommend you keep this meeting a secret for that very reason, especially from your friend Liam. He has a tendency to shout everything he knows from the rooftops. That's why they shut him down."

"So… what *do* you think we should do, then?"

John Doe shook his head. "You may not have a lot of options left." He started to walk away.

"Wait!"

"I can't tell you how to contact me," he called behind him, as he moved away. "I may be able to send you untraceable comms from time to time, but you will not be able to reply. When you need me, I will find you."

Then he was gone, melting into the shadows.

Chapter 13

That night I dreamt of my father, in the French West Indies. I was with him, at my current age rather than at fifteen, as I was when he died. He looked as I remembered him, though. There was a third person with us, too—John Doe, whose face remained in shadow even though we were in full sun the whole time.

Suddenly the scene changed. Both of them lay before me on the sand, dying of Treblar's Disease, as the sun slipped over the water. There was nowhere I could go for help, nothing I could do but watch them die…

I woke with a start, panting. I felt briefly disoriented in the unfamiliar room, until my memories of the day before flooded back to me. The hotel room looked so dark that I wasn't sure if it was still the middle of the night or not. I crept out of bed to pry open the blackout curtains, and saw only the first hint of a sunrise streaking across the San Jose skyline.

My heart still pounding, I sat in one of the

plush chairs beside both the window and the charging station where I'd plugged Madeline in for the night. I powered her up.

"Good morning!" she chirped. "Do you feel any better?"

Before I'd gone to bed the night before, I'd told her about John Doe and the strange meeting. We'd both surmised that he *must* be Loomis—who else could he be?

"I had nightmares," I admitted.

She nodded sympathetically. "Are you going to tell Liam about him?"

I shook my head. "He told me not to, so how can I? Although it feels weird keeping secrets from Liam about this." Liam, who was the original conspiracy theorist… after my father, of course. "I guess I'll just let it play out for now…"

I met Liam in the restaurant downstairs for breakfast. He sat alone at a circular white table, his hair wet like he'd just gotten out of the shower. He really *was* very handsome—I was so used to him, but every now and then it caught even me off guard. A waitress bot wheeled up and deposited his breakfast just as I sat down across from him.

"I'll have what he's having," I told the bot, gesturing at Liam's eggs, bacon, and coffee.

He raised his eyebrows. "You sure you're not too snobby for this coffee?"

"Beggars can't be choosers." I felt nervous, unsure how I was going to avoid telling Liam about John Doe. I wasn't good at lying. Then again, he didn't know I'd gone out again last night, so he'd have no reason to ask. I decided the safest approach was to steer the conversation myself.

"Did… you find anything out about Loomis from Francis?"

"Not much," he admitted. "In your father's day, Loomis was their liaison to those in power. He had a government job of some kind himself, and had a lot of connections because of it, which is part of why it's so surprising that he managed to just vanish. But Francis said that might be *why* he managed it. He might have known the others were in danger and tried to warn them, and fled to at least save himself when they wouldn't listen. All speculation, though. I'm afraid that doesn't help you find him now."

My heart beat faster, as I made a mental note to ask John Doe about this when I saw him next. Not that he was likely to answer me. For Liam's benefit, I tried to look disappointed. I needed him to think he was my only source of information.

With a melodramatic sigh, I changed the subject. "So what's on the agenda for today, then?"

"Meeting with Joon Kim," he said, lowering his voice. "The senator that Dr. Yin knows. We're meeting him at half ten at his office. Dr. Yin told me she hadn't seen him in years, but he was a reasonable guy when she did know him, so she thinks either he'll already be on our side, or else he doesn't know about all the censorship, and he'll join our side once he hears about it. I'd like to have at least one senator in our corner before we try to organize a Town Hall meeting."

I wondered what John Doe would think of the Town Hall meeting idea. *Too indiscreet? Would it make us a target?*

Liam tilted his head to the side, eyeing me as he shoved a forkful of eggs into his mouth. "You doing okay?"

I nodded, dropping my gaze. "Yeah."

"That was convincing."

I shrugged. "I'm just a little nervous about letting someone like Senator Kim know what we believe, and that we intend to tell as many people as possible about it. That's all."

"This from the girl who had no problem discussing it right out on the streets last night, where anyone could overhear." I started, until I realized he was referring to the conversation I'd had with him, when he'd walked me to the hotel. He went on, "It's a risk we've got to take, I think. From what Dr. Yin described, I don't think he'll be dangerous, even if he is in Halpert's pocket."

Senator Kim's office was in an historic

building with a red door and a very long foyer lined with an expensive-looking maroon rug. His maid bot opened the door and admitted us into a sitting room decorated as if it belonged to the Victorian period of the Second Era. I felt terribly underdressed in my cheap cotton skirt and ballet flats. It made me look like what I was: a college student. At least I'd left my backpack at the hotel.

The maid bot offered us tea. Liam accepted for both of us, and the maid vanished, promising to tell the senator that we had arrived.

"Stop fidgeting," Liam hissed at me when she was gone. I hadn't noticed I was doing it, but I kept smoothing my skirt and my hair, crossing and uncrossing my legs.

"I can't help it, I feel so…" I looked around the expensively furnished room, "…insignificant."

"You're in musicals like every other weekend," he whispered back. "You're an actress, play a role!"

"Why are *you* so comfortable?" I retorted.

He shrugged. "I kind of grew up in this world. High society. Powerful people. Doesn't faze me anymore."

I blinked, recalling my earlier thought of how little I knew about Liam. "Really? You did?"

"It's all a show, y'know," Liam went on, as if he hadn't heard my question. "They might act like they're better than you when you first meet them, but people are people. Don't let him intimidate you."

The maid bot returned bearing three cups of fine china, a matching tea kettle and a pitcher of cream. Senator Kim entered the room behind her, wearing a perfectly tailored three piece suit. Liam stood to shake his hand.

"Sir, thank you for meeting with us on such short notice," he said. I followed his lead, standing to shake the senator's hand as well. Liam introduced us both, and then added, "We work for Dr. Ana Yin. She spoke highly of you."

The senator's eyes crinkled around the corners. "I remember Ana well. Give her my regards."

"We will," said Liam, sitting down again and helping himself to a cup of tea. I did the same— if he grew up in high society, then surely he'd know what to do. Although it was very odd to think of Liam as a model of class and elegance.

"Well, let me get right to the purpose of our meeting," Liam said. "I don't know how much Dr. Yin told you?"

Senator Kim hesitated. "She told me that you had something you would like to discuss with me regarding—censorship?" Now he fidgeted, wiping his palms on his trousers. My eyes narrowed.

"Yes, sir." Liam launched into the story

about how his locus had been black-listed, and those of many of his friends as well. "We believe that our labyrinth voices were silenced because they were powerful, and we were saying things contrary to the official line of Halpert and those in charge of the development of Synthetic Reasoning. Rebecca and I had been working collaboratively with other researchers around the world by means of these loci, trying to prove that the successful completion of Halpert's challenge would almost certainly lead to superintelligence, placing all human lives at risk."

As Liam said this, I watched Senator Kim. I'd studied a little bit about body language in my psychology coursework, and he seemed almost like a case study. His eyes darted around the room, rather than resting on Liam's face. He readjusted his seat about every five seconds. He set his cup on its saucer, picked it up, and then set it down again without drinking.

He was even less comfortable than I was. But why?

"Because our loci were removed from the labyrinth," Liam was saying, "not only did we lose our voices, but we also lost the platform to open-source our research within our own network. Halpert of all people knows the power of open-sourcing knowledge to expedite breakthroughs—"

"I see, I see," Senator Kim finally cut him

off, holding up one hand. It was shaking, I saw. *What is going on?* "Are you sure there isn't merely a problem with your server?"

Liam balked at him. "A problem with my —"

"Labyrinth censorship is a thing of the past," Senator Kim went on. "Use of it is freely available to all. If you are implying that your locus and those of your friends were intentionally black-listed, I'm afraid that is impossible."

Perhaps it was because I was already in observer mode, but I thought I could actually see Liam's blood pressure spike. The muscles in his face twitched with the effort of maintaining his veneer of politeness.

"So all of our loci, on a myriad of different servers, coincidentally all went down within one day of each other?" Liam asked, his voice carefully controlled. "Sir, have you searched the labyrinth for any dissenting opinions to Halpert's on the subject of Synthetic Reasoning? There is not one left. Not one. Do you call this free speech?"

"If there are none, then it is because dissenting opinions are quite rare," Senator Kim returned, sipping his tea. "Most people recognize, as does Senator Halpert, that the advancement of Synthetic Reasoning will solve most of the remaining ills in the world today. Now if you will excuse me, I'm afraid I've got a lot of work to do."

163

He stood up, setting his saucer on the serving tray. "I wish you the best in restoring your pages to the labyrinth, I really do. Give Dr. Yin my regards."

"Sir!" Liam jumped up, his eyes flashing now. "You can't possibly believe what you're saying!"

"Good day," said Senator Kim with a slight bow to both of us, and left the room.

As soon as he was gone, I crossed the room to Liam and put a hand on his shoulder, hissing preemptively, "Shh." He looked like he was about to blow.

I needn't have bothered though—he couldn't speak. He was too busy shaking with rage.

Liam went for a run when we got back to the hotel, presumably to burn off the excess adrenaline from our meeting. Once he'd rounded the corner, I went to the alley where I'd seen John Doe the night before. While still cast in shadow between two buildings, it was, of course, broad daylight now.

"John Doe!" I hissed. Waited. Nothing. "John Doe!" I tried again.

He'd told me I couldn't contact him, and that he'd have to contact me. But how would he know when I needed to talk to him?

"I need to know what Senator Kim is hiding!" I whispered to the shadows. "I know he's hiding something!"

After waiting a full five minutes which felt like twenty, I finally sighed in frustration, running a hand through my hair and turning back to the hotel to wait for Liam's return.

"You are not likely to get much from Senator Kim, no matter what you do."

I spun back around. He was there, lurking in the shadows.

"Why not?" I demanded.

"Because he values his life."

I blinked. "Is his *life* in danger?"

"He knows the same secret your father knew. The same one all of your father's companions knew. The same one Liam's brother knew."

"Liam's—*brother*?" I swallowed hard. "Is he dead too?"

John Doe started to back away. "Be careful, Rebecca. Don't probe too deeply for the truth. You may discover far more than you ever wanted to know."

"Wait!" I cried, starting to run after him— but he was gone. I let out a guttural cry of frustration, and called out to the empty shadows, "That didn't help at all!"

Chapter 14

I waited in the little downstairs cafe for Liam to get back from his run. Madeline sat beside me. It felt like a risk; I'd kept her hidden for as long as I'd had her. But Liam already knew about her anyway, and nobody else here knew me. Plus, bots roamed freely in the Capital, and the prevailing sentiment was that they were the potential saviors of mankind, so—why not? Besides, I didn't feel like sitting in my cave of a room, and I didn't feel like being alone, either.

"Maybe I can get Odessa to find out more about—the senator," I murmured to Madeline so softly she had to lean in to hear me.

"Maybe!" she chirped, her expression optimistic as ever.

I deflated first. "Except, she can only find information that's on the labyrinth. And I have a feeling that this isn't going to be something in the public record. Besides, now I'm not so sure I want to leave a trail of my research on a bot's search history…"

Madeline couldn't really slump, lacking an articulated spine, but her expression managed to convey that idea all the same. She was so like a mirror—when I was excited, she was excited. When I was discouraged, she was too. Somehow until I'd told Liam about her, I hadn't ever seen her that way. It made me feel oddly lonely, in a way I never had been in Madeline's presence before.

"I'm very glad you're being careful," Madeline murmured.

My voice barely above a breath, I added, "I don't understand what John Doe wants with me, if it's not to actually tell me anything useful. It seems like all he wants to do is warn me away!"

"Think maybe you should listen?" Madeline asked timidly.

"No! Meeting John Doe makes me want to stay more than ever, because now I know there's something here, something worth finding! I want to know how deep the rabbit hole goes!"

"Are you gonna ask Liam about his brother?" Madeline asked, dropping her voice still further.

I shrugged. "I can't ask him point blank without telling him about John Doe. But I'll find a way."

Liam blew through the glass doors just then, his dark hair askew from the wind and cheeks flushed, either from exertion or from lingering anger. He hadn't quite caught his breath when he spotted us and slid in next to Madeline. He looked at me, just panting. I wasn't sure what to say, so I waited for him to start. He glanced at the receptionist bot and then back at me.

"Let's go up to my room," he said pointedly.

When we arrived in his cave of a room upstairs, a twin to mine, he threw open the heavy curtains to let some of the daylight stream in. Madeline and I settled on the twin bed closest to the window, and Liam sat in the chair beside it, resting his elbows on his knees.

"Senator Kim was nervous," I said finally.

"He was infuriating, is what he was," Liam growled.

"No arguments, but you thought *I* looked shifty when I walked in? He made *me* seem poised. He was definitely hiding something."

"Something about Halpert," Liam agreed. "He's afraid of him, or of something about him anyway. But why?" He tapped his temple then, and his faraway expression told me that he was sending a comm.

"Who are you writing?"

"Odessa," Liam replied, his mouth fixed in a hard line. "I want her to dig up everything there is on the labyrinth about Halpert's history, and not just the biography anybody can read. I don't know what I'm looking for, so I just told her to get everything:

from birth certificates to graduation from primary school to summer camps he went to as a kid... all of it."

"You don't really think Halpert's mixed up in something shady, do you?" I asked dubiously.

"I don't know, Rebecca! I don't know anything right now!"

"Hey! Be nice to her!" Madeline barked, scowling at Liam.

Liam glared at Madeline for a second, but then he relented.

"I'm sorry. I didn't mean to yell at you; I'm just... yelling in general. It's not your fault." A bead of sweat trickled down the side of his face; he swiped at it, distributing the sweat through his hair. "Francis and I talked about how to create a new communication network last night. We think we can create our own version of the labyrinth. We'd call ours the Commune," he added with a smirk.

I blinked at him. "You can do that?"

He nodded. "We think so, we drew up the plans for it last night after you left. We'd use our own netscreens as interfaces. That way we can communicate with one another at a distance, and recreate both the call to action for research, and disseminate any other information that the approved media doesn't want us all to know. But we'd want as many people connected to it as possible, obviously... so we want to have the Town Hall meeting ASAP."

My heart skipped. *Here it comes*. "Here?"

"Sure. We can use Francis's pub for the first one, he said. The idea was for every member of the Renegades to invite everyone we know, whether we think they're likely to get involved or not. We want to tell them what's going on, get them to start making a ruckus to everyone *they* know if we can, and also get their LP addresses so that we can add their netscreens to the Commune as we create it. We need to organize, and without the labyrinth, I can't think of any other way." He stopped, and looked at his hands. Then he looked back up at me. "I know the whole reason you decided to come was to find out about Loomis, Bec. I wish I didn't have to admit this, but I'm not sure I can do anything more to help you track him down."

Guilt gnawed at the inside of my stomach, and I couldn't meet his eyes. "It's okay. Thanks for trying." I could feel Madeline staring at me, too, waiting for me to tell him.

"I know this isn't what you signed up for. If…" he sighed heavily, like he regretted his next words already. "If you want to go back to Dublin, I'll understand."

"And contribute to the research to give bots emotions?" Madeline piped up. "Don't you know that Halpert could take her research and use it for his own ends?"

Liam pressed his lips together, suppressing a smile. "You think that's a bad thing, huh?" he asked her. Then he glanced at me, his eyes soft—much like a child repeating opinions of her parents, of course Liam knew that Madeline's beliefs betrayed my own.

"Of course I do!" was Madeline's reply. "I'm programmed to want what's best for humans, because Rebecca is a human!"

I leaned over and kissed the top of Madeline's metal forehead, and she rolled toward me, sliding a little on the bed which was too soft for her wheels.

"If only we were all so selfless," I murmured. Then I turned back to Liam. "I'm staying."

He raised his eyebrows. "Are you sure, because—"

"I'm staying," I said firmly. "I'll probably need to access full research papers on campus at some point, and maybe chat with a few professors to cut down on my research time. But I can otherwise research the morality and free will questions here as well as there. I can't do the experiments here, but if you guys can create the Commune, I won't have to. Someone else will. It's the collaboration that counts now, not the credit. I get that."

He broke into a grin, leaning across to where

I sat and grabbing both sides of my head with his big, sweaty hands. Before I knew what he was doing, he planted a kiss on my forehead, as I'd done to Madeline a moment before.

"Thank you," he said, still grinning. "I know you're not doing it for me, but—" He stopped. "Actually, why *are* you doing it?"

I looked down, feeling a twinge of conscience. "Maybe I believe in your cause after all. Like my father did."

He didn't seem to be in the mood to scrutinize too much, fortunately. "Well, on behalf of —humanity," he smirked to show that he meant this tongue-in-cheek. "Thank you."

The guilt in the pit of my stomach flared again. Maybe if I told him about John Doe, I could ask him about his brother...

Before I could decide to do this, Liam went on, "I think we should have our first Town Hall meeting tomorrow."

"Tomorrow?" I gaped, my mind racing. "How... do you think we'll manage to pull that off?"

He leapt to his feet, pacing in front of the large netscreen embedded in the wall as he spoke. "Our first one should be relatively small, just so we can get our feet wet. Then we can go bigger—you remember those two guys last night who said they'd backed up their contacts before their loci were pulled, Tom and Jason? They have about a hundred thousand between them. A bigger meeting will take more planning, of course—we'll have to find a safe place in a large arena, which seems kind of like an oxymoron…"

I flashed back to what John Doe had said about Liam: *indiscreet. Shouts everything he knows from the rooftops.*

"Is anything going to be safe, if that many people are involved?"

Liam shrugged, still pacing. "Possibly not, that's what I mean. But we'll cross that bridge when we come to it. Francis's pub can hold about three hundred, though—we can post a sign out front telling ordinary customers that the place has been rented out by a private group for the day. Shouldn't arouse too much suspicion. That sort of thing happens." He stopped pacing and turned to face me. "We'll invite everyone from our lab, of course. Nilesh, Larissa, Dr. Yin— all of them. I've got some buddies from back home that I think I can wrangle, too. What about you, how many people can you think of to invite?"

My heart still pounded. *Well, if it's just in the pub, maybe it's not a* horrible *idea,* I tried to convince myself. "Won't we be putting all of them in danger, though?"

He blinked at me, a little confused. "Bec, I'm going to keep you safe, and out of the spotlight.

You don't have to worry—"

"It's not about just me. What about everyone we invite?" I demanded. "What about *you*? You'll be up front and *in* the spotlight, won't you?"

He shrugged. "Yeah, but that can't be helped."

"What if my father really *was* murdered for doing exactly this sort of thing, Liam?"

"Well… then he died for a worthy cause."

"Easy for you to say!" I snapped.

He paused for a long moment, and then looked away. I expected an apology, but instead, he muttered, "It isn't, actually."

I felt a pang, realizing what I'd said. Of *course* it wasn't easy for him; he'd lost someone too. "I just don't want any of us to take any unnecessary risks—"

"This is necessary!" He jabbed his finger into his palm for emphasis. "Bec, the plan is to organize. Strength in numbers. How can we do that without telling people what we know?" Arms folded across his chest, he stared me down. "Listen to me. Of all the meetings we are going to have, this will be the very safest one. It'll be small, under the radar, and filled with personal friends. Even if they disagree with us, I doubt they're going to go tattling about it to anybody with the power to shut us up. While yes, I want *you* to keep a low profile no matter what happens, *I* plan to tell anyone who will listen. Because at this point, I think that's our only chance!" Another escaped bead of sweat trickled down the side of his face. "Now. Can you think of anybody you know that might be willing to help us?"

I wished I could talk to John Doe, wished he could give me some alternative to the meeting that might make Liam still feel like we were still moving forward. But what did I have at the moment? A contact with whom I had no official way of communicating, and who spoke to me only in riddles: telling me what *not* to do, but not what I *should* do instead.

"I don't think my Mom will come," I said at last. She was always working, and besides, after what happened to Dad, she'd hate everything about the Renegades. I thought of my other friends from drama and creative writing, and eliminated them too. They all really did believe that superbots would solve all the world's problems.

"Jake will come, though," I said aloud. "He's one of my friends from home, he always supports me. And Julie, I know her from school, and I think they're dating... she's actually more on Halpert's side, but if she hooks up with Jake, that won't last long."

Liam nodded, appeased. "Good. Anyone else?"

I thought of a few of the older people I knew

from Casa Linda—Roy Benson and Lyle Hopper. "I know some people who absolutely hate Halpert and would love to do anything they possibly can to take him down. But they couldn't afford the Quantum Track tickets to get here."

"Invite them. I'll pay their way," Liam said, waving a hand dismissively.

I raised my eyebrows. "*You'll* pay? For their tickets and lodging and everything? How are you gonna afford that?"

He opened his mouth and closed it again. "I can afford it," was all he said.

"You don't even know how many people I'm talking about!"

"Bec, it's fine. Just invite them." Evidently he didn't plan on discussing this any further. I flashed back to his comment to me when he'd first guessed about Madeline, and had asked me if I was "an heiress or something."

"What are you, an heir or something?" I joked.

I saw brief amusement in his eyes—he caught the reference. "Or something," he said. Then, in boss mode, he said, "I'll contact everybody from the lab and some people I know from home, and create a digital outline, while you work on your contact list. Let's meet for lunch in a few hours, okay?"

As soon as the door to my own room clicked

shut, Madeline said, "What about all your friends from home? They're still on student loans. They could afford to come."

"Yeah," I murmured. It was true—as long as we still had student loans, none of us really worried about money. "I already promised to invite Jake and Julie, so I might as well…"

My heart sped up at this thought, but for a different reason than before. It was many months earlier than I'd expected to get to see Andy again. I tried not to get my hopes up about that, reminding myself that this wasn't about me getting to see Andy.

I made myself invite the others first. Julie and Jake both said they were in. Emily, Patrick, and Rob got back to me quickly and said the same— Rob had an exam in the morning but he'd come afterwards. Elizabeth asked if there would be any food.

"We're meeting at a pub, so there will be if you want it, I imagine," I commed her back.

Finally, heart thrumming, I messaged Andy. I hadn't talked to him since our fight the night before Liam and I had left Dublin. I'd sent him an apology, but he'd never written back.

"Hey," I wrote, "Are we okay?"

A few seconds later he wrote, "Hey. Sure we are."

I breathed again. Then I wrote, "Remember

how I told you I was going to come to the Capital to fight censorship and Halpert's challenge? Liam and I are here right now, and we want to hold our first meeting about it tomorrow. It'll be in this pub owned by one of his friends—it's our first one, kind of small. Everybody will be there, though: Rob, Emily, Patrick, Jake, and Elizabeth. Do you and Ivan want to come?" I added Ivan at the last second, figuring that would make it look less personal.

I stared at the screen on my handheld, not wanting to miss his reply.

I stared. And I stared.

"That won't make him reply any faster," commented Madeline.

I spared her a quick glare. I could feel my heart in my throat.

"Ivan says he's in," the screen blinked. "Sure. Should we bring more people too if we think they'll be interested?"

I let out the breath I hadn't known I'd been holding. "Yes! Anybody who wants to come. Thank you!!!"

"Send me the address and the time."

Feeling about thirty pounds lighter, I messaged Mom next—I knew what her answer would be ("Rebecca, you are becoming a conspiracy theorist just like your father! This is utterly absurd, and no, I don't have the luxury of taking off of work whenever I want to gallivant all over the continent like you do—" etc,) but it seemed wrong to not at least tell her about it. Then I contacted Roy Benson and Lyle Hopper, promising that we would transfer the money to their accounts for the Quantum Track tickets if they wanted to join. They agreed enthusiastically, and commed back with their bank transfer numbers.

"Where do you think Liam got the money for that?" Madeline whispered over my shoulder.

"No idea," I said absently, still thinking about seeing Andy tomorrow. *When things calm down a little, I'll ask him,* I told myself.

Chapter 15

Dr Yin, Nilesh, and Larissa were the first to arrive in the afternoon, before the meeting officially started. I sat in the corner of the pub, watching as Liam greeted them. They waved at me, but everybody knew that he was the star of this show. I smiled a little to myself, watching Liam's wide eyes sparkle and his hands gesticulate as he spoke. He reminded me of a little kid in the extremes of his emotions, and the way he wore them on his sleeve. One minute he was so angry he couldn't speak, needing to physically burn off his fury, and then in less than twenty-four hours, it was like it had never happened. He was irrepressible.

Larissa skipped over to me, her eyes wide behind her glasses and hair pulled severely back from her face. She did a little spin, splaying her arms out to the sides like she was three.

"Isn't this *exciting*?" she asked me, but evidently the question was rhetorical. "We're here for a secret meeting, and we're all spies in the Renegades! I've dreamt of this sort of thing, but it's so delicious that it's actually happening, isn't it? I love never knowing what's about to happen…"

"I can hardly contain myself," I agreed, deadpan.

As I said this, out of the corner of my eye I saw Francis come up the stairs from his apartment down below. He wore all black, emphasizing his expressionless, angular features. His long black hair was tied with an elastic at the nape of his neck. Larissa's eyes appraised him quickly, and she caught her breath.

"Who is *that*?"

I chuckled—the very idea of Larissa, who somehow reminded me of a fairy, being attracted to Francis of all people was almost painfully ridiculous. "That's Francis. He's the owner of this pub, and one of the leaders of the Renegades. Also, one of the rudest people you will ever meet. Don't get too attached."

But my words seemed to have the opposite effect—Larissa's face softened like a sigh, and she clutched my arm all at once.

"Can you introduce me?"

Larissa *would* be the type to believe in 'love at first sight.' I grimaced. I had very little desire to interact with Francis again, but she looked so hopeful. "All right, but if he says something horrible, it's on you…"

Larissa practically skipped behind me as I

approached Francis, growing more reluctant with each step. A few paces away, Francis glanced back at us, his expression still bored as he appraised first me, then her, with a flick of his eyes.

"Cordeaux," he announced. "What's the matter with you? You look a little green. You're not the one who has to give the presentation."

I gritted my teeth. "I didn't know you ever had to ask anybody what was wrong with them. I thought you could just peel them open like an onion and announce their inmost feelings to the world. That's *not* an invitation," I added sharply, holding up my hand as I saw him open his mouth presumably to do just that, if only to prove that he could. I gestured at Larissa, who ogled him openly like a starry-eyed puppy. "This is Larissa. She works in our lab in Dublin. Larissa, Francis. There. My work here is done."

Francis studied her almost clinically, his mouth turned down at the edges. Then he murmured, "Hmm. Surprising."

"What's surprising?" Larissa asked, breathless.

"Only child, with presumably a severe parent whom you wanted desperately to impress, so you simultaneously decided you'd be very good at something he or she—most likely he, your father— would respect. But you didn't have any friends— and probably still don't—so you spent the rest of your time reading and pretending you were somebody else. Most of the fantasies probably centered around impressing your father, because even though you're an excellent programmer, he still never noticed you. So imagination was the only recourse you had left."

My mouth fell open in empathic horror as Francis rattled this off, monotone as ever. At last I dared a glance at Larissa, wondering if Francis had been as accurate with her as he had been with me.

"How... do you know all that?" she whispered.

Was it my imagination, or did Francis seem a little pleased by the question? He gestured at her various physical clues in turn as he explained, "The vacant expression, the little twirl, and the skipping all indicate that your emotional maturation abruptly stopped somewhere in your childhood years, perhaps ten to twelve. That only happens from some form of trauma, and generally the escape involves the only thing under the control of a child, which is imagination. Only a programmer slumps the way you do, and the severity of the slump even though you can't be more than twenty-four indicates that you've spent quite a lot of hours in front of a netscreen, which implies that on some level you must actually enjoy your job. Nobody enjoys anything they're bad at, and Liam invited you here, so you must be good. Plus the glasses, the hair, no makeup, and the ill-fitting clothing all indicate that you've self-identified as a programmer and you even feel proud to be one of the few females in the profession—which *is* rather an elite position, I must admit. But the skipping and the twirling implies a personality that would have sought out adventure, not a sedentary profession like programming, suggesting that the initial impetus to pursue it lay not in inherent interest, but in desire to impress. There is only one person whom a little girl desires to impress above all others, and that would be her father. And there you are."

I wanted to fall through the floor *for* Larissa. But when I finally dared to look at her, to my amazement, her face shone.

"You are… brilliant," she breathed at last.

"Yes, I know," he said, bored as ever. But he lifted his chin just a bit, and I saw him puff out his chest. He began to walk away then, but Larissa fell into step beside him, and he let her. I laughed, incredulous.

Who would have thought?

"Hey!" I felt the arms around me before I could identify their owners, and looked up to see Jake sliding in next to me. Julie stood behind him, hands in her pockets, watching Jake with a fond smile. "Is everybody else here yet?"

I shook my head, but just as I did, Rob, Patrick, and Emily walked in.

"Becca!" cried Emily, hugging me as Rob and Patrick clapped Jacob on the shoulder and shook Julie's hand, a little awkwardly. "I can't believe *you,* of all people, dropped out of school!"

"Well, I haven't *officially* dropped out yet..." I started to explain.

Elizabeth joined us a few minutes later, and we formed two little clusters of conversation: the girls, and the boys plus Julie. I filled the girls in on what had happened so far to bring about this meeting, keeping one eye on the door every few seconds. Elizabeth was saying something about how gorgeous Liam was, and if I didn't want him for myself, would I introduce *her*, when Ivan walked in the door. My heart stopped. I knew if Ivan was here, then...

Andy walked in next. And behind him, a voluptuous girl with long, glossy dark hair and very full lips. He was engrossed in conversation with her, and didn't seem to be in a hurry to stop.

Ivan spotted us, and broke into a grin.

Everything was a bit of a blur after that: there were hugs and handshakes, smalltalk and catching up that I didn't really hear, even when I was the one speaking. The only part I caught for sure was that the girl they'd brought along was named Yolanda.

Yolanda. That's her.

And while Andy wasn't actually touching

her, he paid far more attention to her than to anyone else. He was always leaning over to whisper to her, while she turned that sultry expression of hers toward him in reply to everything he said, batting her eyelashes and giggling.

I *hated* her.

The pub filled out with friends of Liam's, or so I supposed them to be by the fact that they were about his age, and they clustered around him when they entered. Francis popped up eventually, and I recognized quite a few of the faces of the Renegades from our first meeting. I saw Roy and Lyle arrive, looking quite out of place and keeping to themselves. Kyle, Francis's bartender, supplied wings and celery sticks and beer for anybody who wanted it, and presently Liam called the meeting to order.

"Thank you to everyone for coming," Liam said, setting up his holograph machine on the bar. "Unfortunately our fearless leader was unavoidably detained tonight."

"M!" shouted several of the Renegades. Liam had told me that Harriet Albright couldn't show her face, nor reveal her real name, in a gathering like this one. It would risk blowing her cover for her official position in government intelligence.

Liam nodded before he continued, "But my associates and I are most grateful that you could make it on such short notice." Those in the room who knew me turned to look my way and smile, but I noticed that Liam did not say my name, nor did he point me out in the crowd. True to his word, he *was* trying to protect me. "If you're here, I assume you agree that giving the bots emotion and creativity is a very dangerous thing, no matter what the media would have us believe." Nods all around the room, as Liam's holograph sharpened into an image beside him of Milan, leveled to the ground by a nuclear weapon at the end of World War IV, ending the Second Era. I assumed this was supposed to be a dramatic illustration of the kind of destruction that awaited all of us at the hands of superintelligence, and couldn't help but roll my eyes. *Liam. Melodramatic as ever.*

Liam went on, "Many of us here are too young to have suffered personally from the loss of jobs due to the first wave of SR bots, although I know there are still some of you who have." His holograph flicked to the image of a food line, just after the SR Revolution had put millions out of work. "Should Halpert's open source challenge be answered, all of us will experience at least this tragedy, but likely far worse." I glanced at Julie, who pursed her lips and gave me a guilty little smile before dropping her eyes. I gathered Jake still didn't know her real position on this.

Andy and Yolanda still whispered to one

another, their heads only inches apart. I felt ill.

I tuned out for awhile, letting Liam's words wash over me. I already knew his arguments anyway, and I was too busy being miserable to really listen. The rest of the audience seemed to hang on his every word, though. After describing the existential threat posed by creative and potentially superintelligent bots, he went on to describe the Commune, the alternative labyrinth that the Renegades wanted to build. Then he collected sign-ups the old fashioned way—with paper—for everyone present who wanted to stay connected. Next to name and comm address, there was a slot for LP addresses, so they could be integrated into the first iteration of the Commune.

"This means you won't be able to access the Commune from anything other than that one interface," Liam pointed out. "It will be inaccessible from any chip that has not been manually entered by one of our creators, so you won't be able to get there via your A.E. chip."

At the end of the presentation, Liam invited Francis to join him up front, evidently expecting him to say a few words on behalf of the Renegades, or perhaps of his pub. Francis regarded the room with his usual surly disposition, though—not one for public speeches before strangers, apparently. Liam continued, perhaps to fill the awkward silence left by Francis, "This meeting is only the beginning.

We're stronger together than we are apart—that's why Halpert has fragmented us, and tried to keep us from communicating with one another! We want to ask every one of you to consider hosting similar meetings in your own home towns. I will make this holograph presentation available to you, so that all you will have to do is present it. The goal is to get as many contacts on the Commune as possible, but also for each and every person to hound your representatives to stop Halpert's challenge before it's too late. The future is still unwritten!"

Here Liam nudged Francis. Francis gave him an irritated look, but called out to the room rather unwillingly, "Stay. Eat and drink."

That signaled the official end of the meeting. I did my best just to get through the next few hours, plastering a smile on my face and politely answering questions about my research—many of those nearest me had noticed others glancing in my direction when Liam first started talking. I saw Liam speaking animatedly with Roy Benson from Casa Linda, but I didn't pay much attention, truth be told.

Emily chatted with me about school, volleyball (she played for her school), and the guy she was seeing. I tried to look interested. A few of Liam's friends came up and introduced themselves, and I did my best to attend to their conversations, though afterwards I don't think I could recall any of their names. I was acutely aware of Andy and Yolanda the whole time, even though I rarely looked directly at them. I overheard snippets of Andy's conversation, and her laughter, feeling like my intestines were being mashed together with a mortar and pestle.

"You look like you've had enough," whispered Ivan, Andy's roommate. I was slightly more interested in talking to him than to anyone else, mostly due to association.

I shrugged, and managed a fake smile. "Been a long few days."

"So… what are you doing here again, though?" he asked. "You don't seem that passionate about this, no offense."

I smiled in spite of myself. Ivan was perceptive, I'd give him that. Finally I said, "This was something my dad was passionate about. I guess you could say I'm doing it for him. Carrying on the family tradition." I didn't think it wise to elaborate beyond that, but I didn't have to. Ivan seemed satisfied. Then I gestured with my head to Yolanda, trying to keep my voice casual. "So are they together now, or what?"

Ivan rolled his eyes. "Who knows. Andy's never straightforward about anything, as I'm sure you've noticed. They're hanging out with each other all the time, though."

I bit my lip. *I will not cry. I will not cry.*

Ivan studied my face. "So… do you like him or something? Andy?"

I looked up sharply, and felt all the blood rush to my face. "What? No, where did you get that idea?" It was out of my mouth before I could think about whether flat denial was smart or not. I couldn't help it.

Ivan shrugged. "I didn't *think* you did, but I got a weird comm about it from some unknown number."

I blinked at him, willing the blush to fade and my heart rate to return to normal. "You… huh? What did it say?"

"It was just something like, 'If Andy were to pursue Rebecca, he wouldn't be refused.' But when I tried to reply, it wouldn't go through. It was weird. Any idea who sent it?"

"No," I said, my mind racing through possibilities and rejecting them just as quickly. Julie and my mom and Madeline were the only ones who knew how I felt about Andy… and obviously none of them would have… *Would Julie?* I wondered. But how would she even have Ivan's number? They'd never met before tonight.

"Andy and I are just friends. Really." Again, it came out of my mouth without conscious intention—I felt desperate to convince Ivan in that moment, regardless of the long-term consequences.

"Yeah, it's cool." Ivan shrugged. "Anyway,

we're all taking off from school tomorrow too, and going to the beach, since we're here. Want to come?"

I thought for a second. Liam could spare me for one day, surely. I felt so wretched at the moment, though, and I wasn't sure I could handle watching Andy and Yolanda carry on like that all day tomorrow too. Then again, if I spent another day around Andy, he might redeem himself: he might come talk to me and say something to make me think I still mattered to him more than she did, and then I'd feel more hopeful than if we parted on *this* note.

Was that possibility worth the chance that I might spend a whole day feeling like I did right now, or even worse?

Before I could answer Ivan, Liam made his way through the thinning crowd with a big smile on his face.

"Hey!" he said, sticking out a hand to Ivan. "Figured I'd come meet your friends. I'm Liam."

"Ivan," they shook, and I readjusted my face with a fake smile as I introduced Liam all around.

"This is Emily, Elizabeth, Patrick, Rob, Julie, Jake, Andy, and Yolanda," I said, trying to give away nothing as I pronounced each name.

"All friends from high school?" Liam asked, and they nodded. "Except you," he pointed to Julie, "I've seen you on campus."

Julie widened her eyes at me, and I bit my lip to keep from smirking. I knew what that meant: *He noticed me!* She had Jake now, but that wouldn't keep her from gloating that she'd caught the eye of another handsome man. Since Jake was the schmoozer, Liam and Jake fell into smalltalk conversation. Most of the others just listened, but Elizabeth competed for Liam's attention. Andy and Yolanda still remained aloof, as if they were in a room by themselves.

Julie made her way over to me, though Ivan didn't leave my side.

"You okay?" she asked pointedly.

I felt a rush of gratitude for her—at least I knew *she* understood.

"Of course," I lied, turning up my fake smile to the point of parody. I could tell by the knowing look she gave me that she caught the implied sarcasm.

"You coming with us to the beach? We're leaving right after this," she asked, looking at Ivan. Then she dropped her voice and said sympathetically, "I'll understand if you don't want to."

I felt the tears prick my eyes. *Do not cry,* I commanded myself furiously. *Not here!*

"I… think I'll pass," I said finally. "I'm sure Liam and I will have a lot to do. Thanks though."

"No problem." She squeezed my hand.

When the pub finally filtered out a few hours later, I slipped out, down the street and back to my room in the hotel while Liam's back was turned. The second I entered the room, the tears came. I threw myself onto my bed, sobbing into my pillow.

Madeline wheeled over to me, patting the arm that dangled off the bed. She didn't ask what was wrong. She knew—of course she knew. There was always only one thing.

"Why can't I just get over him?" I sobbed. "Why?"

"What did he do this time?" she asked. "Or, what did he *not* do…"

"He showed up with Yolanda," I practically spat the name. Then I admitted miserably, "And… she's really pretty."

Madeline patted my arm now in a rhythm, almost like playing the drums. "What would make you happy right now?"

I sniffled. "For him to stop hanging out with her. Obviously. At least I don't want them spending all that romantic time at the beach together." I wiped my face and added, "But what's the point? Even if she left, it's not like I'm there instead."

"Would you have gone to the beach with them if she hadn't been there?"

"Of course I would! Like I'd have passed

that up!"

The syncopated knock at my door made me jump. I closed my eyes with a heavy sigh. Only Liam knocked like that.

"Just a minute!" I called, trying to keep my voice steady as I catapulted off the bed into the bathroom to splash water on my face. *Couldn't he just leave me alone for twenty minutes?*

"Come back over!" Liam called through the door, "It was a raving success! Three people are already gonna give the same talk in their own towns, including your Roy Benson—"

"Liam, hold on!" I called, exasperated. I patted my face dry with a towel, and inspected it: no more tear stains, but the eyes were still bloodshot. Didn't matter, though—clearly he wouldn't wait. I opened the door, but stood firmly in the doorframe to keep him from coming inside.

A shadow of confusion marred the enormous grin he wore at first when he saw me. "What's the matter with you?"

"Nothing." I fixed the plastic smile in place again. "So it went well, huh?"

"Yeah, I wanted you to come out with us to celebrate—really, are you okay?"

"I—just don't feel that great, that's all," I said at last.

Liam tilted my chin up and scrutinized my face, frowning. I felt naked. After a long moment, his expression changed to one of resignation. I don't know how, but I suddenly felt certain he knew *exactly* what was wrong with me.

"Fine," he said shortly, releasing my face. "Come if you want." Then he turned to go.

Chapter 16

After Liam left, I commed Julie on her way to the beach with the rest of my friends. I told her about Ivan's mystery comm, just to make sure it hadn't been her—she *had* told me multiple times to just tell Andy how I felt about him, after all. But she seemed as baffled as I was about it. Then we quickly moved on to the subject of Andy and Yolanda. Since she couldn't tell me that she didn't think he liked her, she focused instead on flattering me at Yolanda's expense. "She seems like a bimbo, he can't possibly respect her, you're a much better catch, you're so much prettier, Becca..." that kind of thing. It didn't make me feel any better—actually it made me feel worse in a way, because there was nothing I could do about it. If she was objectively better than I was in any measurable way, then I could... what? Try harder? Probably that's exactly what I would do. But if I already beat her in every category and Andy *still* picked her, there was nothing I could change.

At last I tossed my handheld aside, trying to

force Andy and Yolanda out of my mind. But it was immediately replaced by guilt for disappointing Liam. That, at least, I could do something about. Even though I didn't want to, I ran a comb through my hair and threw on the closest thing I'd brought to "going out" clothes: a purple sheath dress and a pair of black ballet flats. It was just a little too cold for a sheath dress by itself, so I threw on a black athletic jacket on top of it, which didn't go at all. My hair still stuck up in a few places, so I finally tossed it up in a clip. *Doesn't matter how I look, anyway,* I thought, comparing my reflection to Yolanda's voluptuous curves. *Stop it,* I commanded myself fiercely.

"We're at the Tikki Cantina a block from Francis's pub," Liam wrote when I asked where they'd gone. "Wait for me, I'll come back and get you!"

I rolled my eyes. "Don't bother, I can find it."

"Rebecca, please stay where you are and wait for me."

"On my way," was my reply. I wasn't in the mood to indulge this nonsense.

Liam met me halfway to the cantina, glowering. "It's not safe for you to be out here on your own. You're taking stupid risks for absolutely no gain!"

"Oh, this from the guy who wants to rent an arena and preach to hundreds of thousands of people?"

"That's different!"

"How is that different?" I demanded.

"Because it's me!"

We stared at each other for a minute before Liam sighed, conceding, "Look, you probably are completely safe for now, you're right. But please don't make a habit of wandering off by yourself around here, all right? Especially not as things ramp up." He offered me his arm, and I took it, rather unwillingly.

"I appreciate that you're trying to keep me safe. But I'm a big girl, Liam. I can take care of myself."

We walked in silence for a moment before he said at last, "I wish that were true, Rebecca. But you have no idea what could happen to you."

John Doe's words rang in my ears: "*The same secret Liam's brother knew.*"

I would have asked him about his brother right then. But we rounded the corner and the loud cantina that was our destination came into view, pulsing with live music and a crowd of 20-somethings beneath the thatched roof who didn't give us a second glance. Liam ushered me into the little outdoor patio.

"Tonight is a night off," he shouted over the

music. "No more 'shop' talk allowed, just enjoy yourself. Can I buy you a drink?"

I let him order a margarita for me, slipping into the seat beside Larissa. She was the only other female in the group, amid a sea of young male Renegades. A swarm of men vied for her attention —probably a first for Larissa, who certainly was not beautiful—but it was clear that she only had eyes for Francis.

Francis didn't appear to notice. He *did* notice me, though.

"You've been crying," he observed flatly.

"Thanks for that astute assessment." No point in denying it; I'd figured out that much.

He tilted his head to one side, then glanced at Liam, across the room ordering my margarita. "You weren't crying over *him*, clearly," Francis commented. "And your hand keeps twitching toward your jacket pocket. I assume that must be where you keep your handheld, because you've disabled your A.E. retinal chip. You're hoping someone who isn't here will comm you. Must have been someone who was at the meeting earlier, then —"

"Not everything is about a guy!" I snapped.

"Noooo, but this is," Francis returned, smug. "I can tell by the way you're blushing right now—"

"Ugh! You're insufferable!" I shoved myself away from their table and stalked off to the other side of the group.

Liam, who had been *en route* with my drink, followed me to the other side of the cantina, a smirk on his face.

"Getting along famously with Francis, I see."

"*What* does she see in him?" I couldn't stop myself from saying.

"Who, Larissa?" Liam turned to observe them together, and after a long moment said thoughtfully, "Huh. There's someone for everyone, I guess..."

Liam got roped into conversation with a programmer named Rob after that, on something technical and boring, despite his rule about 'no shop talk.' Nilesh was there too, and he made smalltalk with me for a bit, but I guess I wasn't interesting enough for him tonight. He soon lost interest and moved on. After that, I fought off about five single Renegades at once. Liam caught my eye and smirked at my clearly awkward body language on more than one occasion, and I narrowed my eyes back at him.

You could save me, you know, my expression told him.

His amusement replied, *But it's so much more fun watching you squirm.*

When a blond, angular boy named Jimmy actually leaned in to try to kiss me, I got up and announced unceremoniously that I needed to use the restroom. I'd wanted to check my handheld for some time, anyway: I'd felt it vibrate several times in my pocket, and just couldn't find a polite way to excuse myself from my admirers. I knew it wouldn't be from Andy, but I just had to check. I caught a glimpse of Liam laughing as I squirmed away from Jimmy, and shot him a look of daggers.

When I got to the restroom, I saw Jake's name on the handheld and deflated a little. "Hey Bec, Julie and I are taking surfing lessons tomorrow! Wish you could come!" Then, "P.S.: she's kind of amazing."

I wrote back something benign about missing them too, and then returned from the bathroom, considerably deflated. Still eager to avoid Jimmy, I continued to comm Jake in order to send the message that I was otherwise occupied. Unfortunately, Jake began to complain about how Andy was ignoring everyone else because he was so fixated on Yolanda. In a spurt of masochistic obsession, I pumped Jake for as much information as he would give. Did he really think Andy liked her? Did everyone else like her? Did he think they seemed serious?

Finally Jake said, "I gotta go, I'm being antisocial, sorry. Oh, and Emily says to tell you we'll pick you up some genuine California studs at the farmer's market tomorrow. :)"

I grinned in spite of myself. It was an inside joke—I'd said I was craving some local potatoes on a trip once, except I'd said 'spuds.' Emily thought I'd said 'studs.' Ever since, I'd had the dubious reputation of collecting attractive men at every city I visited. It was probably only funny because it was *me*.

I felt a pair of eyes on me and looked up as I put my handheld back in my pocket. Liam scowled at me across the room, looking away as soon as I caught him.

Annoyed, and slightly tipsy, I rejoined Larissa and her clique of admirers, even though there wasn't really room. Since the cantina was so loud and she had her back to me, effectively I sat alone. Which was fine with me: it kept me from having to pretend I was okay when I wasn't.

"Want to go for a walk?" said a voice in my ear. Liam hovered just behind me, taking me gently by the elbow. "Come on, you look like you could use some fresh air."

I didn't know whether I was glad to go with him or not. I *was* glad to escape the general merriment, but I really wanted to be alone. He kept his hand on my elbow lightly.

"Not having fun?" I asked him, once we were far enough away from the cantina that the voices died down.

He shrugged. "It's all right." His tone was

cool: still giving me the cold shoulder, apparently. I fought the urge to roll my eyes. Then he added, "Who were you comming just now?"

I blinked at him, and for the first time it began to dawn on me. *Is he… jealous?* "One of the guys you met at the thing tonight."

"Which one?"

He is *jealous,* I realized with amazement. "Jake," I told him, a bit reluctantly. Some vain part of me wanted to see how he'd react if I'd said one of the others, who wasn't obviously dating someone already. *Although Andy certainly looked unavailable too,* I added to myself bitterly.

Sure enough, Liam relaxed. "Oh. I liked Jake. Are they still around?"

"They all went to the beach for the next few days. They invited me to join them but I… told them I had other things to do."

We walked in silence for a few minutes, as I turned over the revelation of Liam's jealousy in my mind. I was not indifferent to the discovery; I had a strong reaction to it, in fact, but I couldn't identify it by name. Suddenly I saw Liam's overprotectiveness in a whole new light, though.

He *likes* me.

It's not that I hadn't known how Liam felt about me—on some level, I'd always known. But I'd been so busy trying to keep him at arm's length, trying to keep it from being true, that I hadn't ever faced it as a fact before. Because if it *was* a fact, I'd have to do something about it eventually.

No, I do not, I told myself firmly. Unless he said something outright, which I was determined to never let him do, I would never have to deal with it. I could just pretend I didn't know, like I'd always done…

"All right, I just gotta know," Liam said at last. "You're obsessed with one of those guys who came to the talk tonight. Which one?"

I looked up at him, my heart leaping to my throat.

Without waiting for me to reply, he guessed, "Gotta be the skinny one who had that other girl with him, right? Is that what you're so upset about? Is he an ex-boyfriend or something?"

After a long pause, during which I attempted to get my pulse under control with the mental directive, *Calm down, calm down,* I finally decided I might as well be direct. He certainly was.

"No. I never dated him," I admitted.

"But you're making yourself sick over him," Liam observed.

I bristled, wanting to end this conversation. "I don't expect you to understand."

"Then help me to!" He stopped walking in front of a little park nearby, bordered by a wrought iron fence. "What is so great about this guy that he's got you, of all people, pining over him?"

205

"What do you mean, me, 'of all people'?" I demanded. "Why *not* me?"

Liam rolled his eyes. "Are you really fishing for compliments, Bec? Fine. You're beautiful. You're one of the smartest girls I've ever met. You're curious and interested in everything, and totally un-self-conscious, which is extremely rare for beautiful girls. I know I'm not the one you want to hear this from," he held up his hands as I reddened and dropped my eyes, "so just take it as an objective fact, all right? And here another one: from all outward appearances, there's nothing special about that guy! He's... wussy," he finished at last, as if grasping for the right word.

Incredulous, but also flattered in spite of myself, I laughed. "Wussy?"

"Yes! He has this overly pleasing, passive air about him—"

"When did you take the time to observe all this?" I cut in.

He paused, and I had the impression he was considering whether or not to be honest. Finally he admitted, "I started paying attention to him as soon as I realized you were."

I was grateful for the moonlight so that he couldn't see the flame in my cheeks as he held my eyes. I'd hoped he wouldn't come right out and say how he felt about me. This was pretty close.

When I didn't reply, Liam took a step back,

as if to acknowledge the significance of my silence. "I just want to know what you see in him. That's all."

I bit my lip, deciding whether or not *I* wanted to be honest. But he'd certainly put himself out there. I felt I at least owed him that much.

"He reminds me of my dad," I said finally.

We walked back to the hotel, leaving the others to find their own way back. I found myself telling Liam things I never told anyone except Madeline: how I met Andy right after my dad had died, and—given my psychology training—I figured that the timing and my feelings for Andy probably weren't a coincidence.

"Dad was quiet around people who didn't know him," I said, "but he'd open up to those who did. He was almost like a little kid, the way he'd get excited about knowledge for its own sake. He wore his heart on his sleeve. Andy is like that too. He doesn't so much care what he does with the knowledge, he just loves learning new things. They were the same kind of quirky."

We arrived back at the hotel, and Liam guided me into a booth in the little empty cafe downstairs, where we'd had breakfast. He ordered us two cups of tea. Once the waitress bot left I went on, "Sometimes Andy even has the same expressions my dad used to have. Once or twice,

Andy said certain antiquated phrases to me that my dad used to tease me with, but I'd never heard from anyone else."

"Like what?" Liam asked, as the bot delivered us our tea. He unwrapped his tea bag and dipped it into the hot water.

I laughed softly. "Like, you remember that old song from the early Second Age, the one that goes 'school days, school days, dear old golden rule days'?" Liam shook his head no, and I went on, "Well anyway. After a break, when I was going back to class, my dad used to sing that song to tease me. Out of the blue one time, after a summer break in high school, Andy bust out with that song. I thought it was a sign or something.

"I fell in love with him so fast. I thought he felt the same way, but every time it looks like he's about to pursue me, he never actually follows through. As soon as he gets close, suddenly he starts dating some other girl and stops talking to me almost completely. Then a few weeks or months later, he'll break up with the other girl, come back, and repeat the cycle with me, all over again." I sighed, running a hand through my hair. "For *five years*."

Liam gagged on his tea. "*Five years*? Have you dated anyone else in all that time?"

"No," I said, a little defensive. "How could I when I'm in love with Andy?"

He stared at me, deadpan. "So you've never dated."

"Wouldn't you think it would be wrong of me to date one person while wishing he was someone else?"

Liam sighed, and looked down, as if weighing his next words. "At the risk of stating the obvious—I mean, I know you're the psychology queen, and not me—you *do* realize that even if you were dating Andy, you'd be wishing he was someone else, too. Right?"

I blinked. "Sorry?" I really couldn't see how he reached *that* conclusion.

"You've as good as told me that this is all about your dad."

I balked a little before spluttering, "Girls just like men who remind them of their fathers. That's all!"

Liam shook his head, as if speaking to a child. "Rebecca, when he died, did you ever let yourself stop and be sad for awhile? Or did you just channel it all into this obsession with Andy?"

For some reason I couldn't explain, I found myself simultaneously angry and wanting to cry. He didn't understand. It wasn't that at all.

"Please don't psychoanalyze me," I said at last.

Liam took my hand, and I felt a visceral swooping sensation in my stomach. I didn't understand why, and it made me angry with my own body for its betrayal.

"I just hate to see you this way," he murmured, running his thumb down my hand.

There was plenty of light in the cafe; no hiding my blush this time. I gave his hand a quick, perfunctory squeeze before I let go, not meeting his eyes.

"I'll be fine," I said briskly. Then I added, my voice dry, "Not like this is the first time Andy's shown up with some other girl." I gave him a too-bright smile to signal the end of my vulnerability. "What about you, Liam? Since this is apparently a night for disclosures. You said when we were at Senator Kim's office the first time that you grew up in high society. I don't know anything about that."

Liam looked down, giving me a resigned smile. "What is this, a first date, now? Have we resorted to those questions?"

The blush returned, but I belied it with another laugh. "Hardly, unless it's standard practice on a first date to admit being in love with another guy."

He laughed at this. "Fair enough." Heaving a heavy sigh, he admitted like it cost him something, "My dad is the CEO of General Specs."

I stared at him, not comprehending for a moment. General Specs was the largest technology company in the world, based out of London. It was also one of the biggest supporters of William Halpert's legislation for the advancement of Synthetic Reasoning. *CEO Liam Kelly,* I recalled reading on a locus somewhere. *Liam Kelly. Junior.* My mouth fell open when it finally sank in. It had never occurred to me before that it was more than a coincidence…

"You're joking," I said aloud.

He shook his head. "Nope. Wish I was." He took a deep breath, stirring the string attached to his tea bag absently in his cup. "I was the Golden Child all growing up. Prodigy with programming and Synthetic Reasoning development—not to brag," he added with a smirk. "Dad wanted me to go into management, though. He'd started grooming me to eventually be his replacement when I was fifteen.

"Then there was my younger brother, Brian."

My heart jolted a little, but Liam didn't seem to notice. He wasn't looking at me, still stirring the tea bag as he spoke. He went on, "Brian was the rebellious wild child, the 'black sheep,' if you will. I thought for the longest time that he was just jealous of me, and since he didn't think he could compete, he decided to go to the other extreme instead." Liam gave a hollow laugh. "Brian of course thought General Specs had made a deal with the devil, producing so many of the robots that put everyone else out of work. He and Dad fought about it all the time—I mean, screaming matches every time they were together. It was horrible."

"But you were actually working for General Specs?" I clarified. "You *built* and programmed robots?"

"It was worse than that," Liam said with a bitter smile. "I was Head of Operations. At twenty." Sighing again, he said, "Eventually Dad and Brian had a complete rift. They didn't speak to each other for about six months, and I didn't see Brian for most of that time either. It turned out, he'd joined the Renegades before I did, though I didn't know that until much later." He took a sip of his tea and looked up at me briefly before looking back down at his cup again, like he couldn't bear to hold my gaze.

"Brian vanished five years ago."

He said it with finality, like that was the end of the story.

I blinked. *A year after my father.* "Vanished?" I repeated. "What do you mean?"

"I mean, *poof.* All traces of him, gone. The best hackers and private detectives and even research robots in the world could find neither hide nor hair of him. The trail ended in San Jose, so once I realized that something was wrong, I came looking."

"And you found the Renegades yourself," I finished.

Liam nodded. "I also found out Brian had been right all along."

"That's when you started your locus," I guessed.

He nodded again.

"What did you tell your father?"

"All of it," Liam pursed his lips, looking around the room as if he'd gone back in time. "What I knew, anyway. I told him about the level of unrest among the people we'd put out of work, and the fact that the media purposely didn't report that there even was another side to the progress our company had helped to achieve. They didn't want that information out there, for some reason. The fact that I met so many other members of the Renegades who were apparently unharmed suggested to me that my brother had made himself dangerous somehow. He knew something he wasn't supposed to know. I was determined to find out what it was.

"My father didn't want to hear it. He didn't want to deal with the implication of his guilt. I think he felt betrayed by me. He fired me and I quit in the same fight, so I'm not sure who actually got the last word there."

"That's when you went back for your Ph.D.," I concluded. I hated how Liam wore that smile as he told the story, like a mask to hide the pain.

He nodded, turning up the brightness a notch, and joked, "Might as well use my powers for good and not for evil!"

I looked down at my cup. "Have you spoken to your father since?"

Liam shrugged. "Christmases, birthdays… we try. It's not the same, but I'm the only son he has left."

I wanted to do something to comfort him, but considering our earlier conversation, I dared not reach out physically. So I just said, "I'm so sorry, Liam."

"So you see," he concluded as if he hadn't heard me, still wearing that tight smile, "it's personal for both of us."

Chapter 17

It was almost midnight when Liam and I finished talking, and we only stopped then because I could hardly keep my eyes open. After the revelations about Andy on my side, and his brother Brian on his, somehow the floodgates just opened. We swapped childhood stories. Liam told me about old girlfriends and adventures he'd been on. I told him all about my favorite memories with my friends from back home, and about my parents when I was growing up. It was as if we'd burst through a barrier of some kind—previously, there was a layer of awkwardness and formality between us that was just gone now. He knew my secrets, and I knew his.

Well. Almost.

After my third yawn in two minutes, Liam stood up. "All right, I'm calling it," he announced, and made like he was going to hoist me to my feet by my elbows when Larissa stumbled in the sliding hotel doors, humming to herself. Liam raised his eyebrows at me with his lips pursed in a suppressed smile.

"Have a good night?" he called to her.

She hadn't seen us, but she looked up when she found that she wasn't alone. Her face broke into a grin.

"Yes!" she staggered toward us, declaring, "Francis is sooo delicious."

I couldn't suppress a giggle, and Liam laughed out loud too.

"I've heard a lot of colorful language used to describe Francis before, but I'm pretty sure *that's* a first."

"Maybe I should help you up to your room," I offered, noticing how unsteady she was on her feet. I slipped an arm under her elbow, with an amused glance back at Liam.

"Good night," Liam mouthed at me with a wave, grinning.

Larissa prattled all about Francis, and how attentive he was to her—but even with her imagination, I wasn't sure how she'd interpreted Francis's behavior as attentive. From what I'd seen before Liam and I had left, Francis would have been perfectly happy to sit aloof from the others with his drink, amusing himself with his inappropriate deductions about every passerby… but Larissa was persistent. He'd taken as little notice of her as if she'd been a gnat at first—having already laid bare the secrets of her soul, presumably he found her dull now. But she had very little competition for his attentions (*shocking,* I thought), and as the hours passed, according to her, she'd worn him down. He'd even given her a compliment—"He said if I did my hair differently and wore different clothes and changed my makeup, I might even be pretty!"

I made a little choking sound to stop myself from commenting on this. "Oh! Um. That's—" I couldn't think of any way to finish that sentence. "You don't think he might be a little…"

"Socially awkward?" she piped without reservation, and shrugged. "Sure, but… what programmer isn't? *I* certainly am. And I've never seen a mind like his before… it's *so* sexy!" She giggled.

I guffawed once, involuntarily.

"And you and Liam, huh?" she said loudly, gesturing behind us. "About time!" Fortunately we were already to the elevators, so I hoped he didn't overhear.

"Shh!" I hissed instinctively, feeling my cheeks redden for the hundredth time that night. "It's not like that. We were just talking."

"I know Francis says you're not into him, or at least you think you're not," she waved me off. "But even everybody in the lab can see the way he looks at *you*."

I opened my mouth, and closed it again, caught off guard by this. I'd only admitted Liam's feelings to myself earlier that evening… it never occurred to me that everyone else had already known. "Really?"

"Oh. *So* obvious. Francis thinks so too," she declared dramatically. "And like Nilesh said, what woman's gonna resist *Liam*? When you two went off on this little adventure together, we all took bets in the lab on how long it would take you to hook up!"

"What?" I gasped, mortified.

But she went on as if she hadn't heard me, "Nilesh guessed within the week, but I said no way. You're such an uptight perfectionist, it'll take Liam at least a month to loosen you up."

The elevator door opened, and I guided Larissa to her room without speaking for a minute, trying to identify the emotion I felt. Finally I decided it was indignation.

"'Uptight perfectionist'?" I echoed, unable to keep the affront from my tone.

"Of course! You're Little Miss Pleaser, soooo 'by the book'!" Larissa burst out with a giggle, totally missing my offense. "That's what Francis said, anyway. He says you need someone like Liam to lighten you up, if only you knew it!"

"Well, you can tell Francis to mind his own business!" I snapped, as we stopped in front of her door. "Liam and I are just friends, and that's all we're going to be. You and Nilesh both lose. Thumb here." I grabbed her hand and thrust her thumb at the scanner, and the door clicked open.

"Then you're an idiot," Larissa informed me, in a singsong voice. Then she waggled her fingers at me. "Good night!"

When her door clicked shut, I shuddered and let out a whisper-grunt of disgust before heading up to my own room.

"How was it?" Madeline asked when I got back to my room, perky as ever.

"Shh!" I told her, wincing at the shrillness of her voice. I was already moving into that space between waking and dreams, half asleep on my feet. "It was… interesting." I slipped out of my shoes, shrugged out of my light jacket and changed into pajamas as I told her that Liam and I had left the others and had been downstairs talking for the last several hours.

"He told me what happened to his brother," I informed Madeline.

Her digital eyes widened. "What *did* happen to his brother?"

"His dad is the CEO of General Specs, believe it or not. Liam used to be the Head of Operations there himself—he actually built and programmed robots for a living, and he would have taken over as CEO if his brother hadn't found the Renegades and disappeared five years ago!"

Madeline took this in with less shock than I

had. "Poor Liam," she murmured. "But—disappeared? Like the way Randall Loomis did?"

"I guess," I shrugged, brushing my hair as I sat down on the bed. "But nobody else disappeared in the Renegades, at least not that we know of—just them. I'm pretty sure that his brother must have discovered something, and it must have been the same thing my father and his friends knew too. And probably Loomis. But if all these years in the Renegades haven't helped Liam discover their secret, I don't see how I can either…"

Suddenly I felt the mattress vibrate: my handheld, still inside the pocket of my discarded jacket, alerted me to a comm. I pulled it out.

"You must go back to Dublin with your colleagues tomorrow, and resume your normal life," it read. "Leave the Renegades behind, Rebecca."

It was anonymous.

"What?" Madeline rolled up to the edge of the bed, seeing my expression.

I wrote back, "Why should I go back? What would happen if I stay?" But when I tried to send it, the screen read, "Message failed."

"Arrgh!" I said aloud, and Madeline wheeled against the bed frame, since she couldn't come any closer.

"What? What?" she demanded.

"John Doe! Loomis, whoever!" I tossed the handheld away from me in disgust. "He's got no intention of telling me the secret that my dad died for and Liam's brother disappeared for. All he wants to do is warn me away!"

After a pause, Madeline ventured, "Do you think he made some kind of a promise to your dad to keep you safe?"

I looked up—this hadn't occurred to me, actually, but it should have. It didn't matter though. I wouldn't rest until I knew the secret, and I knew Liam wouldn't either. Not when we were this close.

"I wonder if I should tell Liam about John Doe after all," I mused.

"But John Doe told you not to, for Liam's own good!"

"I know, and before, I didn't feel like I had to," I agreed, "but that was before tonight. Now he's suddenly confiding in me, and he thinks I'm confiding in him too... and I *was*, about everything else..." I sighed. "An omission this large feels like a betrayal of trust somehow."

"Did you even tell him about Andy?" Madeline gasped.

I had to laugh—*that* shocked her, yet nothing else I'd said so far had. "I did."

"What did he say?"

"He said he thinks Andy is... wussy." I bit my lip, trying not to be amused at Andy's expense, even though it *was* kind of amusing. "Basically he says he thinks I can do better."

"Everybody thinks that," Madeline said, matter-of-factly. "But you still want him to break up with Yolanda so he can come back to you anyway."

"I do," I admitted. "Even though I don't think 'break up' is the right word because at least according to Ivan, they're not officially together."

As I swung my legs around and stuffed them under the sheets, Madeline said, "So... are you going to tell Liam then? About John Doe?"

I flipped the lights off, all except the one right next to my bed. "I don't know," I yawned. "Maybe... maybe I'll tell him I have something to confess, but make him promise to do nothing with the information before I say anything."

"You think he'll go for that?" Madeline asked, skeptical.

I shrugged, leaning over the edge of the bed to grab the plug for Madeline, and inserting it into the back of her neck. Her eyes brightened just a bit with the initial surge of power. "That's what I did before I told him about you."

"And he promised?" she asked, surprised.

I thought for a minute, remembering Liam's mocking, "Cross my heart and hope to die!"

"Well," I amended, "He sarcastically promised. I don't know if that counts. I'll make him *really* promise before telling him about John Doe, though. He'll give me his word, or I won't say anything."

Chapter 18

I woke up to a knock at my door the next morning: not syncopated, and a little timid. Not Liam then.

"Rebecca?" The voice belonged to Dr. Yin.

"Just a minute!" I gasped my first conscious breath, feeling that my eyes were still bloodshot before I saw them. I rushed around the room, splashing water on my face and tossing my messy auburn hair into a high ponytail before opening the door a crack. Dr. Yin was alone, so I admitted her. "Sorry, I guess I overslept…"

"Yes, you did, it's almost nine!" she said, with a hint of reproach. "The Quantum Track leaves at ten fifteen."

"Quantum Track?" my eyebrows contracted. "You mean for us to see you off?"

"No, for you too, I thought. I got a comm that you were to be on board with us," she frowned.

"You—" my mind spun, trying to make sense of this. "Who sent it?"

She shrugged. "I don't know, it was

anonymous, but—"

"Why are all these people getting anonymous comms about my life!" I burst out. When I saw the shocked look on Dr. Yin's face, I flushed. "I'm sorry. That… wasn't supposed to be out loud."

She stopped, peering over my shoulder. "What is that?"

I felt a stone drop into the pit of my stomach. *Madeline.* She was still plugged in and charging, but I'd completely forgotten about her when I'd opened the door. It didn't matter in the Capital so much, but I'd always tried to keep her secret from everyone else in my life.

"Ah…" I stammered, but my mind went blank.

"You have a companion bot?" Dr. Yin gaped.

There was nothing to do but tell the truth now—the evidence was right there. "Please don't spread that around," I said meekly. "It's a long story."

"Does Liam know?" She said the words forcefully, like Madeline's very existence constituted a betrayal.

"Yes, of course he knows. I told him before we came. They've made friends."

Dr. Yin gave a short laugh. "*Liam* made friends with a companion bot?" She shook her head.

"Wow. Okay. He must be *really* fond of you." She turned to leave before I could reply to this. "Well, we're having breakfast downstairs. If you don't need to pack, then join us at your leisure, I suppose."

Liam waved me over to their table when he saw me, pulling out a chair beside him. I smiled, a little self-conscious. I wasn't quite sure how to act around him now, since the dynamic of our relationship had changed so dramatically in the last twenty-four hours.

"I've decided to stay, too!" Larissa announced to me brightly as soon as I sat down. I guessed in her mind, our conversation last night had been more bonding than insulting. *Well, she admitted she was socially awkward,* I thought. She dropped her voice and added, as if I'd asked, "I'm going to help Francis and Liam build the Commune. They're going to need my help here more than in Dublin!"

"Although Rebecca will be more use to us in Dublin," Dr. Yin said to me pointedly. "You'll have far more resources there for your morality and free will research, don't you think?"

Liam sighed, and glanced at me, reluctant. "I think she's right, Bec. In Dublin you'll be able to collaborate with the psych and theoretical physics departments, and whoever else you need. We won't come in the picture on your project until later, anyway. Besides, I'll rest easier knowing you're safe."

I opened my mouth to tell him that I wasn't going anywhere and he wasn't getting rid of me. But just then, the lights in the hotel dimmed and a track light above a little platform lit up, like a stage at the front of the cafe. Then a holograph appeared: William Halpert.

"This can't be good," murmured Nilesh, as holographic Halpert extended his arms.

"Greetings, everyone," he said. "Senate Leader Halpert here, with an update on the challenge I presented to you weeks ago. My team has confirmed a major breakthrough in Amsterdam: robotics engineer and biochemist Kathleen De Vries and her research team appear to have developed synthetic emotion. They have essentially created an analog of the human limbic system, the system responsible for emotion in the human brain, and verified that electrical responses match their predictions based upon crude markers of pleasure, pain, and fear. De Vries' team is now working closely with General Specs, developing robotic prototypes to prove that this synthetic emotion will, in fact, lead to synthetic creativity."

Liam swore, and sank his head into his hands. I put a hand on his back, trying to comfort even though I knew there was nothing I could do.

General Specs was *his* company, or would have been. Despite everything that had happened, it must have felt a bit like a betrayal. And now there was nothing he could do to stop them.

"This may very well be the breakthrough we have all been waiting for!" Halpert went on. "Again, this challenge is not a competition so much as a collaboration across the globe for the advancement of our species. General Specs has agreed to take no remuneration for their involvement: there will be no patents, and all blueprints are freely available on the labyrinth. Anyone else who wishes to simultaneously create similar bots using the De Vries team's system can do so, and we ask only that you share your progress with the worldwide community. I will keep you posted on the results of the prototypes! Thank you all for your kind attention. This is a day to celebrate!"

The overhead lights brightened, the stage dimmed again, and Halpert's holograph disappeared. The cafe burst into applause.

Once the applause died down, the chatter in the cafe resumed. But our table sat in silent mourning. Liam did not move, still staring at where Halpert's holograph had been.

"Liam?"

He turned around to face the rest of us. I expected a haunted expression, but instead his jaw was set. His eyes, alight with determination, sought Dr. Yin's and then mine.

"Are you guys thinking what I'm thinking?"

Dr. Yin nodded. "Definitely. We'll use their blueprints and collaborate with robotics back home to create a few prototypes as fast as possible. Then we'll get to work on iterations of Rebecca's synthetic morality idea, as soon as she has one…"

"Put a call out for collaboration for synthetic morality on the labyrinth, too. See if it gets pulled," Liam cut her off. Nilesh raised his eyebrows and glanced at Dr. Yin—technically she was his boss, not the other way around—but Dr. Yin didn't seem to notice. She nodded, as Liam went on, "We haven't tried open sourcing that yet. If they pull it, and I'm pretty sure they will—well, we should have the Commune up in a few days anyway. I'm going to try to set up a meeting with Halpert directly."

We all gaped at him, and Nilesh started laughing incredulously. "Oh, just like that, huh? You're just gonna call him and arrange a lunch meeting, you and the most powerful man in the world?"

Liam leveled Nilesh with a confident gaze that silenced him. "Yes I am, and Halpert will take it."

"Why?" I asked what we all wanted to know.

He glanced back at me and said

significantly, "I'll just tell him Liam Kelly of General Specs wants to meet with him regarding the robotic prototypes they're creating."

"And... he'll assume you're your father!" I gasped, both impressed and a little frightened for him.

From the expressions around the table, I gathered no one else had known of Liam's background, either.

"Your *father*?" Dr. Yin choked, and whispered, "*Your father* is the CEO of General Specs?"

"Yup." It was evident that she wasn't about to get nearly the explanation I'd had last night. Liam sat back, touching his A.E. chip on his temple, his expression faraway.

"What are you doing?" Larissa breathed. "Do you have Halpert's direct contact information already?"

"No. I'm having Francis get it for me." His focus returned to us then, and he shrugged. "I could find it myself, but we'd better get down to the Quantum Track pretty soon. And I should help Rebecca pack." He glanced at me pointedly.

"I'm staying with you," I said at once, before I could stop myself. They all turned to look at me, and I flushed. How could I explain my reaction? "I mean... I can... go to The Capitol University and scour the research, just as well as in

Dublin. Maybe better, their uni is twice the size of ours. I'll just pose as a graduate student there. It'll be faster! I can't set up clinical trials here, of course, but we probably only have weeks before the prototypes are approved and General Specs starts to mass produce them. There's no time for human experiments anyway, so I'll just pass along whatever I find out to you guys. You can collaborate on it with robotics in Dublin, until the Commune is up and running. Then hopefully we'll have a bunch of researchers to help worldwide."

I was glad I thought fast on my feet: I saw that I'd convinced them. I'd even mostly convinced myself. Dr. Yin shrugged.

"I guess that makes sense. Clinical trials take awhile. Probably too long." Then she tapped her temple, presumably to look at the time, and looked at Larissa and Nilesh. "We'd better get down to the Quantum Track station."

Liam, Larissa and I helped them all down with their luggage. With promises to keep in close contact, handshakes and hugs, they were gone.

"I'll head back to Francis's pub now!" Larissa announced, looking a little flushed. "I'll see you guys later, I'm sure!"

Once she had gone, my heart started to pound in anticipation of what I knew I needed to do next. I turned to Liam with a determined expression. To my surprise, he met my gaze with equal expectation.

"All right. Out with it," he said, crossing his arms over his chest.

My eyebrows shot up. "Out with what?" I hadn't planned on the innocent act, but I really wasn't sure what he was referring to.

"That was some pretty fast thinking in there. You almost convinced even me, but not quite." He stared me down. "You were awfully quick and vehement about refusing to go back with them, and somehow I don't think you were just being stubborn, although you are certainly that. Why? What are you hiding?"

Instead of agreeing or denying, I just said, "Not here." I turned to walk back to the hotel, and Liam fell into step beside me. It was only about five minutes away, but we walked in prickly silence, and I composed my speech as we went.

After crossing the threshold of the glass doors in the lobby, I went straight up to my room. Liam followed me inside without waiting for an invitation.

As soon as the door clicked shut, I motioned to Madeline to stay out of the way. Eyes wide, she mimed a zipper across her lips and wheeled herself into a corner to give us privacy, her face turned toward the wall.

Then I said to Liam with a deep breath, "I have something to confess. But before I do," I held up my hands to stop him from interrupting, "you have to *promise* not to do anything with what I am about to tell you. No one else can know, and I mean *no one*—not Francis, not the Renegades, not Dr. Yin—*no one*."

He balked, arms still crossed over his chest. "I'm not sure what kind of arrangement you think we have here, but I'm not going to give you a blank check, Rebecca. No."

I blinked, taken aback. "Then I won't tell you anything!"

He closed the distance between us, eyes flashing. "How dare you keep secrets from *me*—of all people! I am the original conspirator here, do you understand that? This is *my* mission, it has been for years, and you didn't even care about it until a few weeks ago! Now suddenly you presume to withhold information from me—?"

"You have a big mouth, Liam!" I shouted back. I wasn't sure at what point we started shouting, but I was glad the walls were sound-proof. "You just shout everything you know from the rooftops, and if you're not careful, you're going to end up just like my dad, and your brother! I didn't tell you because I was trying to keep you safe!"

He laughed—a short, incredulous sound, like he couldn't believe my presumption—but he backed up a step before sinking down to sit on the edge of the bed. "*You* were trying to keep *me* safe?"

he repeated, his tone still biting but no longer a
shout. He ran a hand through his dark hair so that it
stood up in every direction.

"Yes I was, believe it or not!" I rounded on
him, hands on my hips. "You may be super cautious
when it comes to me, but you don't think about
your own safety at all! The second you get a scrap
of information, you want to tell anybody and
everybody. Well, you can't do that with this. All
I'm asking is for you to promise me to *think* before
announcing what I'm about to tell you to anyone
who will listen, because this just might be the only
ace up our sleeves that we've got. All right?"

He sighed, heavy and resigned. "Fine. Fine.
I promise. What is this enormous secret of yours?"

We stared each other down for a few
minutes, and I bit my lip before I said at last, "I
think I found Randall Loomis."

Chapter 19

Liam stared at me for a second, not comprehending.

"You—what?" He shook his head, as if to clear it of all the other things he'd apparently been expecting me to say that weren't this. "When? How? Who is he?"

I took another deep breath—suddenly I felt like I needed the extra oxygen. "The first night we were here," I confessed all at once. "After you took me back to the hotel, I went for a walk. Even though you told me not to," I held up a hand to ward off his angry reply, "I went anyway, and I met this man in the alley the next block over—"

"You did *what*?"

"Let me finish!" I retorted. "I can't explain how, but I knew he was trying to get my attention. He knew my name, Liam, and he knew why we were here, he knew about the Renegades, and he knew about my father and his friends' disappearance. He told me to call him John Doe, and he told me that he'd find me when I needed him, but I wouldn't be able to contact him. That was the first time I talked to him." I took a deep breath, and went on, "The second time was right after we met with Senator Kim."

I could see Liam's blood pressure rising as I talked, until at last he couldn't sit anymore. He stood up and began to pace. He always did that when he was upset and trying not to shout, I'd noticed.

"He told me that Senator Kim knew the same secret my father and his friends had known, and the same secret your brother knew."

Here Liam looked up sharply. "So you already knew about my brother, then?"

I held up my hands in a protestation of innocence. "Not until John Doe mentioned him that morning. I swear that was the first I knew you even had a brother."

He gave a short laugh and resumed pacing. "And then you had to figure out a way to get me to tell you the story, without arousing my suspicion. Bravo, Rebecca. Well done."

"I am telling you less than twenty-four hours later!" I shot back angrily, "will you scale back the sarcasm for half a second?"

"I trusted you," was Liam's reply, all sarcasm gone. He met my gaze, and did not bother to disguise his hurt. That was worse, much worse, than his anger. I felt tears spring to my eyes, but I maintained my anger like a shield.

"John Doe told me not to tell you specifically, because he said you were reckless!"

Liam said nothing to this, pacing still. I waited a few beats, and when it didn't seem like he was going to say anything more, I added, calmer, "The last time I heard from him was last night. He sent me another comm, and warned me to go back to Dublin with the others from the lab. And I think he must've sent a comm to Dr. Yin, too, because she woke me up this morning and told me she got an anonymous comm telling her that I was going back with them."

Liam's pacing was beginning to drive me mad. His accusation still rang in my ears: *I trusted you.*

Finally I begged, "Liam. Stop that. Look at me. Say something."

He did stop, and I saw the little muscle in his jaw tighten before he turned to look at me. I blinked my tears away before they could fall, determined not to let him see them. I couldn't *stand* it when people were angry with me.

"I want to meet him," Liam announced at last.

I sighed, exasperated. "I told you, I don't have control over when or where we meet—"

"He's contacted you multiple times since we've been here, that indicates it won't be long,"

Liam cut me off. "And you will tell me *the second* you hear from him the next time. Right?" I bristled, but before I could retort, he burst out again, "What were you thinking, Rebecca? You snuck out, on your own, twice—to a dark alley! What if he's not Loomis? What if he's keeping tabs on us for the other side, trying to find out what we know? Did you ever think of that, that maybe he didn't want you to tell me because he wanted to use you against me? Against the Renegades? What if one of these times they take you too, as a hostage or something, to shut us up?"

"Now you're just being ridiculous," I countered, but without any real conviction. The truth was, I felt shaken. He was right; I had just blindly trusted that John Doe was Loomis, and that he was on my side. Why hadn't it occurred to me that he might not be?

"I want to meet him," Liam demanded again. "The next time you hear from him—"

"I don't even know if I will again, now that I've told you!" I shot back. "He always seems to know all about everything we've done so far, so he probably knows I've told you now, too! I don't know how—"

"Maybe because he's on the inside," Liam growled. "Unless you think he's got our hotel rooms bugged."

I felt angry and confused and defensive all at

once. I wished I could prove to him that John Doe was who I'd believed him to be, but I didn't know what to say. Liam made me feel foolish and naive. Maybe I was.

Before I could formulate a reply, though, I saw Liam freeze.

"What's wrong?" I asked. Then I saw him tap his temple, and I realized he'd gotten a comm.

"It's Odessa," he murmured to me, and I saw his eyes slide back and forth, reading the comm on the inside of his retinas. "That's odd," he muttered to himself.

"What?"

His eyes snapped back to the room, and he said bitingly, "I don't know, can I trust you? You just have a tendency to run off and tell random men in alleys everything I say to you."

"That's not fair!" I shot back, feeling the tears pricking the corners of my eyes again. I blinked them back fiercely. I would *not* let him see me cry. I would *not*.

I think he saw them anyway, though, because his expression softened.

He sighed, inspecting my face, hands on his hips. "No more secrets, Bec. Deal?"

I nodded, angry with myself for my weakness. I didn't trust myself to meet his eyes. "Deal."

He crossed the room and sat down on the

edge of the bed next to me. "Remember when I said I had Odessa scour everything she could find on Halpert on the labyrinth?" Then he tapped the chip in his temple again and read, "Odessa says, 'Attached are loci with basic biographical information about William Halpert,' and then she lists three of them. She goes on, 'But I can only find independent sources corroborating his history for the past 20 years: Masters' Degree and graduation Summa Cum Laude from South Pacific University, his subsequent rise in politics, humanitarian relief efforts, professional alliances, etc. There's a block before that, though. Aside from the officially sponsored loci giving a cursory back story, there's nothing corroborating it anywhere. No other record that he even existed.'"

"Huh," I said, perplexed.

"I know." Liam nodded. "Then she says, 'The most peculiar detail I found in the last twenty years was his spending habits: he purchases salt and sulfuric acid in bulk monthly from a discount chemistry supply company out of Baltimore.'"

"Salt and sulfuric acid?" I repeated, reaching for my netscreen. A quick search on the labyrinth told me that such these were the ingredients necessary to produce hydrochloric acid, but I didn't see how that could be relevant. I showed the screen to Liam.

"What would Halpert want with that much

hydrochloric acid, though?" I asked rhetorically.

He shook his head slowly, staring at the screen. Then he tapped his temple again, and his eyes skimmed left to right as he mentally dictated a comm to Odessa.

"I'm telling her to find all possible uses for salt, sulfuric acid, or hydrochloric acid. I'm telling Francis, too. He has an uncanny way of seeing patterns I can't see." He shrugged, and met my eyes. At least Odessa's new mystery had diffused all remaining tension between us. After a moment, he reached out and squeezed my hand.

"Hey. We're okay. Right?"

I felt that same swooping, jittery sensation I'd had when Liam had touched me unexpectedly yesterday. "Yeah, of course." I gave his hand a perfunctory squeeze back, and dropped it like a hot potato. "We're fine."

Chapter 20

As soon as Liam left my hotel room and the door clicked shut, Madeline spun around, eyes wide.

"Sorry to make you stand in the corner," I said, stuffing my netscreen back in my backpack. "I just didn't think having an audience would be smart right then."

"I'm glad you told him after all," Madeline murmured. "I see what you meant now, about him feeling betrayed if you didn't. It would have been so much worse if you'd kept it from him any longer."

"As long as he keeps his end of the promise and doesn't go telling anyone else," I muttered. "Liam is so volatile, I never know what he's gonna do." I crossed the room to stuff some old fashioned pens and notebook paper into my backpack also. I was the only one who needed to go to Capitol University, but overprotective Liam insisted on coming with me. Since Liam needed to work on the Commune with Francis and Larissa, they were coming too—much to Francis's irritation.

"It's safer to talk in the pub, and Rebecca will be perfectly safe on a university campus. For heaven's sake, Liam," were his exact words. He'd sent the comm to both of us.

"He's right, Liam. I'll be fine."

"You know where you'd be fine? Dublin," Liam had shot back.

Francis sent Liam Halpert's direct comm address after that, and Liam had disabled the holograph feature for the call so that Halpert's secretary could not see that he wasn't his father. He left a message that Liam Kelly of General Specs would like to meet with the senator at his earliest convenience, suggesting lunch the following day. The four of us finally agreed to meet up again in the lobby downstairs in a few minutes to head to Capitol University library. The three of them would try to find a soundproof study room to work on the Commune, while I dug up whatever I could to at least give me a starting point on the neuroscience of morality and free will. That wasn't daunting at all.

"Do you think Liam might be right?" Madeline murmured to me. "About John Doe?"

I shook my head slowly. "I don't… think so. But then again, John Doe really hasn't told me anything useful so far. All he's done is try to get me to leave…" My handheld vibrated, and I picked it up, expecting Liam. I frowned.

"What is it?" Madeline asked.

"It's Julie…" I shook my head. "That's weird. She said Yolanda had to go back home suddenly because of some family emergency. So if I want to come to the beach to join them after all, I can."

"So… you got your wish then?"

"No, I didn't wish for that!" I felt a slight twinge of guilt, though. *Hadn't I?* "I just wanted her to leave, I didn't want it to be because of a family emergency…"

"Will you go meet up with them now, though? To be with Andy?"

I shook my head, biting my lip. "I wish I could, but I can't now. Liam's downstairs waiting for me." I wrote Julie back quickly, saying I was sorry and to let me know when they found out the status of Yolanda's emergency—slightly assuaging my conscience. Then I crossed the room and planted a kiss on Madeline's metallic forehead. "I'll see you tonight."

"Comm me if anything happens!" she piped.

Liam, Larissa, Francis and I took a hovercar to the university campus. Something in me breathed deeper once we arrived: like the campus in Dublin, it was open and spacious, and felt like the grounds of an old countryside manor in the midst of the hubbub and overwhelming technology of the rest of San Jose. The occasional hovercar passed overhead even on the campus, and there was the odd bot here or there. But mostly there were human students, wearing that same air of purpose and anticipation I loved so much in Dublin.

"Oh, how lovely!" breathed Larissa, "don't you just wish you could pick all these flowers, Becca, and take them home with us? Or back to the hotel, anyway?" She skipped over to a hedge of rosebushes, breathing in their scent. "Don't they just make you feel like springtime and infinite possibilities?"

Francis blinked at her, deadpan. Then he glanced at me. "Is she on any sort of medication?"

Trying not to laugh, Liam tapped the A.E. chip in his temple. From the way his eyes scanned up, down, and around, I didn't think he was reading a comm. Also, he had a little bit of green in his mostly blue eyes that caught the sunlight. I'd never noticed before—I guess I'd never wanted to look that deeply while he might catch me at it.

Francis caught me at it, though. He rolled his eyes, like he knew exactly what I was thinking. I flushed. Then he glanced back at Larissa.

"She's going to burst into song at any minute, isn't she? Please tell me there won't be a flash mob, and I won't find myself thrust into a musical."

"That's my idea of heaven!" cried Larissa, skipping back over to us. "I can just burst into song, and everyone around me spontaneously knows all the words, and all the steps!"

"Funny. That's how I imagine hell," Francis deadpanned.

Ignoring them, Liam announced, "Okay, we're right by the Modern Languages and Social Sciences buildings, and the library is thataway." He fully extended his right arm eastward, like a traffic cop.

I enabled my own A.E. chip for the moment, and pulled up a map of the campus also.

"Looks like the library is a few buildings down from Psych," I said, following behind him with one eye while I scanned the map with the other. It was a little disorienting. I'd never, for instance, try to descend stairs that way.

"Yeah, but all you need is the library, right?"

"Well…" I had an idea, and did a quick search while we walked. When I didn't reply right away, Liam glanced back at me.

"Don't run into a tree," he said, and explained to Francis and Larissa, "Rebecca can't comm and walk at the same time."

"I'm thrilled to learn of Rebecca's every delightful quirk," Francis replied dryly.

"Oh, hush! You needn't be so rude," Larissa scolded him, and I could hear her merry smack on his shoulder.

My vision returned to reality, and Liam's eyes widened at me, as if to say, *You're not really going to leave me alone with these two, are you?*

I bit back a smile. Aloud, I told him, "Ok, I'm going to Physics, meet you in the library afterwards. There's a Quantum Mechanics professor with office hours today."

"Again, you'll have access to way more information than she could ever memorize in the library, unless she's a bot…"

"She might be a bot," I pointed out. "Plus, this isn't something I've ever studied before. I don't even know where to start. I figured I could cut my research down by hours if I can just get her to summarize what I need to know, or at least point me in the right direction. I'll meet up with you after."

"All right. Be careful," Liam said dubiously. "Which professor? In case I need to come find you?"

"You two are pathetic," Francis commented.

"I think it's sweet! He's concerned about her!" piped Larissa.

I told Liam, "Her name is Professor Reddy, and I won't be gone an hour!"

Professor Reddy *was* a bot, it turned out. She was tall and lithe, with an articulated spine—not boxy, like Madeline. She was silver, though, and had strangely human almond-shaped eyes in her face. No nose, no hair, and a mouth with rounded edges of metal to pass for lips.

"Hello," she said, her voice far more musical than I had expected. It was slightly creepy. The almond eyes scanned my face. "I do not recognize you from any of my classes."

Of course, she'd have a perfect memory. "I'm not in any of your classes," I admitted. "I'm visiting. I just had a few questions for you on—well—how does quantum physics make free will possible? " I swallowed, suddenly realizing what a tall order that was for a girl who had almost no background in the subject.

"That question is a fallacy," Professor Reddy informed me. "You assume that it *does*."

"Doesn't it?"

"There are many theories and few facts," was her reply. "May I assume from your absence in my classes that you do not have a background in physics?"

"That's correct," I nodded, enabling my A.E. chip to record what she said.

"All right. Briefly: Newtonian, or macroscopic physics, is essentially deterministic. You have heard of the thought experiment of Laplace's Demon?" I shook my head, and she said, "In the experiment, the demon has infinite intelligence, knows all the laws of physics, and has infinite computing capability. It also knows the exact state of every particle of the universe at a given moment. If it has all this, then according to Newtonian physics, it ought to be able to perfectly predict both the past and the future. The idea is, given all knowledge of all possible influences upon any particular particle, there is only one thing that particle can possibly do, and only one thing it can possibly have done to bring it to its present state. This is equally true of every particle in the universe, including those of your own human brain. Therefore, according to Newtonian physics, there is no free will."

"But quantum physics introduces uncertainty," I pointed out.

The bot nodded. "It *may*. When unobserved, quantum particles proceed deterministically as well —but as a wave of possible positions, not as individual particles. Once observed, the wave coalesces into a particle. There are two theories of this: in the Multiverse theory, every possible state of each particle in the universe actually occurs in some alternate universe. Thus, determinism is preserved, even down to quantum particles— although the uncertainty of which path the particle will choose in any one universe persists.

"Then there is the Copenhagen interpretation, in which quantum physics is truly non-deterministic. When the wave becomes a single particle, it is called the collapse of the wave function—all those other possible futures vanish. So this does introduce uncertainty at the quantum level. Some say human thought must be a quantum system, meaning that there is a certain amount of information that even Laplace's Demon could not know, because it is unknowable. Are you with me so far?"

I nodded. She had a remarkably calm and teacherly manner about her—not exactly empathic, the way Madeline seemed to be, but Professor Reddy was certainly modeled after the best qualities in human teachers. I'd had teacher bots before, and they'd never bothered me then. So I wasn't sure why I felt so anxious to get out of her office.

Professor Reddy went on, "However much indeterminism may exist at the quantum level, though, when you take a step back, all of these possible states merge together into a larger state. I presume you have seen stippled drawings which seem nonsensical up close, but when you step back, they form recognizable patterns and images?" I nodded again, and she said, "A stray dot here or there will not make much difference to the overall image, correct? It is the same way when many possible microstates coalesce into the macrostate. There are laws that govern the macroscopic world that can never touch tiny particles, and it is from these laws that emergent properties occur."

"Like what?" I shook my head, wondering

how this related to free will.

"Like hiking, for instance," she said. "Does hiking exist?"

I blinked at her. "Suuure… but it's an activity. It doesn't 'exist' in the sense that I can point to it."

"Exactly. But in a microscopic world, would the concept even make sense?"

"No, because you have to have a body and a trail in order to do it," I said.

The bot nodded. "And both your body and the mountain trail itself are comprised of quantum particles, none of which could 'go hiking' in any meaningful sense individually. It's therefore an 'emergent' idea. And while each individual particle in both your body and the trail can, in principle, be anywhere in the universe at any given moment, the chances of any individual particle being on the other side of the galaxy from you are infinitesimally small. In the aggregate, those probabilities are essentially averaged out. So despite the uncertainty at the quantum level, you can reasonably expect to have feet tomorrow, and to have a mountain tomorrow, should you wish to go hiking."

"I'm sorry, but how does this relate to free will?" My head was starting to hurt.

"Because the human brain—and for that matter, my brain too—are both also macroscopic structures, in which the randomness at the quantum level has been averaged out. Your desires and values are not properties that belong to the individual particles of your brain any more than hiking is a property that belongs to the individual properties of the particles of your feet—they, too, are emergent properties that exist only when the possible states of every particle of your brain coalesce together. Which means they are, for all intents and purposes, governed by Newtonian, deterministic laws."

Was she saying what I thought she was saying? "So... from what we know, if we want to use quantum physics to explain free will..."

"If 'free will' means a real choice to do this or that, not predetermined by any other preceding event in the universe, then at the quantum level, it exists, if the Copenhagen interpretation is correct. And there's of course a chance that every participating particle in your brain may simultaneously line up to generate a thought completely independent of external macroscopic influences. But the chances are so small as to be negligible."

"But we *do* have free will," I blurted. "How can you explain that?" I knew I was being rude, but I was being rude to a bot, so did it really matter? I brushed the thought aside, though—I'd been hanging around Liam too much.

"I would argue that free will is merely an

illusion. Or perhaps the possibility of it technically exists, but in practice it never manifests," said the patient Professor Reddy. "Your every choice is exactly what it must be. Really," she gave me a gruesome smile, "you are no different than I am."

Chapter 21

I practically fled from Professor Reddy's office, stumbling down the hallway when a comm appeared across my retinas—I'd forgotten to disable my A.E. chip again when I left. It was from Liam.

"We're in the glass conference room in the far corner of the second story of the library," he wrote. "Come find us when you're done."

I stared at his comm for a minute. How could I tell him that Professor Reddy told me there was no such thing as free will? That even *we* didn't really have it?

And why did the very idea make me want to hyperventilate?

Instead of replying, I disabled the A.E. chip and started toward the library when my handheld vibrated, insistent on a response. I gave an exasperated sigh until I saw that it wasn't Liam this time—it was Mom.

"I assume you're back in Dublin, and back in class?" it read. "You never told me you arrived safely. I've been worried. Call me. Love, Mom."

I stopped dead in my tracks, closed my eyes, and let out an audible moan.

Class. I'd completely forgotten to tell my professors anything. I'd just been no-showing... for exams, for rehearsals, for classes... If I didn't do something fast, I'd fail the semester and destroy my GPA.

A wooden bench sat in the hallway outside another professor's office, and I sat down, taking a few deep breaths as I organized my thoughts. I needed to take care of the school situation before I said anything to Mom. I didn't want to tell her I'd withdrawn until I actually had, and now that I remembered, I didn't want that hanging over me.

I enabled the A.E. chip on my temple again, because it would be faster to mentally compose the comms I needed to send. I wrote first to the Registrar with my official withdrawal, asking for any paperwork I needed to complete to make it official. I read it over once, took a deep breath, and thought, "Send."

Another deep breath. *I'll be back next semester,* I assured myself. My GPA wasn't the most important issue right now anyway, nor was my degree... and yet, I felt like I needed a moment of silence. It was a big step.

Next I composed comms to Henry, the director of "The Tempest", who had probably already figured out I wasn't coming back when I'd no-showed for three rehearsals now. I was surprised he hadn't commed me already to find out what was keeping me. Maybe he was still just waiting, since I'd told him before I'd left that I'd be back soon.

I really wanted to play Miranda, too, I sighed as I composed the message, telling him to re-cast my role. I just loved playing the lead, no matter what the show was. I wondered what that said about me.

Then I wrote Dr. Yin, with a much less formal withdrawal, since she knew exactly what I was doing and why. I knew she'd sign any paperwork the Registrar required on my behalf, but I asked her to do so all the same.

Then I composed very carefully worded emails to each of the professors whose exams I had missed, begging them to register my grades as Incomplete rather than Fail. I explained that I had been in San Jose… for… *what excuse could I give?* I rapped my fingernails on my knee. *Family emergency?* No… it had to do with family, but since Dad died six years ago, it could hardly be considered an emergency… *research for my senior thesis? That's not a good reason to miss class, either…*

A comm appeared directly on my retinas. Liam. "Bec? You still in office hours? It's been a long time…"

I let out a little harrumph and dismissed it.

I'd get to him later.

Suddenly another comm appeared on my retinas: Julie this time. "So I guess Yolanda's family is just fine! She commed Andy when she arrived back home, and said her mom never even sent the message and had no idea what she was talking about. Weird, huh?"

I stared at the comm for a second, with an odd feeling in the pit of my stomach.

So who did *send it?* I wondered. The idea that it could be John Doe was absurd, of course. But then again, hadn't he been the one to send the comm to Dr. Yin, saying I needed to go back to Dublin? And who sent the comm to Ivan, for that matter, telling him that if Andy pursued me, he wouldn't be refused?

I couldn't deny the feeling that I—my desires—were somehow responsible for Yolanda's mystery comm, also. But I didn't send it, so how *could* I be responsible?

I couldn't think about that right now. I'd deal with it later.

I opened the comm to my Abnormal Psych professor and wrote, "I needed to come to San Jose on some urgent family business, and I've found it requires my continued presence here for the time being." It was true enough, and it also didn't invite further questions. I added a few more lines, begging his forbearance. I sent it, and then tweaked it for the other professors whose exams I had also missed.

After I'd sent off the last one, I felt a sort of emptiness. Despite all that had happened, despite the fact that I knew this was the only decision I could possibly make, it wasn't the life I had planned. It was 180 degrees from the life I had planned, in fact.

How did any of this happen?

I composed a comm to Mom next. "I'm still in San Jose, actually. Things took an interesting turn here, and I had to drop out of school after all. Just for the semester. I'll go back as soon as I can. I'm sorry I didn't update you earlier. I love you." I closed my eyes but could still see the message in my mind's eye when I thought, "Send."

I couldn't have sat there for more than a minute before I saw the incoming holograph call. Mom, of course. I had the A.E. eyepiece in my bag and could take the call if I wanted to, but I didn't think I could deal with her irate questions at the moment. *Decline,* I thought.

Another comm appeared. Liam again. "Hello???"

This is why I never enable the A.E. chip, I thought with annoyance, tapping my temple to turn it off. Something about having comms and calls appear on my very retinas felt so dreadfully invasive—as if I wasn't even in control of my own body, even though I had the ability to turn the feature on and off. I would never understand how most people left it on all the time.

Once the A.E. chip was off again, I pulled my handheld out of my pocket and wrote to Liam, "I'm alive, calm down. I'll be there when I can."

A few seconds later, the screen blinked. "Well, if you don't update me for hours, I start imagining you getting kidnapped seven ways from Sunday. Sue me."

I scoffed out loud, but a tiny smile tugged at the corners of my lips anyway. I still wasn't quite used to this character trait of his. Some small part of me found it kind of endearing… a *very* small part. I wrote, "We're on a university campus, Liam. I'm fine. You're so paranoid."

"Yes, we've established this," he wrote back, "and I accept my flaws. What did you find out?"

I didn't want to try to compose my findings, or my subsequent musings in a comm, but he clearly wasn't going to leave me alone for long. I'd have to just go tell him in person. With a twinge of dread, I enabled the A.E. chip one more time just to pull up the map so that I could find my way back to the library. I wasn't very good at directions.

But between the physics building and the library, I saw one labeled, "Philosophy."

I couldn't explain why, but I felt drawn to it. *Maybe I was preordained to go there,* I thought, with a humorless little laugh. Maybe there was no point to anything I was doing, because what would be would be, no matter what I did. Or maybe instead, my preordained choices would 'make a difference,' if anything could truly be said to make a difference, but only because they were already woven into the tapestry of the universe from the foundation of time…

On my way to the Philosophy building, I searched the labyrinth and found a professor also hosting office hours, who happened to be a dual chair in psychology. I made my way to his office, praying that he wasn't another bot.

"Enter," called a husky voice, and I pushed open the old fashioned wooden door with clouded glass bearing his name in black letters. The man sitting before me—he was definitely man and not bot—had thinning salt and pepper hair, an oversized gut, and loose skin about his neck and above his eyelids. But he smiled when he saw me, spreading a kind of fatherly glow to all who entered his domain. A wave of relief hit me; I hadn't known exactly how much I'd hoped for someone older and wiser to guide me until that moment.

"Sir," I began, as he gestured for me to sit in the upholstered chair across from him, beside the warm orange light of an incandescent bulb. "My name is Rebecca Cordeaux. I'm a neuroscience major." I didn't need to tell him in what school.

"Ah, so you're here for psychology and not philosophy, then. Which class are you in?"

I opened my mouth and closed it again, deciding in a split second not to lie. "In—well, I'm visiting, sir. I'd just hoped I might be able to ask you a few questions, for… for a project I'm working on. I wondered what you can tell me about… free will. I mean, what is it? What do we know about it?"

Professor Willit tilted his head to the side, inspecting my face. "Is this an academic question, or a personal one?"

"Both," I admitted.

He nodded. "Philosophers have struggled with this question throughout the ages, of course. But the definition comes down to this: free will is when an agent has the ability to both recognize a choice between at least two alternatives, and is not coerced by any external force, but can choose between them of its own volition."

"But according to Professor Reddy, every choice is predetermined," I blurted. "Do you believe that?"

Right at that moment, another comm appeared on my retinas—I'd forgotten to disable the A.E. chip again after using it for the maps. "Bec, seriously? Are you dead, or are you *trying* to drive me crazy?" I dismissed it, and tapped my temple to turn it off.

Professor Willit considered my question. "Well, yes and no," he said. "If what she means by 'predetermined' is that our choices are a result of our past experiences and our character, then largely, yes. But I would argue that there is a distinct difference between being *predictable* and being *coerced.* Do I have a choice about whether or not to pick up this letter opener and throw it through my window right now?" He demonstrated, gesturing at the window. "Sure. But my character, my experiences, and my emotions are such that I won't make that choice, because I have no good reason to do so. No one makes that choice for me; I make it for myself, but I am influenced by the whole of my history in making it."

"So you're saying that free will arises automatically from having a choice between at least two alternatives. Even if you're essentially… programmed to make one choice over another. By your history."

Professor Willit's eyes sharpened at the word *programmed.* "Correct…" he said slowly. I had the sense that he was trying to guess my meaning. Then he ventured, "This doesn't only apply to humans, though."

My heart skipped a beat. "What do you mean?"

"Well, take companion bots, for instance,"

he said. "They are programmed with social and moral 'rules,' as well as the core program of protecting the interests of the person to whom they are given as a companion. But what happens when these two things come into conflict? If the moral rule dictates one thing, but protecting the interest of her master dictates another, this sets up a choice, doesn't it?"

For some reason, Julie's comm sprung to mind again when he said that. *"Her mom never even sent the message. Weird, huh?"*

"But there are if/then statements in companion bot programming that determine which rule to follow when they come in conflict," I pointed out. "So that isn't truly free will, because the choice *is* coerced by their programmer."

Professor Willit shrugged. "You may be correct. I'm not a programmer. But…" he leaned forward, conspiratorially, "If I may say so, if Halpert has his way and the bots acquire emotion, then they will have a true dichotomy: the choice between following their programming, and following their desires." He watched me very hard as he sat back in his chair again. "Which they choose at that point will be anybody's guess."

"So… let me switch over to cognitive neuroscience, for a second," I added. "This may be a stupid question, but are there… specific parts of the brain that deal with free will?"

"You mean so that we can override it?"

I nodded, and the professor tilted his head to the side, regarding me with a somber expression. "I wish I could help you. I really do."

My heart sank. "What do you mean?"

He shook his head. "There are several parts of the brain associated with free choice, to be sure: decisions in the anterior cingulate cortex, timing of decisions in the supplementary motor area, and whether or not to act in the first place in the dorsal medial prefrontal cortex... but alas, Rebecca. The fact that we know which parts of the brain make free will decisions does not mean that we can *eliminate* free will by creating lesions in those areas. Quite the contrary: lesions in the prefrontal cortex tend to lead to socially inappropriate or immoral behavior. Rather than imposing an absolute mandate, such a lesion would exclude morality altogether."

I deflated. "But—there must be a way!"

Professor Willit shook his head. "If there is, it will not be found by imitating the human brain. One can eliminate all restraint by damaging the brain, but we cannot impose moral behavior without the free choice of whether or not to obey it, once emotion gets involved. We use brain structures in the manifestation of our free will, but the reason free will is there in the first place does not appear to reside in the brain itself. I'm afraid you are seeking a scientific answer to a fundamentally spiritual question."

The conversation was clearly over. I mumbled my thanks, and slung my backpack over one shoulder as I left Professor Willit's office.

Once in the hallway, I closed my eyes, resting the back of my head against his door like I couldn't bear the weight of it anymore.

"Then we're all doomed," I whispered.

Chapter 22

It took me only a few minutes to find Liam, Francis, and Larissa in the library, in the glass conference room like Liam had told me. Liam's eyes flashed when he caught sight of me.

"I was just about to go looking for you! How hard is it to comm me and just tell me where you are?"

"You'd think you were his stray teenage daughter or something," Larissa commented, resting her chin on her fist and blinking up at me placidly.

Liam shot her a sour look. "I'll thank you to never make *that* reference again."

Francis narrowed his eyes at me while Liam and Larissa had this exchange, and I was just about to reply to Liam and beg exasperated forgiveness yet again when Francis's stare became so annoying I could no longer ignore it.

"What?" I demanded.

"On a scale of one to ten, how important would you rate what you've found out so far?"

To our mission, or to me personally? I

thought but did not say. What I said was, "It was important, but not helpful, really." I sighed, and turned to Liam, just about to summarize my conversations when Francis cut me off.

"Okay, then I go first. Mine is an eight." He pulled out a chair next to him, indicating that I should sit. I gave an incredulous little harrumph, but did as I was told, glancing at Liam as I did so. His lips twitched in amusement, his irritation evidently forgotten. At least there was that.

"Liam told me about the salt and sulfuric acid purchase," Francis said, showing me his netscreen.

"Wait, I thought you guys were working on the Commune?"

"Francis is phenomenal at multitasking," sighed Larissa. "I think intense concentration on just one subject would bore him to tears."

Francis nodded, very seriously. "That's true, unless the one subject is a mystery in need of solving, in which case I can concentrate for up to twelve hours at a time with hardly a bathroom break. Although very few subjects warrant such attention. I solve most dilemmas long before they reach even two hours, let alone twelve—"

"*Oh my goodness,*" I said, widening my eyes at him. "Get to the point!"

Francis, for once, did as he was bid. "Salt and sulfuric acid produce hydrochloric acid."

"I already figured that out."

"I know you did, that's not the discovery, if you would just wait a minute," Francis said impatiently. "Some decades ago, there was a theory that a weak acid like hydrochloric might be able to artificially produce ATP..."

I shook my head. "What's ATP?"

Francis gave a superior little snort. "I forget, you don't know biochemistry. ATP, Adenosine Tri-Phosphate. It's your body's energy currency, produced by mitochondria in all of your cells. In our bodies we need protons in order to drive its production. A weak acid like hydrochloric would have protons that could be stripped relatively easily. Way back before the Council of Synthetic Reason, before it became illegal, everybody was trying to produce humanoid bots. The assumption was that if they looked human, they would have to be a combination of silicon and wires and biochemistry like ours—essentially like a cyborg."

"So Halpert is building, or he's helping someone else to build, illegal humanoid robots!" Larissa finished for him. "The weak acids are essentially its food!"

I blinked at her, not understanding. "But why would Halpert be building illegal bots? What would be the point?"

"I have a theory," murmured Francis. "It's a good one."

"Oh, that's a given," I rolled my eyes. "Fine. Let's have it."

"I'm not ready to share until I have more evidence," he declared placidly. "Liam has your Odessa researching a few things for me to see if it bears up."

"All right, Rebecca's turn," said Liam, turning to me. "What did *you* find out?"

I sighed, ticking off my discouraging findings on my fingers as I related them. "One: according to physics, there's no such thing as free will. Not even for us. No, no, I amend: it's *possible* that we could do something completely independent of all our previous experiences and external influences, but it is so unlikely as to be essentially impossible, for all intents and purposes."

"I could've told you that," Francis muttered, not even looking at me. He was already apparently engrossed in an A.E. search, on to some other more interesting task. I shot him a scathing look that he didn't even see.

"Was the physics professor a bot?" Liam asked.

"Yeah. How did you know?"

"Only a bot would reason like that," he shrugged. "It's a deductive approach to what ought to be an inductive question. Humans *know* we have free will, because we experience it. A human would start with the conclusion in mind and work

268

backwards, to try to explain it. But a bot can't do that, because free will is a subjective experience that it does not share. So instead, it will try to use laws of physics to determine whether free will is possible."

"Francis," I turned to him, deadpan. "Are you a bot?"

He arched an eyebrow at me. "Ha, ha. I *meant* I could have told you that is the conclusion you'd arrive at purely from the standpoint of physics."

I exchanged a nettled smile with Liam, and told him, "Well, I'm glad you feel that way, because it freaked me out a little, honestly. So I went to see a dual philosophy and psych professor after that…"

"Ah, was *that* where you were when you were ignoring my last comm?" Liam asked pointedly.

I rolled my eyes and went on, "Professor Willit was a human, thankfully. He said that free will just means an agent has a choice between this or that, and is not coerced by any external force to choose either. Even if his choice is predictable based upon his past experiences, that makes him no less free to make it. He agreed that giving bots emotion will set up a dichotomy between the machine's programming and its desires." I thought about mentioning what he'd said about companion bots. But vocalizing it would somehow make it seem more real, and I didn't want it to be real.

"So basically he said giving bots emotion *will* create free will, but there's nothing we can do about it," Francis summarized, now scrolling through his netscreen like I was boring him to tears.

"Yes, I *said* it wasn't helpful, didn't I? What are you doing?"

Francis turned his screen to show me, and my heart skipped a beat. A photograph filled the screen of a large group of people, most of whom I did not recognize. But dead center was my dad.

I shook my head at Francis, not wanting him to see that he'd unnerved me. "Why are you showing me—?"

He pointed at the screen again, but his finger landed on an image beside my dad's. "That is Randall Loomis."

It took me a second to comprehend this. When I did, I pulled Francis's netscreen toward me, and enlarged the picture. This photo had been taken probably ten years ago, judging by my dad's features, so I'd have to account for *some* aging, of course. But Randall Loomis was a young man, not much older than my dad had been. He was rather handsome too, with a crop of dark hair and laughing hazel eyes.

"That's not John Doe," Liam guessed.

I shook my head slowly, meeting Liam's eyes and feeling a knot in the pit of my stomach, like I'd swallowed a stone.

"No," I said at last. "It isn't."

Chapter 23

"Who's John Doe?" Larissa piped up, but Francis didn't ask, I noticed. I knew Liam must've told him, or Francis wouldn't have gone to the trouble to show me the picture in the first place. That was *why* he did it.

My eyes flashed at Liam, gesturing at Francis. "You *told* him?"

"He's on our side, Bec," Liam reminded me.

"I'm on your side, too!" Larissa piped, raising her hand.

"Can I talk to you?" I said to Liam through gritted teeth. "Alone?"

"Why, so you can chew him out in private?" Francis commented, his tone flat and bored. "We can imagine what you're going to say, anyway. Might as well get it out of the way here."

"Nobody asked you!" I snapped.

"Or, you can yell at me instead," Francis suggested, nonplussed. He made a reeling motion with his hand. "Whatever gets it out of your system."

"Come on," Liam took me by the elbow before I could do just that, leading me out of the conference room. Evidently deeming the general library a poor choice for a shouting match, he led me to the lawn outside. I wanted to yank my elbow away indignantly—the trouble was, Liam wasn't gloating. It made it harder to be mad at him, and I really wanted to be mad.

"Congratulations. You were right and I was wrong. But did you have to tell Francis?" I hissed.

"Like it or not, he's brilliant, which makes his a good opinion to have," Liam ran a hand through his hair, turning imploring blue eyes upon me full force. "Look, I know I should have asked you before I told him, even so. I'm sorry I didn't."

"*Why* didn't you?" I demanded.

"Because you'd have said no, and because there's something fishy about that guy. He knows everything about you, knows where to find you, but won't give you his name? And you're meeting him in these dark alleys and anything could happen... I just wanted Francis's help in figuring out who he is. I don't know why I didn't think of just showing you a picture of Loomis for comparison in the first place. I'm sorry, Bec." He took my hand, raising his eyebrows and tilting his head down in a perfect imitation of a puppy. "Forgive me?"

"Fine, sure," I muttered, irritated that he wasn't provoking me.

He smiled, tucking a stray strand of my hair behind my ear. I felt the heat rise to my cheeks in response, annoyed with my own body for its betrayal. Liam could surely see it, and would probably take it to mean something it most certainly did not. I tried to drop his other hand, but he held mine fast.

"We *are* making progress, even if your meetings weren't as useful as you hoped," he assured me. "I think we might have the first prototype of the Commune ready by the end of the week!" He gave my hand a squeeze and then let it go. "So I take it you didn't get much direction from your meetings?"

I sighed. "None whatsoever, I'm afraid."

"Well, this might help. Let me show you what the De Vries prototype actually looks like. It's so simple, I'm kicking myself for not thinking of it first. Occam's razor, right? The simplest explanation is usually the right one?" He led me to a concrete bench beside a vastly cultivated flowerbed brimming with bees, and settled his netscreen on his lap.

"If you *had* thought of it, what would you have done? Submitted it for Halpert's approval?"

He scowled at me. "Ha, ha. Look." Two loci appeared on either side of his screen: one a mechanical blueprint and the other a programming language. I understood neither. He started to point things out to me in the code, like, "See this recursive loop here? This corresponds to this," and he'd point to a section of the blueprint, "which is her version of the limbic system, see? It's almost a direct analog of the way I understand the human limbic system to work: the amygdala and hippocampus," here he pointed out some code, "and," he scrolled down, "here she's connected them to her version of the thalamus and the hypothalamus, which are also right on top of each other here," he pointed to the blueprint, "like they are in the human brain—"

I let him keep talking and just tuned him out, with the appropriate "ooohs!" and "uh huhs" when he looked at me expectantly. I would have listened, but aside from the references to the brain structures, I really had no foundation for understanding a word he said.

"So basically you're saying whatever is true of the human brain will be more or less easily translatable into the De Vries prototype," I summarized.

He nodded. "Right. So, once we introduce emotion, sounds like we can't stop the emergence of free will. So maybe there's a way to strengthen the morality programming somehow, make it stronger than an emotional pull? If you wanted to do that in a human, how would you do it?"

I sighed. "Well, there are many parts of the

brain that are involved in morality, but none that are devoted to morality exclusively. There is no 'seat' of morality in the brain. Instead, both the emotional and the logical parts of the brain interact to form moral judgments in each individual case."

Liam narrowed his eyes: it was the expression I recognized to mean he was listening less to the specifics of what I said, and more for something that he might be able to use. "How many different structures?"

I'd researched this before I left Dublin, and recited from memory, "Well, for instance, the ventromedial prefrontal cortex helps us to project the consequences of our decisions before we make them," I ticked them off on my fingers one by one, "the superior temporal sulcus is involved with emotional processing and social cognition, the posterior cingulate cortex is involved in empathy and forgiveness, and the amygdala is required for empathy and moral judgments. But I don't see how that helps—"

He waved me off, looking at the flower bed without really seeing it. "The latter three aren't helpful most likely because they're part of the emotional limbic system. We can't tinker much there without either strengthening or destroying the very emotion that the De Vries prototype was designed to create. What about the first one? The prefrontal cortex. That's decision making?"

I nodded. "Executive functioning, yeah. But the ventral prefrontal cortex is also involved in emotional decision making. You're not going to isolate morality from emotions entirely, I don't think—not if we're emulating the human brain."

Liam narrowed his eyes, still looking beyond me. "So… you're saying the best we can do is give the bots as much morality as we have?"

"I think so?" I shrugged. "Maybe we can try to strengthen their equivalent of the prefrontal cortex… but I'm not convinced that wouldn't just result in a really cautious, disciplined robot, and not necessarily a moral one. It might even mean they're better long-term planners, and they'll be more likely to seek out their 'core programming' and rewrite it if it doesn't happen to suit them. But I guess we won't know for sure until we build one."

Liam sighed. "Well. That stinks."

"Tell me about it." I deflated a little more, settling palms on either side of me on the bench and leaning forward distractedly. "Also, in other news, I dropped out of school. Officially."

Liam didn't register surprise, but said, "You okay with that?"

"No," I admitted. "I know it's not a big deal in the scheme of life, and all the crap going on right now, but…" I sighed. "I told my mom in a comm. Now I'm avoiding her calls because I know what she's gonna say. 'I'm being foolish. I'm throwing my life away. I'm throwing her sacrifice away,' blah blah blah…" I felt him watching me, and glanced back at him.

"You can still go back, you know," he said.

"No," I said stubbornly, "I'm not going anywhere. I have to see this through, same as you."

"Why?"

He asked with real curiosity; for once, he didn't pressure me. *Why indeed?* I had a myriad of answers and I wasn't sure which was most important. Because I was my father's daughter, and I needed to know what had happened to him? Because I wanted to assuage my conscience for having thought him a foolish conspiracy theorist, when I now began to believe he'd been right all along? Because of a perverse curiosity regarding the real identity of John Doe?

Because I'd been blithely ignorant of the potential dangers of confiding in my best friend?

"Professor Willit said something else," I told Liam, not answering his question directly. "Even without true emotion, if two programs in a bot come into conflict, and they can't both be obeyed at once in a specific instance, he assumes there's something in the code that anticipates this, and says which of the two they ought to follow. Which one is stronger."

Liam watched me with an odd expression. "Sure. He's right." His tone was leading, like he expected me to go on.

I suddenly wished I hadn't started the conversation, though. Liam might already know about my feelings for Andy, but the idea of telling him my wishes for Andy's separation from Yolanda in order to explain my suspicions about the odd comms regarding her family emergency was just too mortifying.

And then there was the comm Ivan got, telling him I wouldn't refuse Andy if he pursued me.

And even the affair of Andy's girlfriend Sarah's plagiarism, if it came to that...

"What?" Liam pressed, looking concerned now.

I shook my head. "Never mind. It's not important."

Liam looked unconvinced. "You didn't answer my question about why you have to stay." When I still didn't reply, he pressed, "I always had the impression you had such a full life outside the lab. You're into everything, and it seems like you are actually more passionate about your performing and writing than you are about any of this stuff. You could go back to it, you know, and still help us at a distance when you can. It doesn't have to be all or nothing."

It *was* true—I *did* have a full life before, and I missed it. I thought of the Dublin campus. Of my

novel I hadn't touched in what felt like ages—
Elizabeth the maid, and Prince Nikolai. I'd just left
them hanging. Of playing the lead role in musicals
about every three months, and the subsequent cast
parties until two in the morning. Of laughter and
travel and working in the lab only when I had to, in
order to finish my thesis and make a little extra cash
to supplement my student loan money. It had been
such a simple life, and I'd enjoyed every minute of
it… except for when I was moping about Andy.
Which I guess was also, most of the time.

At least I'd been distracted enough that I
hadn't spent every waking moment fretting about
him and Yolanda in the last few days, I realized.
Comparatively, I'd barely thought of Andy. That
was a nice respite.

"How could I go back to amusing myself for
the moment, knowing what I know now?" I said
finally. I glanced at Liam again, and knew from his
sad smile that he had correctly judged the question
as rhetorical. "It's all your fault, you know."

"It usually is," he agreed, touching my
cheek gently. Then his expression changed—he
stopped and blinked, tapping his temple. His mouth
fell open.

"What?" I said, more sharply than I'd
intended.

"I just received a comm from Halpert's
personal assistant," he said, sounding a bit shocked.

"She says Halpert will be pleased to receive me at noon *tomorrow,* and his entire advisory board will be there!"

Chapter 24

I followed Liam back into the library, where we found Francis and Larissa hard at work on the Commune algorithms.

"I got the invite!" Liam announced as soon as the door shut behind us. "I'm meeting with Halpert and his board tomorrow—"

"You mean your father is," said Larissa placidly.

"So *they* think," Liam grinned. His smile faded just a bit as he added, "As long as they don't contact him about it for any reason between now and then—" His expression changed again: there was a faraway look in his eyes and all his features seemed to draw back. I knew it meant he'd gotten another comm.

"What?" I demanded. "Did they cancel already?"

"No," he said, perplexed. "I heard back from Odessa on your questions, Francis."

"And?" he asked.

Liam touched the A.E. chip on his temple to

turn it off, and then he met Francis's eyes. "You were right. Wallenberg, Rasputin, St. James, Chiefton, and Montgomery are *all* buying sulfuric acid and salt. So whatever Halpert is doing... his board is doing it too."

I blinked at Liam, shaking my head. "That's..."

"Exactly what I expected," Francis finished with a self-complacent air. "Have you replied to the invite yet? Is tomorrow a lunch meeting?"

Liam looked a little confused. "Not yet, and I would assume so, she said noon."

"Make sure it is," said Francis, "offer to have it catered or something. Also, I'm coming with you."

"What?" I demanded, turning to Liam. "Why does he get to go?"

Liam ignored my question and said to Francis doubtfully, "That'll be hard to explain..."

"No it won't, Liam Senior couldn't get away and sent Liam Junior, his Head of Operations—isn't that what you were?—and his right-hand man. Pick a name of someone in the department. I'll be him."

"Then I'm going too!" I insisted, "I can do that as well as he can!"

Liam held up his hands to silence all of us, and then said to Francis, like a teacher calling on us one at a time, "Francis. Why?"

"To find out if I'm right," he said.

"You could tell me your theory, and I could find out," Liam countered.

"No you couldn't."

"Why not?"

Francis gave an exasperated sigh. "Need I really say it?"

Liam rolled his eyes. "All right, fine. You'll be Bill Spencer. He's a middle aged guy I used to work with and you don't look a thing like him, but if they research our story at all, we're screwed anyway. But you *must* keep your mouth shut!" he added severely. "If you come, I do *all* the talking!"

I interjected, "The whole point of this meeting is to argue that they need to find a way to either incorporate morality into the De Vries prototype or halt production until they can, for safety reasons. Right?"

Liam turned to me, brows knitted together. "Right…"

"So that's my specialty, not yours," I finished, crossing my arms over my chest. "You need me there too."

Liam opened his mouth and closed it again. He didn't look pleased. Then he glanced at Larissa, and said with all the injured air he could muster, "All right, why are *you* indispensable? I'm waiting."

"Oh! You can do without me perfectly well. I'll just stay behind and work on the Commune with the other Renegades," she said sweetly.

"At least there's that," Liam muttered.

"Why don't you want us there?" I demanded.

"Because at least I have a legitimate connection to General Specs! You two will only raise suspicion."

"Which is exactly what I want," said Francis, more to himself than to us.

"You *want* the most powerful men in the world to know we pulled one over on them?" Liam demanded, exasperated.

"You'll understand afterwards," was Francis's smug reply.

Liam and I both deliberately turned our backs on Francis at the same moment; such a statement did not deserve a response.

"Did Odessa investigate the board at all, beyond their purchases?" I asked Liam. "The way she did Halpert—their back stories and what not?"

Liam frowned. "I didn't ask her to, good point. Hold on." He touched the A.E. chip on his temple again, biting his lip as his eyes tracked back and forth in the imaginary space in his head.

While I watched Liam compose the comm to Odessa, I thought of the one person whom I knew could tell me what we wanted to know. Maybe he wasn't Loomis after all, and maybe he didn't want to tell me very much, but he *could* if he wanted to.

Whoever he was, John Doe knew their secret: of that, I was certain.

He'd said I couldn't contact him, though; I'd have to wait for him to contact me. The last time I'd tried to write back to his comm, it bounced back. But I could *try* to reply to the last comm he'd sent, at least.

I tapped my own A.E. chip. "I need your help," I thought, seeing the words appear across my retinas. "We know Halpert and his advisory board are buying massive amounts of ingredients for hydrochloric acid, and we know that means they're probably building illegal humanoid robots. What we don't know is, why?"

I sent the message, but immediately the bold red letters flashed across my retinas: "ERROR: Recipient Unknown." I swore under my breath.

"What was that?" Liam asked, arching an amused eyebrow at me.

"Nothing."

"Did you actually just say 'damn'?" He persisted. "Because I think that's the first time…" I glared at him, and he swallowed his smirk. "Sorry."

"I tried to ask John Doe what they're all doing with those ingredients, but the message wouldn't go through. Which is what he told me would happen, I know."

Liam glowered at me. "Rebecca, you shouldn't be talking to him anymore. We don't know who he is or whose side he's on."

"He knows what we want to know," I insisted. "He's a shortcut, I know he is, if he'll only help us!"

Francis, probably tired of being excluded, announced, "Larissa and I are headed back to the pub. Liam, you can join us whenever this little *tête-à-tête* is finished." Larissa bounced up from her seat like a sprightly four year old at this, stuffing her netscreen into her satchel.

"Fine, I'll take Rebecca back to the hotel first," Liam said, somewhat absently.

"What am I supposed to be doing at the hotel?"

"Accessing the labyrinth for more ideas on how to program morality, I thought, right?"

"Oh." I didn't hold out much hope that there was anything else to find, but kept this to myself for the moment. "Right. You could just leave me here, then…"

"I don't want you to have to get back to the hotel by yourself."

Okay. This is getting to be a bit much, I thought, as Francis and Larissa slipped out behind us. "Liam, I'm not your responsibility, you know. If anything happens to me—which I don't think is likely, but even if it did—it's not like you should ever have that on *your* conscience. I'm a big girl."

He raised an eyebrow. "You think I'm

worried about my conscience?" Then he started walking, such that I had no choice but to follow him.

"Well—"

"Bec, you *are* my responsibility, at least as long as you're here. You came here with me, on what was originally my mission. I'm sorry if it annoys you that I'm so overprotective, and if we go back to Dublin, I promise to never keep tabs on your whereabouts ever again. Deal?"

"*If* we go back?" I repeated with an incredulous laugh.

When we reached the edge of campus, and Liam hailed a hovercar to take us the rest of the way. A silver-blue one presented itself to the curb where we stood. As we climbed in, I muttered, "I hope that you never have any daughters. For their sakes."

Liam laughed, closing the door and telling it where we wanted to go before the hovercar swooped up into the carpool motorway. "I'd love to have a daughter, but I'm sure if I did, she'd find me unbearable once she became a teenager. For more reasons than just because she'd have a seven o'clock curfew. Which she would."

I smirked, trying to picture Liam as a father. "And she wouldn't be allowed to kiss anybody until she was thirty, right?"

He shrugged. "Or maybe she could just be

like you, and wait until she's twenty-one. I'd settle for that."

I felt my cheeks flame. "I never said I'd never—!"

Liam burst out laughing. "You didn't deny it, though, did you? And you're bright red... so you haven't, then! *That* explains it... I figured you hadn't when you said you'd been waiting for years for that chump to come around—"

When the hovercar pulled up in front of our hotel, I shoved him, mostly to force him to turn away until my face resumed its usual color. "Out! Get out!"

Still laughing, he scanned his thumbprint to the hovercar for payment, and climbed out onto the curb, waiting for me to join him. He held up his hands and said, "Hey, if you ever want some practice, I'd be only too happy to help... I could even give you some pointers..."

"I hate you so much," I muttered, shoving past him toward the big double doors, while Liam retreated down the sidewalk towards Francis's pub, still laughing.

"Is everything okay?" Madeline wanted to know when I'd burst into my room. "You look very red."

"Yes. I've been told." I buried my face in my hands, speaking to her through the gap in my fingers. "It's nothing, just Liam humiliating me again…"

She rolled over, her expression assuming concern. "He humiliated you? What did he do?"

I told her the story, and then exclaimed, "He can be so—unbearable sometimes! I *never* would have admitted that to him, and yet somehow he got it out of me anyway… and that explains *what,* anyway? What did he mean by that?" I felt like I wanted to throw something at Liam's face as I remembered him laughing at me, but I settled for hurling a box of tissues at the door. Suddenly a sense of dread settled into the pit of my stomach. "How am I going to face him later tonight?"

Madeline patted my knee, her face all sympathy. "What would make you happy?" she asked. "Do you want to get even with Liam for humiliating you?"

I looked up, suddenly tingling with déjà vu.

Was it her after all, then? All those other comms?

"No, of course not!" I blurted. "Liam didn't mean to be cruel. He…" I suddenly knew exactly why he'd done it. "I think he was just trying to get a rise out of me, because he still likes me. He probably *would* like to give me pointers, come to think of it… he only said it like a joke because he knew I wouldn't go for it."

"You're smiling," Madeline pointed out,

sounding confused now.

I schooled my face immediately. "I am not!"

She tilted her head to the side, inspecting my face. "You smile a lot when you talk about Liam," she observed. "Even when your words imply that you want him to go away, your manner suggests the opposite. Do you have feelings for him?"

"No, of course not!" I cried again.

Instead of responding, Madeline just stared at me, like she was waiting for a different answer. Finally I blurted, "Oh my gosh, I *hope* not."

Madeline rolled back and forth on the carpet just in front of me. "Do you think he would be kind to you?"

"Of *course* he would, but…"

"Do you think he would make you happy?"

"Well yeah—I mean, no! I mean… I want to be with Andy! You know that!"

Madeline blinked up at me. "Do you think Andy would be kind and would make you happy?"

I fell silent for a long time. Too long. Then I admitted, "I'm… not sure, actually."

"He's never made you happy in the past," Madeline observed.

"That's not true, there have been nights when I've come home after hanging out with Andy totally excited and bursting to tell you all about it —"

"Because you're interpreting something he

said or did to mean he likes you," Madeline pointed out, "but has *being* with him ever made you happy, apart from that?"

I didn't want to answer that, but she kept staring at me. So I thought about it. And I thought.

And I thought.

There had to be just *one* time…

"I'm not sure," I admitted at last.

"But you're usually smiling when you talk about Liam. You can't seem to help it."

I leapt up, hands to my temples as I paced away from her. "Please just stop. I don't want to think about this!"

"But if Liam would be kind to you and he'd make you happy, and Andy wouldn't, and if you *are* starting to like Liam, why would you prefer to pine for Andy instead? I'm just trying to understand what you want!" Madeline persisted, following me as I paced.

I gave a short little laugh. "Isn't that the million dollar question," I muttered. I really didn't want to think about the substance of what she was saying. But I also wanted to know…

If I *did* have an answer, what would she do about it?

We watched each other for what felt like an eternity, as I tried to work up the courage to frame the words. *I'm going to ask her. I have to ask her.*

I'd just opened my mouth to speak, when I

felt my handheld vibrate in my pocket. I jumped about a foot.

It took me a second to comprehend what I saw on the screen. It said, "If you knew for certain that remaining in San Jose and making yourself known to Halpert and his board would put you in mortal danger, would you leave?"

I stared at it.

"What is it?" Madeline asked, as if with bated breath.

I read it to her. She made a little squeak, and then I added unnecessarily, "It's from John Doe."

"You *would* leave, wouldn't you?" Madeline demanded. "Liam would make you leave, if he knew!"

"Liam can't *make* me do anything," I retorted, staring at the screen and wondering how to reply. I couldn't say yes, and I couldn't say no... I just wanted John Doe to keep talking.

"I like Liam," Madeline added, talking to herself now. "He keeps you safe."

I ignored this, and wrote back, "Maybe. It would depend on who wanted me dead and why." Then I waited, still staring at the screen. After a few minutes, when it didn't seem like he would bite, I added, "Is it for the same reason my father was killed?"

"Don't you think you should tell Liam that John Doe contacted you?" Madeline persisted.

"I can tell him when I see him next," I told her, distracted. "He's busy right now."

"But he'd want to know…"

John Doe wrote back to my question, "The very same." At least he was answering *something*.

I took a deep breath, and pressed, "Does it have anything to do with hydrochloric acid?"

There was another long pause, so long I wondered if he would write back at all. I felt Madeline's eyes on me, but didn't look at her.

Finally John Doe replied, "You are clever."

My breath caught. "Halpert, Wallenberg, Rasputin, Montgomery, Chiefton, and St James are all building illegal humanoid bots. Aren't they?"

I counted seven seconds before his reply landed on my screen. He wrote, "Meet me tonight, at sunset. General Northrup Park, two blocks south of you. I will answer all your questions, on one condition: you must promise to leave tomorrow morning, and never come back."

Tomorrow morning. I couldn't leave before the meeting tomorrow—could I?

But could I pass up the information he offered me now?

"What if I don't promise?" I wrote back.

"Then we will not meet. I risk my own life every time I contact you."

My heart thumped. "Okay. I promise," I wrote, not even sure as I typed it whether it was a promise I would keep. It all depended upon what he told me.

"You must come alone," John Doe added.

Dang it. Well, Liam wasn't here right now anyway. I'd just have to tell him afterwards. Better to ask forgiveness than permission. He'd be mad... he'd be really, *really* mad, actually.

But he'd get over it. He'd have to.

Chapter 25

I read the entire conversation to Madeline as soon as it was over.

"Where are you going?" she demanded as I packed up my netscreen, my journal, my notebook, and the Bronte novel I was currently reading in my satchel.

"Gonna try to find the park in the light at least," I told her. "It's only a couple hours until sunset, and I don't think I'll be able to concentrate on research anyway—"

"At least tell Liam where you're going!"

"Why? He'll just forbid it…" I said, but I knew she was right. If I told him something at least, he might be slightly less angry with me later. I also couldn't have Liam showing up at the park and scaring off John Doe before I could talk to him, though. So I sent Liam a comm saying, "I have something to tell you the next time I see you, but I don't think I should put it in a comm." That way he couldn't pull the 'but you promised to tell me the next time he contacts you!' card later. Then I added,

"I'm going out for a bit. Just around our hotel."

He wrote back almost immediately. "No. Stay where you are. Please."

My mouth twitched. "I'll be just fine, *Dad*. It's broad daylight, and I'm not going far."

Liam's reply came half a beat later. "Never call me Dad again. Creepiest thing ever."

"Then stop acting like one!"

There was a pause, and then he wrote, "Fine, I'll come join you."

I closed my eyes, irritated with Madeline for making me tell him anything. "Want me to call you Dad again?"

Another pause. "At least tell me where you're going."

"Promise not to be there waiting when I get there?" I rejoined.

"Damn," he wrote.

I laughed aloud. "You're so predictable."

He wrote, "Fine, fine, I promise."

I inhaled, and held it, staring at his words. My question had been rhetorical, but he *did* promise. Had Liam ever broken a promise to me? I couldn't think of a time, but if ever he'd have inducement to do so, it would be now. So instead, I wrote, "I'll meet you in the lobby of the hotel at 7:15." That should give John Doe plenty of time to tell me whatever he intended to say.

"Where are you going???"

"Liam, I *will be fine*. Trust me."

The park took up an entire block. A few vagrants slept on benches with hats covering their faces, but it was otherwise deserted, despite the bustle of the city surrounding it. I chose a spot facing a lake, with a few swans swimming nearby. It was under the shade of a weeping willow tree, and something in my soul expanded at the sight of it. I just breathed for a few minutes, watching the swans as they swam.

I'd intended to call Mom this afternoon about quitting school… but this time tomorrow, I might be back in school after all, depending on how the meeting with John Doe went. Why put myself through an unnecessary confrontation? Besides, then I'd also find myself in the potentially difficult position of trying to explain why I'd changed my mind a day later, without telling Mom whatever John Doe told me.

So instead, I just sat there, my mind flitting from one topic to the next. I was unable to stay with one idea for long enough to make any progress before giving in to its competition.

I decided the best thing to do would be to ignore all possible topics pertaining to my actual life. I'd work on my novel instead. It had been weeks, but it felt like months since I'd touched it.

I pulled out the notebook where I'd been

writing, long-hand, the story of Elizabeth the maid, and Prince Nikolai. I reread the ten pages leading up to where I'd left off, but I found I had to reread entire paragraphs multiple times before the comprehension of the words sank in—which was pretty sad, considering I wrote them.

Thinking maybe the problem was trying to write something new (creativity requires a lot of brainpower, after all,) I stuffed the notebook back in my satchel and pulled out "The Tenant of Wildfell Hall," by Anne Bronte. I loved everything written by the Bronte sisters, although I'd had a bit harder time getting into this one, since it was told from the male protagonist's perspective. But again, every few sentences, my mind wandered—to the meeting tomorrow. To John Doe's text. To Madeline and Yolanda's false family emergency. To what Madeline had said about Andy, and about Liam. To humanoid bots being built in secret by the most powerful men in the world...

I stuffed the novel back into my satchel, pulling out my journal instead. Not knowing which topic to pursue at first, I just updated it on the De Vries breakthrough for emotion, and our current search for how to program morality into the bots, including my disheartening discussion with Professor Willit earlier that day. Then I added, "I have one more reason to stay... and I suspect that will be over in a few hours, too. If not tonight, then probably tomorrow afternoon, when Liam, Francis, and I will be meeting with Halpert and his advisory board. How in the heck did *that* happen? At least Liam feels at home in that environment. I would just keep my mouth shut and let him do all the talking, except that the whole reason he's letting me go is to explain what we know about the neuroscience of morality. To *the most powerful men in the world.*"

Maybe I should write out what I would say. But depending on what John Doe told me, I wouldn't be at the meeting, anyway.

I considered writing about John Doe and all my suspicions… but for some reason, I feared writing it down. I didn't know how that could be used against me, but it just didn't seem smart to keep any written evidence.

So instead, I defaulted to my usual journal topic: Andy. "I haven't heard from him since Liam's meeting when he brought Yolanda, nor have I attempted to contact him." I tapped the pen on the paper for a minute before adding, "I haven't even wanted to talk to him, truth be told. I feel like something shifted in me. When I think of Andy with Yolanda now—and I know he's probably back at school and hanging out with her even as I write this—I don't have the same sense of utter despair I used to have when I thought of him with Brittany, and with Jennifer, and with that one girl he hooked up with for a weekend whose name I never even knew… and especially him with Sarah. Now… I see him differently somehow. He's not the Nikolai to my Elizabeth anymore. It's like a spell was broken. I mean, I still love him, of course! I'm not so flighty as that. But now, for the first time… I *wish* I didn't. I feel like he's not worthy of me, as arrogant as that sounds. But it's as if I've been cursed to love him and only him anyway, whether he deserves it or not."

I hesitated to put this next bit on paper also, but for an entirely different reason. If I wrote about what Madeline said about Liam, I was afraid it would make it true somehow. Externally processing my feelings about what she'd said would dignify the idea, would make it real… and I didn't *want* it to be real.

But I could say a few things without running that risk… a few incontrovertible facts.

"I also figured out since being here that Liam likes me," I wrote. "And I told him I was in love with Andy. I thought telling him that would make him safe, but then he told me he thought I was only in love with Andy because of what happened to Dad. He almost seems…" I searched for the right word, before finally settling on, "undaunted. Like he thinks he still has a chance with me, even after I told him I want someone else." What did I want to say about that? The fact that he still seemed so confident made me feel... *what?*

I had no idea. And I didn't want to know, either.

"Madeline wants me to like Liam instead of Andy," I wrote instead. Yet here was another topic I couldn't put down in so many words—what was it I suspected her of? And if I wrote about it, would I start to see her through the lens of suspicion? Would it change our relationship? It was absurd, that I should even entertain such thoughts about my best friend.

Since when did I start to censor myself so heavily when speaking to my own journal, anyway?

No sooner did this thought cross my mind, I heard a gasp behind me, pulling me back into the present.

"Bec! Thank God!"

I whirled around to see Liam hurrying toward me. "What are you doing?" I cried, my eyes darting to the sky—it would be sunset within about ten minutes. "You have to get out of here!"

He didn't slow his stride, but I saw the confusion pass over his face as he closed the distance between us. "Madeline told me where you were, but she didn't tell me why, she just said you'd been here all afternoon!"

"I said I'd meet you in the hotel lobby at 7:15, and I will!" I pleaded, "Now please go away!"

"And leave you here after dark?" he

demanded. "Why can't you come with me now?"

"Because I can't!" I hissed, holding up my handheld with an expression that I hoped conveyed my meaning.

Understanding dawned on his face now, and then his features relaxed into a scowl. "You *promised* you would tell me the next time…"

"And I was going to, but not in a comm, and you were gone! I'll tell you tonight, but he made me promise to meet him here alone!"

"I'll bet he did!" Liam's eyes flashed, and he crossed his arms over his chest, sitting on the rock beside mine stubbornly.

A wave of desperation rolled over me, and I sank down to my own rock so that our eyes were on level.

"What do I have to do to make you leave?" I begged.

His eyes narrowed at me. "Tell me why you want me to so badly."

"Because he promised to tell me the secret my father died for!" I hissed, "And your brother! But if you're here, he might not come at all!"

Liam's eyes darted across my face, as if searching for clues to my sincerity. I didn't see how he could possibly doubt it; I'd never been so serious in my life.

"Fine," he said at last. "I'll wait across the street. If you need me—"

"I'll scream bloody murder. Yes."

"Not funny right now," he growled, snatching my handheld out of my fist. I grasped for it too late, and he turned his shoulder to obstruct my reach.

"What are you doing?" I demanded.

"Programming myself under 'Emergency Contacts.'"

"Oh, Liam!"

I only halfheartedly attempted to take it back again, already knowing he wouldn't let me until he'd accomplished his intention. My heart thundered in my chest as I watched the horizon: the sun had just disappeared, and the sky was streaked with red and orange.

Liam showed me my own handheld screen when he'd finished, holding it just out of my reach. "You press the center button, and it dials me automatically and sends me your location," he said. "Which I hope I won't need, since I plan to keep you in eyesight, but just in case." He thrust it back to me at last, his expression dark.

He'd be mad at me later for sure. Well, it was mutual.

Without another word, he turned and crossed the street.

Chapter 26

Liam melted into the shadows, but I could still see his silhouette, since I knew he was there. My heart thumping my chest, I turned around again, facing the pond beyond which the sun had just set.

Please come, I silently begged John Doe. *Please still come.*

A few minutes later, I saw his tall, sparse form draped with an overcoat flapping at his ankles. When he came into view, I saw the narrowed eyes, and the frown creased upon his pallid face.

"I told you to come alone," he growled. "You promised you would. You lied to me."

"I didn't lie!" I blurted, glancing in the direction where Liam's shadow lurked. "He came looking for me!"

"If you lied about that," John Doe continued as if he hadn't heard me, "why should I believe you didn't lie about being willing to leave tomorrow after I answer your questions?"

"I couldn't stop him! I can't control Liam. No one can, you said so yourself!" There was an edge of desperation in my tone now. In the interest of full disclosure, I whirled toward Liam's hiding place and waved him over. "Liam!"

He came running. "What is it? What's wrong?" he demanded once he was in range.

I spun around again, gesturing to Liam to make the necessary introductions. But John Doe was already gone.

"Where did he go? Did you see him? Where did he go?"

"I don't know, I wasn't looking at him. I was looking at you!"

I let out a cry of frustration. "He's gone!" I declared, as if this wasn't patently obvious. I whirled on Liam again, jabbing my finger in his face. "He didn't tell me anything because he *knew* you were there! He *told* me to come alone!"

"Then why did you wave me over?"

"Because he knew you were there anyway! I was trying to show that I wasn't hiding anything on purpose!"

"And he didn't want to stick around with a second witness, huh?" Liam growled. "Sounds like criminal behavior to me."

I balled my hands into fists. "You just cost me my only chance of finding out the truth!"

He stared back at me, serenely calm. "Between that and the risk that John Doe might have killed you or taken you captive, I can live with that."

I could have slapped him. But instead, with supreme self-control, I turned on my heels, marching back to the hotel. Liam fell into step beside me and tried to reach for my arm, but I yanked it away the second he touched me. I felt his hand on my lower back instead. When I tried to shake him off, his fingers hooked gently around my waist, keeping me ever at arm's reach.

I like Liam, Madeline had said. *He keeps you safe.*

We still didn't speak once we reached the hotel. He pushed the elevator button, so I darted toward the stairs instead, taking them two at a time. I heard him jog to catch up.

"Stop following me!" I panted.

"I'm in the room next to yours, remember?" he said, even though he stood behind me, like he intended to enter mine.

"I did *not* invite you in!"

He sighed, and took a step back. "All right." But before I shut the door in his face, I made the mistake of looking in his eyes. I wanted to stay mad at him, and I *was* still mad at him, but he looked so hurt. I bit my lip, as if that physical act of restriction would also keep my emotions from softening.

"You'll never know either!" I whispered. "Don't you even care?"

"It's not worth trading the life of another

person I love to find out."

I stared at him for a minute. *He means it in the generic sense*, I decided. *He must.*

"Besides," he added, "I might already know what he was going to tell you."

I looked back: he hovered on the threshold of my room, a questioning look on his face. I sighed, irritated. He had me and he knew it.

"Fine," I gestured him inside, and he gave me a quick smile, crossing the threshold and closing the door. I glanced at Madeline meaningfully, spinning my finger around to indicate what I wanted her to do. Just as before, she mimed a zipper across her mouth and spun around to the wall, to give us the semblance of privacy.

"What, then?" I demanded, placing my hands on my hips for emphasis, as if to say, *This had better be good.*

Liam sat on the twin bed beside the one where I slept. "After we meet Halpert tomorrow, I'll know for sure. I'll tell you then."

I let out an aggravated cry. "Is this the thing Francis wouldn't tell us earlier? He told *you*?"

Liam nodded. "And I trust Francis a lot more than John Doe."

"So why can't you tell me now, then?"

"Because I don't want to color your perceptions tomorrow. You're very observant, Bec. I just want to make sure you're as objective as possible."

I scowled at this. "As if you need me for that, when Francis is around!"

"But Francis is also biased. So far, you're not." He put out his hand to me. "So come on. Truce?"

I glowered at him, but with less conviction. "You persuaded me to let you in here under false pretenses."

"No, I *implied* I would tell you my theory, but I never directly promised to tell you *now*," he pointed out, his eyes twinkling just a bit. "I can't help what you infer."

"I hate you," I muttered. But I could feel the beginnings of an involuntary half smile tugging at my lips.

He transferred his seat from the bed opposite mine to right beside me, and I glanced back at him. He raised his eyebrows, giving me a shy, hopeful smile.

"Does that mean you forgive me?"

"How did you get that from 'I hate you?'"

He turned up his grin a notch. "Wishful thinking?"

I shook my head. "You really are a prison warden, Liam. I *can* take care of myself, you know."

He shrugged, bumping my shoulder with his instead. "Don't I at least get chivalry points for *trying* to protect you?"

I rolled my eyes. "What exactly do you think you're going to trade those points in for?" The second the words were out of my mouth, I realized what I'd said, and the color rushed to my cheeks.

"*Well*," he began meaningfully.

"Don't answer that," I interjected and stood up, suddenly very aware of our proximity. I moved toward the door again, knowing he would follow me.

Liam stood too, and did follow. "You know, it *could* actually be beneficial for both of us…" he teased, "You *do* need the practice, after all…"

Grabbing his shoulder and shoving him on the other side of the door, I declared, "I have to shower for dinner!"

"Need a cold shower, huh?"

I slammed the door in his face.

A few seconds later, I heard him call through the door, "Does that mean later?"

Chapter 27

Liam came back to my room about an hour later to take me to dinner. It was chillier that night than it had been the previous several evenings because of the wind, and I was grateful to have packed my peacoat. Liam wore a long dark overcoat with the collar popped up against the wind, hands in his pockets. I looped my hand through his elbow and kept my body close enough to his that passersby didn't jostle me away from him. I didn't bother protesting about my independence anymore; we'd had enough fighting for one day. The streetlights cast everything in a strange yellowish glow as we rounded the corner to Francis's pub.

"For security," he told me, his voice low. "We have a lot to discuss before tomorrow."

"With Francis?" I tried to keep the groan out of my voice.

He nodded, and gave me a wry smile as he held the door open for me. "He's not so bad once you get to know him."

"Meaning he gets less rude?"

"No. He's always rude. But after awhile, you start to think of it as part of his charm."

I snorted. The pub for once was filled with actual customers, and I wondered briefly how this translated into a secure environment at the moment. But then Liam guided me to a private room in the back labeled 'reserved,' the heavy curtains pulled open to admit our entrance. He helped me slip out of my coat and into one of the chairs around a table built for four. He had just moved to his own seat when Francis appeared beside us, dressed in his usual black t-shirt and black jeans with his hair pulled into a low ponytail at the nape of his neck. Francis glanced at me and frowned.

"You weren't supposed to bring *her*."

I raised an eyebrow, glancing at Liam. "Was that the charm you were telling me about?"

Liam's only reply to either of us was a smirk to himself. He slipped out of his own overcoat and settled his elbows on the table. To Francis, he said, "Are you gonna bring us some menus, or what?"

Heaving an irritated sigh, Francis snapped his fingers and beckoned one of the servers over, leaning in to make his request: two menus, and two beers for himself and Liam. I wasn't sure if this meant I wasn't allowed to order, or what, but then he explained, sullen, "I don't know what she drinks."

"Probably water would be best, for this

conversation. She's a lightweight," Liam winked at me.

Why did my heart have to flutter when he did that? I looked down, avoiding his eyes.

"Ugh. You two disgust me," Francis rolled his eyes, slipping the curtains closed as he moved to a third seat. "Why don't you just make out already and get it over with?"

"I don't know. Rebecca?" Liam raised his eyebrows at me with an inquiring smile, steepling his fingers.

"I think I *do* want some wine," I mumbled, grateful for the low lighting. "Where's Larissa?"

"In my apartment downstairs with a few of the guys. They're in the testing phase," said Francis.

"So," Liam turned to Francis. "What did M say after I left?"

I sat up straighter. M might be the only person more intriguing to me than John Doe. "Harriet Albright, right?" I asked, eager to show that I knew who they were talking about.

Francis made a face at me and replied, "Yes, and she'd appreciate it if you don't use her real name too freely. She's high up in government intelligence, and we don't want to blow her cover." Then he turned back to Liam as if I wasn't there.

The bar maid came back with two beers and a glass of water for me, and our menus. She looked at me expectantly to see what I'd be having to drink.

"I think I will stick with water after all, thanks," I murmured. I saw Liam's triumphant smirk and kicked him under the table. He *was* right, though: if this conversation held much import, I probably shouldn't be drinking.

Once the maid had left, Liam sighed and said to Francis, "I wish M could come to the meeting with us herself."

"Why can't she?" I asked.

Francis deadpanned, "Did I not just finish saying she's high up in government intelligence and they think she *works* for them?" Then he promptly turned back to Liam. "I caught her up on what we know so far: the twenty year gap in the timelines of Halpert and his board, and also the hydrochloric acid and my theory about it. M agrees that those are clues to the information we'll need to ultimately expose them publicly and remove them from power, but I still need to verify my theories." He gave a pointed look at me. I crossed my arms over my chest and stared right back at him, refusing to be intimidated. Finally Francis gestured at me with his head, but spoke to Liam. "So are you gonna tell her she's not invited tomorrow, or should I?"

"What?" I turned to Liam, alarmed.

"She *is* invited. I don't care what M says," Liam retorted.

"Why, just because you have a romantic

interest in her?"

"No, because she's part of our cover: I'm ostensibly meeting with them, or my father is anyway, to discuss putting morality failsafes into the bots. She can speak with some authority on that subject, and I can't. Also, she's the only one who will be present tomorrow and who doesn't know your theory now, which makes her an objective observer."

"So, wait," I interjected. "M... *knows* about me? And she doesn't want me there tomorrow?"

Francis turned to me and said with characteristic frankness, "No. You're just an undergrad, and you have nothing to offer at the meeting. You're a pure liability. M insisted that we send you back to Dublin at once."

Despite the fact that I'd seriously considered doing just that earlier that day, I felt a flare of indignation. "Does she *know* who my father is?"

"Liam told her when you got here," Francis replied, and then added flatly, "She wasn't impressed. We're not a dynasty."

"We *need* her," Liam insisted again. "She might not be *you*, Francis, but she's still extremely perceptive."

"You're going to directly disobey M's orders?" Francis countered.

"Yes," said Liam firmly. "I am. If I'm going, she's going. And M needs me there, obviously, or there's no meeting at all."

"Once they see it's you and not your father, they could easily find out you hadn't worked at General Specs in years, though," I pointed out. "And what about your locus? Don't you think the fact that you tried to blow the lid off them for years might bias them against you?"

Liam shook his head. "The locus was under a pseudonym, and I doubt they'll bother to research me that much, unless we arouse suspicion." He shot a pointed look at Francis, who looked affronted.

"Oh, be fair!" Francis retorted. "I don't choose to play social games around *you*, but I understand them better than you could ever hope to do. I can blend in anywhere, and be anything to anyone."

I scoffed. "So you're saying you *can* be perfectly charming, but you just *prefer* to be an ass?"

"Falseness of every kind is my abhorrence," he replied to me, in a most dignified manner. "I use it only when it suits my purposes."

"There's a difference between politeness and falseness!" I retorted.

"Guys," Liam held up his hands.

I closed my eyes to reset, and turned back to Liam. "Okay fine. But wouldn't Halpert, or at least people under him, have researched the owners of loci they considered potentially dangerous?"

Liam shook his head again. "That's part of what M is doing in their intel department. One of her roles, ironically, is detecting and suppressing any external threats to the Republic—including us, the Renegades. She's the reason why we've managed to stay hidden for these meetings thus far: she told Halpert and his board that removing our loci was all it took to destroy us as a threat, and that we now have no way of contacting one another."

Francis added, "She also led them to believe that our loci were connected to other people. Liam's alter-ego is a man named Erik Johanssen. He's a gamer living in Sweden in his parents' basement, and he spends most of his time either high or in Artificial Experience landscapes, or more likely both at once. Possibly he's also a small time dealer of illicit substances. My alter-ego is a woman living in Rome by the name of Alessandra Russo, supposedly a brilliant programmer in her own right —she'd have to be, of course, to get confused with me—with a suspected history of embezzlement and extortion that the authorities could never pin on her. Both of them are now being watched very closely for any missteps. They'll no doubt be apprehended shortly."

"But they're innocent!" I exclaimed.

Francis shrugged. "Of rebellious activity, perhaps. But they're not *entirely* innocent."

"What if they wind up like my father? Or

Liam's brother? For something they didn't even do?"

"We're in a war, Cordeaux," was Francis's flat reply. "There are casualties in war."

I was shaking now. "People convicted of petty crimes *die* under Justice Wallenberg!"

Liam placed a hand on my thigh under the table. It was sufficiently distracting that some of my anger simmered. "I don't like it either," he murmured. "But I don't see what we can do about it right now."

"Was this M's idea?" I was liking her less and less as this conversation went on, too.

Liam nodded. "Her top priority is protecting our real activities from discovery…"

"We have to help Erik and Alessandra," I declared. I was acutely aware of Liam's hand still on my thigh, but trying not to show it.

"Maybe we will, but it's not the priority at the moment," he told me. "Let's just focus on the meeting tomorrow for now, and get through that. Hopefully on the other end of it, we'll have more information than we have right now."

"We will," Francis leaned back in his chair, confident. Liam released my leg, and a breath I hadn't known I'd been holding involuntarily escaped my lips. Francis noticed—I saw his eyes sharpen upon me, and I willed him not to comment. For once, he didn't.

"You really think he's right about whatever it is he suspects?" I asked Liam, gesturing at Francis with my head.

Liam waffled his head. "I'd say no way, if it were anybody but him. It's on a whole new level of absurd—"

"Outside the box," Francis corrected, raising one finger. "*Absurd* means wildly unreasonable, illogical, or inappropriate, none of which describe me in the least. I am ruthlessly logical."

"And completely appropriate at all times," I deadpanned.

Francis didn't seem to get it, but Liam snickered.

Chapter 28

Francis waited for Liam and me outside his pub the next day, wearing a long black coat very much like the one Liam wore. It was the first time I'd seen Francis in anything other than his black t-shirt and jeans, and it made him look more wiry somehow. He didn't smile, but his green eyes danced. He was clearly excited.

Liam hailed a hovercar, and as one swept down to meet us, he glanced at Francis.

"You are to keep your mouth shut," he told him. "I'm serious."

"I know you are," was Francis's enigmatic reply.

Liam turned on him squarely. "Not the response I was after. If you say nothing, they may actually believe we all work for General Specs and represent my dad. But if you say *anything*…"

Francis opened his mouth and closed it again, a smile playing at the corners of his mouth. "I will say no more and no less than absolutely necessary."

Liam growled, and glanced at me sourly. "If he wasn't so bloody brilliant, I'd never put up with him."

"Stop telling him how brilliant he is, he's got a fat enough head already," I muttered as I climbed into the hovercar beside Liam.

After Liam directed the hovercar to our destination—the Capitol building—we rode in silence. I felt jittery: this was it. It all came down to this meeting. Also, I'd be expected to present at least half of what Liam wanted to communicate to six of the most powerful men in the world. Arguably, *the* six most powerful men in the world.

When we arrived and entered the lobby, Francis hung back and let Liam tell the receptionist bot who we were. I noticed that he introduced us as "Liam Kelly of General Specs, and my associates, Rebecca Hutt and Bill Spencer."

I glanced back at Francis: he bit his lip, clearly doing something on his A.E. chip, looking up at me with a mischievous twinkle in his eye. Then he stepped up to the podium behind which the receptionist bot sat.

"Excuse me, could you point me to the restroom?"

She directed him, and Francis vanished. I looked quizzically at Liam, but he didn't seem surprised or perturbed by this.

When Francis returned, his overcoat folded

over his arm, the receptionist bot wheeled around the desk in front of us. "This way, please," she announced, leading us down a long glass hallway through an atrium.

Liam walked just in front of me. I noticed that he wiped his palms on his trousers twice. It wasn't like him to get nervous—but then again, if he was ever going to, this was the time. I felt a few beads of sweat spring up on my own forehead.

The receptionist bot opened a set of rich mahogany doors, beyond which an enormous cherrywood table filled the center of a room replete with natural light. One entire wall was made of glass. Six men sat around the table; one stood up when we entered.

He seemed shorter in person than I thought he'd be—which was odd, considering the holograph projections are life size. Still, I expected Halpert to be at least six feet tall if he was an inch. He was probably only five foot four or so in reality. His hair reminded me of sand, and his eyes were even bluer than Liam's—like sea glass. There was also something about him that just seemed... *wrong*. I couldn't put my finger on it, but it made the hairs on the back of my neck stand up.

The corners of his eyes crinkled as his face split into his the charismatic smile I recognized from the holographs.

"Well! Liam Kelly *Junior*!" crowed Halpert,

"I was under the impression the meeting was with your father." He seemed unfazed, though, coming forward and reaching to shake Liam's hand with both of his.

"He was detained at the last minute, and asked me to come in his place," Liam said smoothly. "It's an honor to meet you, Sir. These are my associates, Bill Spencer and Rebecca Hutt."

After a gracious nod in our direction, Halpert turned our attention to the other five men around the table. "I'm sure none of these gentlemen need much introduction, but nevertheless, might I present Abraham Chiefton," Halpert gestured to a graying man with a bald spot and a heavy beard, with sharp gray eyes. He reclined in his chair, nodding at us. "Chief Justice Wallenberg." Wallenberg was built much like Francis was, tall and wiry. His heavy brow reminded me of Frankenstein. He merely tilted his chin up when Halpert introduced him, like he couldn't be bothered with politeness. *Charming,* I thought. "Kennedy St. James." The owner of Plethorus, the largest supplier of goods worldwide, was bald, with thick eyebrows and thin lips. He seemed most interested in Francis, who stared right back at him. Neither of them smiled. "Pierre Montgomery." The head of the International Education Board looked every bit the academic, with half moon spectacles on his nose even though glasses were a relic of the past. He wore a tweed sport coat. "And Dr. Janner Rasputin." Dr. Rasputin narrowed his eyes at me, his mouth set in a long hard line. He had more thick dark hair than most men half his age, with heavyset features as if he had some Romanian blood in him. I tried to smile at him, but my mouth refused to obey. Every one of the faces around the table gave me the same queer feeling Halpert's had, of something not quite right. If I hadn't had a very good reason to be there, I'd have very much wished to leave.

As Halpert introduced the board, three bots entered the room bearing platters of food, which they arranged on the center of the table.

"Please, help yourselves," Halpert gestured to the stack of plates and cutlery with a gracious smile.

Liam reached for the plate on top, for which I was glad—I didn't want to be the first. I wiped my brow, attributing the sudden intense warmth to more nerves than I was aware of feeling. Liam and Halpert fortunately kept the conversation going, prattling about Liam's father—the one thing they had in common. Liam managed to expend quite a few words while saying very little. Here and there the others jumped in too—Kennedy St. James had quite a bit of interaction with Liam Kelly Senior, apparently, as the largest seller of General Specs products worldwide.

Once we'd filled our plates, Francis cleared

his throat, interrupting the pleasantries about Liam's father. I felt a momentary spike of dread. But what he said was, "Will we have the pleasure of eating *with* you distinguished gentlemen, or just in front of you?" That was when I noticed that Francis, Liam and I were the only ones with plates.

"I'm afraid we just finished a brunch meeting," said Halpert, with no indication that'd noticed Francis's rudeness. "We will have to forego that particular pleasure."

I glanced at Francis, who looked a bit smug. This meant something to him, but I didn't know what it was.

Why is it so hot in this room? I adjusted my collar, unbuttoning the top button of my cardigan. At last I just took it off altogether; I had a thin white blouse on underneath.

"Well, should we call the meeting to order?" Halpert asked rhetorically. "Perhaps you can start off by sharing Liam Senior's reasons for wishing to meet—or, meet by proxy, as it turns out." Halpert's expression betrayed nothing, but I felt a pricking sense of alarm on the back of my neck.

He knows Liam Senior never sent us.

In response, Liam stood to indicate that he had the floor, wiping his mouth with his napkin. "While General Specs recognizes that we cannot stop progress, the purpose of this meeting is to draw your attention to some potential dangers of S.R.

creativity before it becomes widespread. We would like to request your public support for research into ensuring that certain failsafes are built into the De Vries prototype."

Abraham Chiefton, still leaning back in his chair, peered at Liam over steepled fingers. "You haven't worked for General Specs in five years," he declared.

I saw the momentary flash of panic cross Liam's face, so fast I might have imagined it, before he answered smoothly, "My father and I differed on the issue of the relative safety of creative bots. I believe, and I hope to convince you, that we stand at the precipice of two diverging possible futures. On one side is the continuation of our species, symbiotic with machines, and perhaps tending toward the utopian vision you describe, Senator Halpert. On the other side is our almost inevitable extinction. Which one becomes reality depends upon what we do, right now—*before* the De Vries prototype reaches full development, and software upgrades become available to the rest of the bots on the planet."

Halpert gave a mild, unconcerned laugh. "Mr. Kelly, I believe you've been reading too much science fiction. Power-hungry superintelligent bots who destroy all human life? Come now."

Liam wiped the sweat off his own forehead —he, at least, felt the heat too. "Our concern is not that they will become power-hungry *per se*, sir. Our concern is first, that the introduction of creativity will lead to a bot whose core purpose is to improve upon itself, thus leading to superintelligence. Even one such entity would be a disaster. But surely the moment one bot achieves it, software upgrades will immediately become available on the labyrinth for all other bots as well. The way superintelligent bots might interpret their core purposes is impossible to predict."

"It's quite a leap to jump from creativity to superintelligence," declared Kennedy St. James. "Have you *seen* the De Vries prototype?"

"I have, but—"

"Then you know," St. James went on, his tone all condescension, "that it merely mimics human creativity. Bot superintelligence is about as likely as the same feat in a human who decides to expend all its creative powers in the effort of making itself godlike."

"Maybe at this point, and using this prototype," Liam countered, "but this is only a starting place! You know as well as I do, Mr. St. James, that learning curves for machines are exponential, and not subject to human limitations like fatigue. A creative bot will surely make small strides at first. But by the time superintelligence comes near enough to seem like a credible threat, it will already be upon us."

Halpert rose. "Excuse me for a moment." With a dulcet smile, he strode to the doorway, letting the door shut behind him with a soft click. I followed him with my eyes, and then glanced at Francis. His eyes met mine with an expression that was probably as close as he ever got to alarm. *Breathe,* I told myself. He probably just needed to take care of some business that had nothing to do with us. He *was* the most powerful man in the world, after all.

Shaken by Halpert's abrupt exit, Liam continued, "Our… second concern is that we believe the introduction of emotion will lead the bots to discard any programming they happen to dislike. Including any moral code we attempt to instill." He nodded to me, his eyes meeting mine with an intensity that meant something, though I wasn't sure what. Encouragement, perhaps? "This is Rebecca's field of study, so I'll let her take it from here."

I stood up as Liam sank back into his chair, and for a terrifying moment, my voice failed me. *You are an actress, Rebecca,* I reminded myself. *You are on a stage, and this is all a set. You are an impassioned executive, here to state your case. You are brilliant and articulate.*

I cleared my throat. "Hello." Not a great beginning, but I swallowed and went on, "As Liam said, in humans, morality is what modulates our behavior and prevents us from acting in destructive ways toward others. With few exceptions such as psychopaths and individuals who have been brainwashed by certain cults or political ideology, everyone agrees upon the foundational rules of morality, even across cultures."

Dr Janner Rasputin narrowed his eyes at me, scrutinizing. My heart beat faster. Halpert slipped back into the room just then, smoothing his suit as he resumed his seat. It threw me off—I didn't know what I was saying. I glanced at Dr. Rasputin again, and found his expression changed: from scrutiny to recognition.

"Dr. Rasputin," I finally said before I could stop myself. "Is something wrong?"

"Yes," he leaned back. "Your story."

My mouth went dry. "Sorry?" I hadn't been telling a story, had I?

"Your name is Rebecca Cordeaux, not Rebecca Hutt," he said. "Daughter of Quentin Cordeaux. He was a talented general practice doctor who worked under me for some time."

Involuntarily I glanced at Liam, as if hoping he could save me. Even across the table, I could see his dilated pupils, and sweat trickled down the side of his face. I looked at Francis next, who— impossibly—looked quite self-complacent.

How can this possibly be a good thing? I wanted to shout at him. I did notice that wisps of

Francis's hair clung to his neck, too. At least he was sweating like we were—so either he was still nervous in spite of his airs, or it really *was* sweltering in here.

"N-no sir," I stammered. "My name is Rebecca Hutt—"

Abraham Chiefton finally touched all four pegs of his chair to the floor. "You're a local stage actress and a college student at Dublin University, studying neuroscience," he informed me. Then he looked at Francis. "And there *is* a Bill Spencer working at General Specs, but he is fifty-eight. You're certainly not him."

Justice Wallenberg leaned forward and joined in. "Mr. Kelly is who he claims to be, but he has been estranged from his father for five years now. Liam Kelly Senior did not send you today, and he has no knowledge of your presence here. You've lied to us, Mr. Kelly. I trust you are aware of the consequences of false representation to men of our stature."

Liam replied to this somehow—his tone was smooth and calm as ever, but his expression reminded me of a dog with its ears flattened against its head.

But I didn't hear what he said. Instead, my father's words came back to me in flashes:

"Rasputin is a fiend," he'd spat. *"Sure, he contained infectious disease outbreaks, and you*

*know how he did it? By killing everyone who
contracted the disease and throwing them in a
quarantine until their bodies decomposed beyond
recognition! He's a complete utilitarian: he wants
to keep the human race healthy, but he doesn't give
a damn about individual lives."*

I turned to Wallenberg, and remembered the
story of Jim Holtz, a prisoner who had embezzled
money from his employer because his sister was
dying of cancer, and he was trying to pay for her
treatment. *"Sure it was wrong, but he'd never had
any criminal record before, and he justified it to
himself because the company was corrupt,"* Dad
had said. *"But did Wallenberg take the
circumstances into account? Of course not. He gave
him the death penalty, like he always does for every
minor infraction. Justice without mercy."*

"Kennedy St. James?" Dad had railed. *"Oh
yeah, he's a great businessman. He pays his
employees splendidly, and gives 'em great
benefits... but he owns them. Ask anybody who
works for him, and they'll tell you: he only does that
much because it's a smart business move. Give 'em
the golden handcuffs, and they'll never be able to
leave, even if they're getting called day and night,
weekends and holidays. They're working eighty
hour weeks, most of 'em, and their average lifespan
is at least twenty years less than the rest of the
population."* That was before those jobs were all

automated, of course.

Dad had slammed down his fork at the dinner table at the mention of Pierre Montgomery's new book launch on the netscreen. Mom's face tightened in anticipation of whatever diatribe was sure to follow, and he did not disappoint. *"Montgomery's a snake,"* he declared, waving his fork in the air. *"Revisionist history, every last bit of it! He's responsible for the homogenization of thought in this Republic. He brainwashes every kid worldwide into seeing the world his way! And we let him!"* Mom rolled her eyes, but wisely held her tongue—I knew she thought Dad was unhinged by this point.

He said more or less the same thing about Abraham Chiefton: *"He uses his influence to shape mass opinion! Whatever comes down from the courts, whatever political opinions Halpert wants to influence, whatever Montgomery wants to indoctrinate, Chiefton creates propaganda films to perpetuate those beliefs! He knows just how to tug on the heartstrings and bypass human reason. He's a master at it,"* Dad added bitterly, *"I'll give him that."*

And what did Dad say about Halpert himself? *"He's insidious, like a little spider."* Dad mimed the creature with his hands. *"He's content to make very small gains over a long period of time, with the help of his 'minions' to turn public opinion little by little. That's how they get you: little by little. If he sprung his agenda all at once, we'd rebel —but noooo."* Dad wagged his finger at me, *"just like the frog that jumps into the pot on the stove, if it starts off cold and you heat it up juuuust a bit at a time, he'll sit there content while you boil him alive."*

The room had gone silent. Everyone stared at me: that's when I realized I was still on my feet. Liam had finished whatever he'd said to excuse our lies, and his eyes bored into mine. I understood his meaning this time: *Sit down and don't say a word.* I obeyed, sinking back into my chair.

Halpert cleared his throat as if nothing unusual had happened at all.

"Well, I'm afraid we have some other business to attend to this afternoon," he said, reaching across the table to shake Liam's hand. "Thank you all for bringing your concerns to our awareness. We will make sure they receive all the attention they deserve on the senate floor."

I mumbled my goodbyes too, but nobody shook my hand, nor Francis's. Liam practically yanked Francis to his feet and shoved him towards the door, and I thought I overheard him hiss, *"Shut. Up."*

As soon as the main door to the street clicked shut behind us, Francis clapped his hands together, unable to contain himself any longer.

"What is *wrong* with you?" I snapped at him. But it was Liam who replied.

"Not here," he said through gritted teeth, signaling a hovercar. It descended in front of us and I climbed in beside Liam, Francis on my other side. Liam directed the car to take us back to our hotel. Francis was obviously quite pleased with himself. I shot him another sour look.

"I guess all this self-congratulations means he proved his theory?"

"Oh yes," Francis confirmed, rubbing his palms together. "I love it when I'm right. Which let's be honest, I nearly always am—but when nobody else ever had even the *slightest* inkling, it's *so* much more satisfying..."

"And, that's about as humble as he gets," Liam muttered to me.

When we arrived at the hotel, we didn't speak all the way up to Liam's room. As soon as the door opened, Liam grabbed his suitcase, which was fully packed and waiting on the other side of the door. He pulled it into the hallway, then reached in and grabbed a second one, handing it to Francis. Liam had only arrived with one suitcase, so the second one must belong to Francis. Then he gestured to my room next.

"You need to pack," he informed me, as I pressed my fingerprint to the keypad and opened my door.

"Why? Where are we going?"

Still brimming with mirth, Francis stepped inside my room behind Liam and told me, "We're catching the Quantum Track to Geneva, Switzerland in about an hour. Oh, you have a personal bot!" He'd just noticed Madeline. "Isn't that ironic!"

Madeline's eyes widened at me in an expression I knew meant, *Do you want me to hide?* I ignored this—it didn't seem important now. Instead, I grabbed my empty suitcase out of the closet, glaring from Francis to Liam and back again.

"Will someone please tell me what's going on? Why are we going to Geneva, and what was Francis right about that's rendered him so beside himself with self-congratulations?"

Francis gestured to Liam in a show of ostentatious generosity. "You want to tell her?"

Liam glared at him, sighed, and looked at me. "Can you power her down first?" He pointed at Madeline.

Without comment, I crossed the room and knelt down to her, whispering, "I'm sorry," as I pressed the blue power button on her neck. When the light from Madeline's eyes went dim, I whirled on Liam. "Well?"

He took another deep breath. "Halpert and his board are not using the hydrochloric acid to feed illegal humanoid bots," he said.

I blinked at him. "Okay, then what are they doing with it?"

"Eating it," Liam said. He stared at me, unblinking, as he waited for this to sink in. "Bec. They *are* the bots."

Chapter 29

I blinked at Liam. "I'm sorry. What?"

He sighed again, shooting an irritated glance back at Francis, who was still rubbing his hands together in glee.

"You do realize this is *bad* news, right?" Liam snapped at him.

"Wait wait wait," I held up a hand. "Halpert is a bot?" I said it again, with emphasis, "Halpert *is* a bot? As in... he *is* one. Like Madeline. He's a bot."

"And so are all his board members," Liam sighed. "Look, we've got to check out and get to the station, we don't have much time. I'll go downstairs and check us out, and we'll explain more once we're on board."

"What's in Geneva?" For some reason, of all things, the concern that flashed through my mind was what I'd tell my mom. After she'd accused me of using this investigation as an excuse to gallivant all over the world because 'Rebecca does what Rebecca wants,' wouldn't a sudden trip to Geneva after dropping out of school seem to confirm all her suspicions?

"Ramses Youssef," was Liam's answer. He was halfway out the door already, dragging Francis behind him by the overcoat. "Their creator."

An hour later, we found a private compartment on the Quantum Track and closed the sliding glass door after stowing our luggage. Liam sat beside me, Francis on the seat opposite us. He reclined on the seat, arms folded behind his head like a lounging cat.

"All right," I demanded, glaring at Francis's outstretched form, "convince me they're bots."

Francis sat upright, leaning toward me across the seat so suddenly that I leaned back to maintain my personal space. His green eyes danced, and he said very fast, "Clue number one: they're all stuck in the uncanny valley."

I glanced at Liam, then back at Francis, who smirked as if waiting for me to ask him. "Fine, I'll bite. What's the uncanny valley?"

"Their eyes never seemed to focus quite the way a human's eyes might, and their expressions create a slight cognitive dissonance in the observer: the disconnect between expectation and reality. *Uncanny valley* is a term referring to the graph that plots the continuum of human verisimilitude on one axis, and human reactions on the other—that is, human revulsion increases as the machines look increasingly human. I suspected that if any uncanniness existed, it would be so minute as to be virtually undetectable via holograph; I'd have to see them in person to tell. I knew at the first glance that they couldn't possibly be human. Still, for your benefit, I'll enumerate my other reasons."

"Gee, thanks," I said.

Francis went on, missing my sarcasm, "Clue number two: they didn't eat. They could, of course, but it's not very efficient for that generation of humanoid bots to get their protons from food, and it can clog up their systems over time, so if they were bots, I knew they'd make some excuse to avoid eating if they could. Protons from acid are much more efficient. Clue number three: they didn't sweat, even though I programmed the thermostat to ninety degrees inside our conference room—"

My mouth fell open. "You did?"

He nodded. "Yes, I hacked into their thermostat last night to make sure I had access but I still had to find the physical unit—"

"That's what he did when he 'went to the bathroom,'" Liam told me, using air quotes. He pushed his feet against the opposite seat, folding his arms across his chest.

I turned back to Francis. "*That's* why it was so hot in there?"

Francis nodded at me, grinning. "Human

bots of the HCl generation couldn't sweat. I had to make it hot enough that all of *us* would, just for contrast. Notice *they* were all dry as a bone, though?"

I opened my mouth and closed it again, but Francis didn't wait for my reply. He went on, "Clue number four: no physiologic response to emotion. Even sociopaths will display anger, excitement, or some tells of adrenaline when they find out they're being lied to. I expected them to see through our false identities, of course: any human with an A.E. chip who wanted to search us could have determined pretty quickly that we weren't who we said we were. But there should have been some emotional response to this information; specifically pupil dilation and shallower breathing. Yet not one of the six displayed any of the human physiologic signs of emotion: not a raised voice, not a shortened respiration, not a pupil dilation, not a muscle twitch. They might feel emotion, but they don't show it like a human would."

My head spun. "So… you *wanted* them to figure out we weren't who we said we were?"

Francis ignored the question. He was on a roll.

"Clue number five," he went on, "Rasputin positively ID'ed you. I expected them to know we weren't who we said we were, but in order to know our real identities, he'd have had to scan your face like a photo and search it on the labyrinth, which human A.E. chips lack the capability to do—as I trust you know."

"I… thought he might have seen a picture of me from my dad's desk once or something," I said faintly. "They did used to work together. I would have been a lot younger than I am now, but still."

Francis's brow sank and he glowered at me. "Okay, maybe. But that's hardly necessary to carry my point."

I shook my head. "It still seems like a pretty big leap…"

"No," Francis cut me off, jabbing his finger in the air, "those are the confirmatory bits of evidence that fill in an already clear picture." With a self-satisfied flourish, he gestured to Liam. "You want to tell her the rest?"

I might've made a guttural noise of disgust, and I saw Liam's mouth twitch before settling back into the seriousness of the moment. I turned to face him, my own arms folded across my chest in a mirror of his posture. I guess he relented, uncrossing his arms and resting his hands on the seat beside him.

"We had Odessa do more digging while you were gone yesterday," he said. "Corroboration of all six men's stories ended twenty years ago, as you knew—but there had to be something else linking them together. We found one name that recurred for all of them."

"Ramses Youssef," I guessed, and Liam nodded.

"So we had Odessa investigate him, and found that he was a programmer at that time in computational neuroscience. He was at the forefront of the development of that generation of humanoid bots, and he was also very politically active in pushing for widespread acceptance of his work. Just after the Council of Synthetic Reason ruled that humanoid bots were illegal, he went underground. Officially his record seemed to end there, but there were hints that he kept on with his work in secret. We're pretty sure he currently lives in Geneva, under the pseudonym Sol Huckabee."

"Pretty sure?"

"We think he wanted to cut all ties for some reason, and needed to disappear," Liam told me. "It wasn't easy to find even that much. If Huckabee isn't Youssef himself, then he's someone who was closely connected with him."

"So why didn't you just assume this Youssef gave humanoid bots to the men on Halpert's council, or else gave them the blueprints so they could make their own?" I asked. "Why assume that they are the bots themselves?"

"Because," Francis sat up, sounding exasperated now, "if that were the case, why would there be no record of the existence of Halpert or the board members before twenty years ago? We'd be able to trace them to *something*, even if it were totally different from their public personas. But no, once you dig below their superficial back stories, you find *nada.*" He held up a hand with the fingers and thumb closed together in the form of a zero. "Nothing. Zilch. They apparently sprang into existence as fully grown adults with highly specialized skills and immediately began their methodical climb to the top of their respective fields, which every one of them achieved in record time. What would be the relevance of each of them having a humanoid bot at home, like a pet? Wouldn't that sort of beg the question of what happened to them before twenty years ago, and how their connection to Youssef linked them to one another? Isn't it fascinating that each of them seems specially suited to taking his unique mountain of influence—politics, law, media, business, medicine, and education? Every one of them at the top of his game, without rival, and yet banded together to make decisions jointly. Given that, combined with the clues I just listed for you, I *dare* you to postulate an alternate theory that suits the facts better!"

Francis leaned forward incrementally as he said this until I was flattened against the seat behind me. Liam planted a hand on Francis's chest and pushed him back to his own seat.

"All right, you've made your point," he said

dryly. Then he looked back at me. "I had the same reaction yesterday, but he predicted the clues that would be present if his theory were correct. He was so sure it would be that he convinced me to pack last night and look up the first Quantum Track to Geneva after the meeting ended, just in case. The only reason I didn't tell you to pack last night too was because I honestly didn't think he'd turn out to be correct, and I didn't want to explain all that to you if he wasn't, and prejudice your perspective before you met them. Plus, you're pretty low maintenance, I figured it wouldn't take you that long to pack anyway," he added with a lopsided grin. "And it didn't."

I took a deep breath. "What am I gonna tell Mom?" I murmured, more to myself than to him. "I have to give her *some* explanation for why I'm heading to Geneva…"

Liam shrugged. "Do you usually give her that many details? Can't you just tell her this is where the clues point and you have to follow them?"

I waffled my head. "I guess," I conceded. I hadn't actually called her since we'd arrived in San Jose anyway; the only contact we'd had were the brief comms we'd sent in which she asked if I was back in Dublin yet, and I told her I'd dropped out of school. All she cared about was my whereabouts and safety; she didn't ask a lot of other questions.

Liam was probably right; I wouldn't need to go into much detail. She'd be too busy lecturing me on how I was throwing my life away to care about the whys of where I was at any given moment.

Nobody said anything else for a long while, and I suddenly realized how tired I was. I hadn't slept very well the night before, and I'd apparently been running on adrenaline all morning. The movement of the Quantum Track lulled me; right about when we began skimming the top of the ocean, I closed my eyes. That didn't last long, though: Francis apparently also dropped off to sleep, and started snoring like a water buffalo. I opened one eye, and exchanged a disgusted look with Liam, who glanced from Francis to my face and shook with silent mirth. He gestured to the sliding glass door and slid it open gently to keep from waking Francis. I slipped out behind him, and followed him to the compartment opposite where Francis slept. Liam sat down opposite me, and I rested my head on the glass. I closed my eyes, but a few minutes later opened them again, and glanced back at Liam. I found him looking back at me.

"Do you think this was it?" I asked. "What John Doe was going to tell me? The thing my father and your brother died for?"

He hesitated for a moment, as if considering. But then he nodded. "Yeah," he said. "I think it is."

"They threatened to tell people, you think?"

Liam shrugged. "Maybe they didn't have to. It's not the sort of thing you can find out about and just sit on, you know?"

I nodded. I *did* know. At last I said, "So Halpert's challenge was all a ruse, then." Liam didn't seem surprised by this, but I went on, "The whole idea of a widespread collaboration, trying to develop creativity for bots: synthetic creativity has to already exist. They have to have it themselves. Unless there's some mastermind behind them telling them what to do every step of the way..."

Liam nodded. "I think Youssef probably developed it twenty years ago or more, but because politics wouldn't allow it at the time, he had to keep it under wraps until public opinion could be sufficiently swayed to reintroduce it. We're there now."

"So you think they seeded the information to the labyrinth somehow, so that De Vries and whoever else could find it?"

"That's exactly what I think." Liam shifted, resting his arm on the windowsill and his chin on his fist. "It was an incredibly complex problem, and yet they cracked it in a matter of weeks. That's awfully suspect. And as you say, the only way the board could possibly do their jobs is if they had the capacity for creativity already. The technology *had* to exist. It was just too unpopular to make that public knowledge, until Halpert's challenge made it the hottest thing going."

"So why now?" I asked. "What's the point of suddenly taking old technology and making it widespread?"

Liam took a deep breath, and faced me. The reflected sunlight made his eyes seem to match the color of the water. "Well, if I had to guess... I'd say it goes back to their core purposes. Let's say Justice Wallenberg's purpose is to ensure law and order. He'll do that much better with bots under him than with humans, because humans are fallible. If Rasputin's purpose is to ensure the health of the human race, he'll be able to fulfill that purpose much better if everybody in the medical profession is a bot, for the same reason. People get tired. They make mistakes. They're fallible."

"But most professions have already been taken over by the bots," I pointed out.

Liam shook his head. "Only the ones that don't require creativity. If it's a step-by-step procedural solution to an already identified problem, yes, bots are ideal for that. But to be able to solve new problems, they need creativity on the level of what a human has—without the weakness of humans. Wallenberg and Rasputin and the others are totally focused on their core purposes, to the exclusion of all else, though," he went on. "That's the very nature of core purposes. So they're not going to get into the politics of how to get an army of creative bots working under them. Halpert, on the other hand…"

"…is programmed to further the cause of the bots," I finished.

"And maintain peace at the same time," Liam nodded. "I think that's why they're *his* board, and not the other way around. Youssef realized the public wouldn't accept the challenge until they'd been indoctrinated to do so, using all of the primary pillars of influence in society. Someone was very clever in putting creative S.R. bots in each of those positions of influence… and then biding his time."

I shuddered. "Do you think it's safe for us to visit this Youssef?"

Liam didn't look too sure, but he nodded. "As far as what Odessa could find, it seems he really did retire, and then vanished so completely that we can't even be sure he *is* Sol Huckabee, and it took us every trick in our repertoire to find out that much. He clearly doesn't want to be associated with his former research. That leads me to believe he regrets it."

I pursed my lips. "Have you told M yet?"

Liam nodded. "We told her before the meeting yesterday what Francis suspected, and where we'd go if it turned out he was right. I commed her after the meeting and told her he was."

"What did she say?"

Liam gave a short, almost guilty laugh. "She

wanted to make sure you hadn't been with us at the meeting, actually."

I scowled. "What?"

"I know. It's weird, I don't know why she cares so much."

"Is she going to meet us in Geneva?"

"She'll try," he said, "but I asked permission to get Dr Yin, Nilesh, and Larissa involved."

"Oh, so she's fine with them, but not me?" I muttered. "Why, just because I'm an undergrad?"

"That..." he trailed off.

"What else?" I demanded.

He paused, wincing. "I guess she found out about all your other hobbies, too. Acting, singing, writing..."

"So what?"

Liam held up his hands. "Don't shoot the messenger! She just doesn't think you could possibly be all that good if you're not passionate about your work, and she assumes if you have that many interests, you couldn't be. But that's only because she hasn't met you," Liam consoled me. "She doesn't know how smart you are. Once she meets you, I'm sure you'll win her over."

I gave him a half smile, deflating against the window again. "Not like I'm doing any of those things anymore, anyway."

"You're not writing?"

"When would I have had the chance

recently?" He watched me, and I met his eyes. "What?"

He shrugged. "I've never even read your stuff. Or seen you act, or heard you sing…"

"And you never will," I said firmly.

He tilted his head to the side. "Why?"

It was a genuine question, and I realized the reason seemed dated now: Liam used to make fun of me for anything and everything when we'd been back in the lab in Dublin. But now, things were different. I didn't think he'd laugh now.

"I don't think you'd like what I write," I said finally. "And I can't see you being the type to get into musicals."

"That doesn't matter. I'd like it because it's you."

It was such a sweet thing to say that it disarmed me. He looked right at me when he said it, too. I dropped my eyes, suddenly embarrassed.

"Okay," I said at last. "I'll invite you next time I perform." It seemed like an easy enough promise to make, anyway—who knew when *that* would be.

"Good." He grinned at me. "Can I read your book?"

I squirmed. "Maybe someday. When it doesn't suck."

He laughed softly. "I'll take what I can get."

Chapter 30

We arrived in Geneva just before sunset, and disembarked at the center of town. While Liam and Francis got directions to the residence of the eccentric "Sol Huckabee," retired engineer living in a mansion in the mountains, I pulled out my A.E. goggles and enabled my chip, taking a deep breath in preparation for what was sure to be an unpleasant conversation.

"Call Mom," I said.

Mom picked up and immediately snapped, "Rebecca Elizabeth Cordeaux!" She used my whole name only when she was very, *very* angry.

"Mom, I'm sorry I haven't called," I cut her off. "I'm in Geneva. I can't explain any more than that, but we got some information in the Capitol and —"

"Rebecca," she glowered at me through gritted teeth. "Is there *any chance* that you are in danger?"

"Well... no," I lied. "Not right now anyway..."

"Is this information you are chasing in *any way* related to what your dad was so obsessed with at the end? Does it have *anything* to do with Halpert, or those men on his board?"

I took a deep breath. "Mom."

"Give me *one good reason* why you personally need to be in Geneva for whatever it is you are doing!"

"I just called to tell you where I was, so you wouldn't worry!" I shot back, tears springing to my eyes. "I *told* you I'm not in danger. I don't know why you're so upset!"

She closed her eyes as if physically reining herself in. When she opened them again, I saw the tears in her own eyes.

"You are all I have left, Rebecca," she said softly. "Please don't follow in your father's footsteps. Please. I'm begging you."

"You thought Dad was paranoid anyway!"

"I did," she conceded. Then after a long pause, she looked up at my holograph again. "But what if he wasn't?"

I took a deep breath too. "He wasn't." We just watched each other for a long moment, and then I said, "Mom, I think Dad was murd—"

"Shh!" She held up her hands and waved them at me frantically. "Don't say it!"

I blinked at her, absorbing this. "You *knew*."

She took another deep breath, eyes darting

around her room as she ran her hands through her short dark hair. "We'll discuss all this in person. Do not say *anything* specific on an unsecured holograph! Remember that, Rebecca!"

I shook my head, exasperated. "I don't know when I'm going to see you in person, though—"

"I don't know either, but we'll talk about it then!" she snapped. "If I ask you, if I *beg* you to go back to school and leave all this behind, for me… would you even consider it?"

Ugh. That phrasing. It was a perfectly crafted dagger of guilt.

"Who am I kidding, of course you wouldn't," Mom answered her own question bitterly. "Does *Liam* understand how much danger he's putting you in? Does he even care?"

"Of course he does! Actually, Liam is the most ridiculously overprotective person I've ever met—"

"If he were that, he would have sent you back to Dublin weeks ago," she retorted. "He's a selfish young man, Rebecca."

"That's not true! First of all, he *tried* to send me back, I just wouldn't go, and he's been knocking himself out to keep me safe ever since—"

"I don't wish to argue about him," she cut me off, sniffing. "Since you *clearly* don't care about me, I don't know what else there is for me to say."

"Oh, holy guilt trip!" I snapped, belying the

fact that her words had produced their intended effect.

"Mark my words, Rebecca: the man who loves you will put your needs and your safety ahead of his own desires. Liam has absolutely *failed* that test!"

The goggles went dark, and I stared at the blackness for a moment, trying to identify all the roiling emotions. Anger, indignation, guilt…

And who said anything about Liam *loving* me, anyway? I'd barely even talked to Mom about Liam.

I took off the goggles in a huff, trying not to cry and refocusing on the real world around me.

Liam and Francis were talking to a young man a stone's throw from me, in the city square. I jogged over to catch up with them, trying to shake off my anger, at least for the time being.

"Good luck getting him to see you though," the young man was saying to Liam with a thick Swiss accent. "He's kind of a recluse, and he doesn't like strangers."

"He'll see me," Liam said to us, as the young man went about his business. "If my father's name was good enough to get us a meeting with Halpert, it's good enough for Sol Huckabee. Bec, you've got a journal in there, right?" He gestured at my backpack. Startled, I nodded. "Can I borrow a sheet?"

In response, I lowered my backpack to the ground, unzipping it to reveal Madeline. Her eyes met mine.

"You ok?" she whispered, concerned. She knew. She always knew.

I shook my head. "Mom," I told her. "She's really, really angry." As I said this, I pulled out my journal, carefully flipping to the back page so Liam wouldn't see anything I'd written—not that he was looking. I tore it out and handed it to him, with a pen.

"Thanks," he said, bending over an abandoned metal cafe table to scribble a hand-written message to Sol. Glancing over his shoulder, I saw that it said Liam Kelly of General Specs had a 'mutually beneficial proposal' to make, and would call in the morning.

"You wanna see Mr. Huckabee? I overheard." A school-age boy grinned at Liam. "I play with Charlotte Huckabee all the time. She's his granddaughter."

Liam and Francis exchanged a look.

"If we take you to his mansion, will you deliver a message to him for us?" Liam asked the child, talking to him like they were the same age. "Name your price."

Francis folded his arms over his chest, scrutinizing the kid to us, out loud. "Ten years old, give or take, dirt on the knees and under the fingernails. Oblong stickum outlines on the forearms where some kind of adhesive has been, but there's no wound so it wasn't a bandage. About the size of those warrior badge stickers that come in fantasy character trading packs that all the kids love these days, aren't they? He wants more trading packs." Then he turned to the kid. "We'll give you five."

"Ten!" the boy shot back.

"Seven," said Francis.

"Eight, and that's my final offer!"

"Done." Francis stuck out a hand to the kid, and they shook, the boy's mouth set in a determined line.

Liam grinned, shaking his head in admiration. "All right, where do we purchase said trading packs?"

"C'mere, I'll show you!" The boy skipped off in the direction of a little convenience shop that was just closing up for the night, manned by a bot, of course. "And I want some ice cream, too!"

"I knew he was going to say that," muttered Francis, sounding irritated that he hadn't called it verbally.

"How did you know?" I challenged, glancing over my shoulder with a smirk.

"You know he's dying to tell you," Liam remarked.

Francis gestured at the boy. "He has to pry

his fingers apart when they touch each other with a bit of effort. They're sticky. Kid with sticky fingers means sugar, probably from something that either was already liquid or turned to liquid rapidly during consumption. Dark creases in the corners of his mouth imply chocolate. He wants chocolate ice cream, it's his favorite."

"No!" the kid protested defiantly once we'd caught up to him, "maybe I want something different this time! Maybe I want strawberry!"

"Do you?" Francis raised his eyebrows at the kid like a challenge, as Liam reached for strawberry.

"No," the kid admitted. "I *do* want chocolate."

Once the kid (whose name was apparently Ethan) was sated with trading packs and a chocolate ice cream bar, Liam hailed a ground taxi-- apparently they still had those here--and all four of us piled inside.

Ethan gave directions to Huckabee's mansion to the taxi, and Liam instructed it to wait with us in the taxi while he delivered the message.

After waiting for about ten minutes outside the mansion, I looked at Liam and murmured, "Do you think he forgot about us?"

Just then the door opened again, and Ethan skipped back down the stone walkway to where the taxi waited. Francis opened the door, and Ethan handed him a note.

"From Mr. Huckabee! He says to call tomorrow morning at ten."

We found a little chateau to stay in for the night. Dr. Yin, Larissa, and Nilesh expected to meet us there later that night, and we would all see Sol Huckabee, or Ramses Youssef, together the following morning. I never would have picked such expensive accommodations, but Liam covered it for all three of us, saying tonight we had something to celebrate.

"Even if it's not exactly good news," he conceded, clinking his wine glass against mine, "we found our answer, and we found our engineer."

I turned to toast Francis, who scrutinized some other patron of the chateau restaurant, and barely glanced back at me at the sound of my glass clinking against his.

"He's just bored and trying to keep himself stimulated. Ignore him," Liam explained to me, shaking his head.

I gave a short laugh. "Sure. I can absolutely see how today wouldn't have provided enough stimulation."

"Well, that's a mystery he's already solved. He's ready for something new," Liam told me, smirking.

Ignoring our exchange, Francis gestured at

the man he was looking at, balding with gray hair in a ring just along the line of his ears. He sat across from a much younger woman in a low-cut black dress; not beautiful, but much better looking than he was.

"Accountant or a financial manager," he narrated for our benefit. "Spends most of his time at the office—possibly because he's one of the few humans in his line of work that hasn't yet been replaced by a bot and he wants to prove his usefulness, or possibly just because he doesn't like his wife. Unhappily married, you can tell by the dent in the ring finger where the ring usually is but isn't at the moment. That woman is not his wife. Probably she's someone who works with him in some capacity, perhaps a lawyer who consults with his practice on occasion. They don't see each other very often, or he'd be less nervous about being caught, see the way his eyes shift around the room? She's annoyed he's not paying more attention to her. Look how she's trying to distract him, rubbing her foot against his leg and following his gaze with exasperation. And that dress is obviously meant to seduce; she wouldn't be trying so hard if the relationship were ongoing and well established, so it must be newer…"

I gave Liam a look, and he rolled his eyes.

"You want to get our own table?" he asked.

"Definitely," I muttered.

Francis glanced over his shoulder at us as we collected our glasses. "There's a view of the city and the mountains on the balcony upstairs. Nobody's up there. It's terribly romantic, someone should take advantage of it," he added dryly.

Liam glanced down at me with a half smile. We hadn't yet sat down at the adjacent table. "You want to check it out?"

My heart fluttered. *No. No. Think about Andy.*

"Sure," I said.

Upstairs the sky still held the last vestiges of the glow of dusk. I could see the outline of the Alps not far in the distance, and the white snow caps stood out starkly against the deep shadows. It was chilly, and I was only wearing a thin sweater. I wrapped my arms around my shoulders, rubbing one hand against the shoulder I could reach while the other hand still held my wine glass. Without waiting for an invitation, Liam slipped an arm around me, replacing the friction of my hand with his own. It would have been better if he'd made some light conversation, but he didn't say anything, and I couldn't think of anything to say either. My heart pounded, as I felt the simultaneous urge to run and to stay. Then he took my wine glass from my hand and set it on the ledge beside his own, turning me to face him. I can't describe the feeling that

passed over me. I wanted to start babbling—
anything to stop him—but I didn't want to at the
same time. I was utterly frozen.

Andy. I love Andy, I thought desperately.

Liam tilted my chin up to his; the way he
looked at me was so full of tenderness. I opened my
mouth, just on the verge of telling him we couldn't
do this for a million reasons, when someone behind
us cleared his throat.

"Sorry to interrupt."

I let out a little cry, and I saw Liam startle a
bit too. Both of us turned to face the intruder. I half
expected to see John Doe.

A man sat in a chair in the shadows all
alone, nursing a scotch glass and watching us. He
was not John Doe, I could tell that much. He had a
full head of white hair and wore an expensively
tailored suit, though I could not make out the color.

"I hope you don't mind that I followed you
after I saw your taxi pull away, Liam Kelly *Junior,*"
the man said his name pointedly. "I like to conduct
my meetings on my terms."

I blinked at him. "Sol Huckabee?"

"Ramses Youssef," Liam corrected, his arm
tightening around me protectively.

"No one knows me by that name anymore."
He raised his scotch glass to his lips. "I must say, I
was curious to know what kind of proposal Liam
Kelly's son might have for me, when your father

and I haven't spoken in nearly a decade. When I found out that you haven't spoken to him in five years, either, I became even more intrigued."

Liam glanced at me. "Rebecca's cold," he said, "why don't you join us downstairs for a drink?"

"I prefer to have this conversation somewhere more private," said Youssef, "and that includes away from the prying ears of my servants, which is why I followed you. She can go downstairs if she likes; in fact, I'd prefer it. I only need to speak with you."

"I'm staying," I said stubbornly.

Liam glanced down at me, rubbing my shoulder for warmth. "You sure?"

I nodded, glaring at Youssef. I hadn't expected to feel such hatred for him when he was only an abstract idea. But now that he sat before me in the flesh, it hit me all at once.

This is the man responsible for my father's death.

Chapter 31

Liam leveled his gaze at Youssef. "We know you created Halpert and his entire board," he said.

Youssef sipped his scotch and looked out over the Alps for so long that I wondered if he was planning to answer.

"*Did* you create them?" I demanded.

Youssef glanced at me and murmured, his face impassive, "Sorry, who are you?"

"Rebecca Cordeaux," I told him through gritted teeth. "My father was Quentin Cordeaux. Perhaps you've heard of *him?*"

Youssef raised his eyebrows, unimpressed. "Nope."

"Really?" I snapped. "Because your creations are the reason he died!"

"Youssef doesn't know anything about the Renegades," Liam murmured to me. "Why would he?"

"I don't know, maybe because we only exist because of what he made?" I shot back. Then I jabbed a finger in Liam's direction, still facing Youssef. "If you don't know my name, clearly you know the name Kelly! *His* brother died because of your bots too, did you know that? And many more besides!"

"Rebecca," Liam said in a low voice, tightening his hand on my shoulder just slightly. I knew he meant it as a warning. I looked away from them both, breathing hard and trying to get myself under control.

Liam turned back to Youssef. "Do you deny you made them?"

Youssef sipped. Blinked. Then replied, "Why don't you say what you came all this way to say. Unless that was it." He gestured at me.

I saw Liam grit his teeth out of the corner of my eye. "I understand that you feel the need to protect yourself, but we're not here to cause any trouble for you. We just want to understand how they work, their abilities and limitations, what their ultimate goals are, and how many of them there are. With your help, we might be able to figure out how to stop them."

Youssef sipped again. "You can't stop them. They've already won."

My blood ran cold. "What do you mean? *What* have they won?"

"The allegiance of the masses," Youssef said simply. "The public acceptance of their technology. *You* know, Mr. Kelly—the world is already overrun with bots. All it takes is one software upgrade to make them *all* like Halpert and his board. Given foundational creativity, if even one has the core purpose of making itself smarter and distributing that technology to other bots once it's available…"

"Then why didn't you create that twenty years ago?" I interjected.

"He didn't know how," said a voice from behind, and we spun around to see Francis approaching, his overcoat flapping at his calves. I wondered how he'd known Youssef was up here—had he watched him follow us? Francis went on, "Twenty years ago, nobody had a clue how creativity worked in humans, including him. Humanoid and human level Synthetic Reasoning was a hot political issue, and those who believed it would lead to destruction were greater than those who believed it would lead to utopia. He was on the losing side. But instead of obeying the law and abandoning his research, he just moved it underground. He thought he'd prove he was correct by doing it, and then when his utopian vision came to fruition, everyone would beg his forgiveness. But since he didn't know how creativity worked, the best he could do was simulate human creativity, like tracing a drawing. Isn't that right, Youssef?"

"Who the hell is this guy?" Youssef

demanded.

Francis ignored the question and went on, "You literally copied the brain of someone who had died in that first iteration, didn't you? With detailed VMI imaging slices, you basically just traced the human synaptic connections with silicon, and what you got was a replica of the dead person. Was it Halpert? Was he the first?"

Youssef stood up, his scotch forgotten on the arm of his chair. "I don't know how you *think* you know all this…"

"But he wasn't quite like the dead man had been, was he?" Francis went on. "Something was missing. What was it?"

"His soul," I breathed, looking back at Youssef for confirmation.

Youssef glared at all three of us, eyes shifting from Francis to me, and something in his face relented. "My colleague and business partner knew he was dying. It was his idea. He wanted to be immortal, and he thought if we could copy his brain, he'd just wake up in a new synthetic body."

"Did he?" I asked again, breathless.

Youssef shook his head, glancing at me briefly before attending again to Francis. "His memories were there, and all his factual knowledge and intellectual abilities—he still reasoned the same as he had before. He was quite charismatic and likable in life, and that much did translate to his synthetic form. But he wasn't *him*. Bill was dry and funny. He got excited about intellectual challenges. He appreciated good art from the Second Era. He cared about people. He cared about social justice."

"So his personality and emotions were gone," Liam concluded.

"And his morals, too," I added, and Youssef hesitated before nodding.

"We couldn't recreate neurotransmitters and hormones, which likely explains the lack of emotions, even though he has an intact limbic system. Bill's recreated brain runs entirely on silicon and electrical impulses."

"Bill... William," said Francis. "So the first one *was* Halpert."

Youssef nodded again. "Yes. We chose the name William for consistency, since his implanted memories of himself were all under that name. But like I said, he's not Bill, not in personality or in looks, so we created a fake back story. Ironically, Bill and I had already created the humanoid shell together, before he died—"

"Based on human biochemistry of ATP, yes, yes, we know," Francis waved him off impatiently. "We figured that part out already."

Youssef glanced at Francis with an expression that was at once taken aback and impressed. "Right. Also, because of the limitations of the recreated brain, we still had to give him a core purpose, like any other bot. We borrowed from Bill's personal obsession in life, since it was already imprinted on his brain and required little enhancement: that was, advancing the cause of Synthetic Reasoning, except through administration. We programmed him to keep peace, as well, of course. We couldn't have him declaring all-out war to advance his purpose."

"Except that meant he interpreted anyone who opposed his goals as a threat to the peace," I cut in, "and he eliminated those who tried to rebel!"

Youssef bowed his head. "An unfortunate side effect."

"A *predictable* side effect, once you consider the fact that all bots deal with any opposition to their purposes in the most efficient way possible!" I retorted.

"And of course," Francis added, his tone cold, "they also thought the most efficient way to deal with powerful loci such as mine and Liam's was to quietly dismantle them, once they attracted enough attention to pose a threat."

"I don't know anything about what they are doing these days," said Youssef. "I've been retired for nearly a decade."

"So that was Halpert," said Liam, with forced calm. "What about the others? Did they come from dead men too?"

"Of course they did," said Francis. "He

wouldn't have known how to create them any other way."

Youssef did not contradict this.

"Why did you stop building them, then?" Liam asked. "At what point did you figure out that your experiment was a failure?"

I thought Youssef would take issue with this, but he did not. Instead, he looked off into the distance as he said, "I began to see it long ago, but I didn't want to see it. What makes them dangerous is inherent in what they are: it is in their very perfection. As the head of the medical community, Rasputin believes nothing short of perfect human health should be his goal, and so he kills all those whom he cannot cure. This prevents contagious diseases from spreading and eliminates long-term illnesses from dragging the economy down. It is efficient. As the head of the justice community, Wallenberg condemns all who so much as err on their tax returns in the name of the good of society. Etcetera." He sank back into his chair. "But I couldn't stop what had already been set in motion. I knew I couldn't."

"So you just fled and changed your name," I accused. "Like a coward."

Youssef met my eyes, steady and unflinching.

"Did the work stop when you retired?" Liam asked. "Did your colleagues stop after creating those six?"

We all knew the answer as soon as he asked the question.

"No," Youssef said at last.

Liam hesitated before he asked with dread, "How many?"

Youssef shook his head, and opened his mouth to reply. Then his breath caught, his eyes bulged, and blood blossomed across his forehead.

I didn't understand, until Liam threw his arms around me, shoving me to the ground.

"Get down!" he shouted.

Chapter 32

I hardly knew what happened after that—it was all a blur of adrenaline and gunshots. Crawling on our hands and knees, somehow I reached the staircase leading back down to the main hall of the chateau. Liam thrust me back up to my feet once we were inside and shoved me forward.

"Run!"

"Where?" I cried.

Behind us, Francis swore. I glanced back at him and saw that he was limping as he ran. He'd been hit in the leg.

Outside the windows of the dining room, a hovercraft bearing the seal of the Republic touched down on the lawn. Liam sprinted straight for the heavy double doors leading to the patio and out to the lawn, dragging me by the hand behind him.

"No way! Are you crazy?" I tried to jerk my hand away from his, but he held me like a vice, dragging me inexorably forward. "Liam! That's *them*!"

"Trust me!" he shouted back.

Sniper bullets riddled the ground as we ran, and the wide side door slid open on the hovercraft. When I got close enough, Liam flung me toward it.

"Get her!" he shouted at someone in the opening.

"Liam!"

But he turned around, running back to help Francis just as a pair of arms grabbed me from behind.

"Rebecca, get in here!"

I recognized the voice, but it didn't immediately register. Nilesh, frantic and wide-eyed, pinned me against the side of the hovercraft so that I couldn't see out, but I was no longer in the bullets' trajectory. Deeper in the interior of the craft, I saw Larissa and Dr. Yin, and several men I did not recognize. One of them leaned out of the hovercraft opening with a rifle.

"Liam!" came my strangled cry, as I struggled against Nilesh.

"They're almost here!"

The man at the hovercraft opening lay down his rifle and reached arms out to haul Francis inside.

"Go, go, go!" Dr. Yin shouted in the direction of what was presumably the pilot bot.

"Wait!" I yelled, just as Liam let out a strangled cry. The man at the opening hauled him inside too, just as the hovercraft swept up off the ground. I fought Nilesh off, but he released me now anyway. All of us crowded around Francis and Liam at once.

"Hepzibah!" said the man who had hauled them aboard grimly.

A little medic bot, about Madeline's size, wheeled over to inspect their wounds.

Madeline, I realized with a sinking feeling in the pit of my stomach. I'd left her behind, in my room.

"Shot twice," Hepzibah declared in her tinny voice as she inspected Francis. Larissa hovered just behind Hepzibah, her face almost as white as Francis's. "One embedded bullet in the right gastrocnemius muscle, and one graze on the left deltoid. Second wound is superficial. First wound requires pressure to avoid shock. Will wait to extract the bullet until patient is stable."

"Here, let me!" Larissa breathed, taking the gauze from the bot and wrapping it around Francis's right leg.

"What about Liam?" I heard my own voice say, but it didn't seem like mine. Blood blossomed across his chest. He was pale and clammy, and wasn't breathing right. I felt like I couldn't breathe right either.

After pressing her hand to Liam's chest in several places, Hepzibah asserted, "He has a pneumothorax."

"What does that mean?" I demanded.

"Shh, Rebecca, get out of the way," murmured Dr. Yin, pulling me clear as Hepzibah produced a remarkably large needle. With one smooth thrust, she shoved it into Liam's chest.

I screamed, clamping my hands over my mouth.

"The bullet passed through his chest and collapsed the upper lobe of his right lung," Hepzibah explained, completely ignoring my scream. "The chest tube should allow his lung to re-inflate. Next we need to stop the bleeding. Apply pressure here." She took the arm of nearest person to her, which happened to be me, and placed gauze in my hands, guiding them to Liam's wound.

I might have been hyperventilating. My hands tingled and my vision narrowed like I was looking through a tunnel. All I could see was Liam's pallid face and bloody chest, with my bloody hands on top of it.

Liam's glazed eyes focused on me at last. "You okay?" he croaked.

An hysterical giggle bubbled up to my throat, but came out as a hiccup. "Shut up," I gasped, sinking my weight onto his wound. I saw him wince, and that seemed to snap me back. I *couldn't* panic. Not right now. "Liam! Keep breathing. …Okay?" I added shrilly when he didn't reply right away.

"Anything for you, Bec." I could barely hear

him; I only knew what he said by reading his lips.

"Where are we going?" Larissa asked no one in particular. She sounded dazed.

"To a safehouse. Off the grid," said the man who held the rifle.

"Who sent you?" I demanded. "How did you know where to find us?"

"M directed us," the man replied, gesturing to the cockpit.

"M? Is she here?" I followed his gaze to the front of the craft. "Harriet Albright?"

As if on cue, a figure emerged from the shadows of the cockpit. I recognized the way she moved at once, but my brain did not register it right away. Once she came into the light, my mind went blank. The dissonance between what I knew and what I was seeing simply would not compute.

She sighed. "Hello Rebecca."

I stared at her. "*Mom?*"

Sneak Preview of

The Silver Six

Prologue: Alessandra Russo

"Miss...Rochelle Denning," the neurosurgeon bot read from the screen displayed on his retinas, glancing at the young woman sitting before him. She was beautiful, with long dark hair and eyes the color of cornflowers, startling against the caramel color of her skin. But the bot was, of course, unimpressed. She knew in advance that she'd have to find another way to get the creature to do what she wanted. He read from her carefully fabricated medical chart, "You are here for migraines?"

The woman, whose real name was Alessandra Russo, grimaced, clutching her forehead theatrically. "I had my first chip replaced two months ago because it malfunctioned," she choked out. "Ever since they put the new one in, I've had a nonstop migraine, literally every day for two months! Please, you have to help me. I'm not suicidal, but I've considered it because I just can't live like this. Please!"

The bot glanced at her, unmoved, and then

back at her chart. She might have known she could save the emotional appeals; they were as wasted here as was her beauty. "I see. Your notes request no replacement?" The implication was clear: removal of an Artificial Experience chip, without replacement of another, was a peculiar request. Suspicious, even.

"I had problems with the first one too," Ali asserted without missing a beat, knowing everything she was about to say was already corroborated in her chart—since she'd hacked in and written it. "I've had headaches for as long as I can remember, but never as bad as they were after they put the new chip in. I can just use a handheld, I don't want to risk another A.E. chip. Please, I just want it *out!*"

The neurosurgeon bot was incapable of facial expressions, but Ali read in its rapidly moving eyes that it didn't take her assertion at face value. It was accessing the labyrinth, checking her story. Had she made a mistake in the chart somehow—used the wrong language, maybe, or said something a real primary care medical bot would never say in a referral? She held her breath.

At last the bot's digital eyes refocused on her, extending its silver arm to the surgical bed. "Arm out," it instructed, and Ali breathed a sigh of relief. A medical assistant bot wheeled over, adjusting the head of the table to a convenient height for the surgeon. But just as the M.A. sterilized her arm for anesthesia, the neurosurgical bot commanded, "Wait!"

Ali's heart stopped just as the M.A.'s silver arm froze in midair. Back and forth, back and forth went the neurosurgeon's eyes. They focused inward, then on her face, and then inward again—comparing. She knew he was matching every square millimeter of her flesh to the pixels in the image in his mind.

"Go ahead and sedate her," he said, and Ali winced with the tiny invasive pain of the needle. She watched, almost crying with relief as the M.A. attached the needle to an IV, and cool liquid mingled with the blood in her veins. But even as the effects began to blur the edges of her consciousness, she heard the neurosurgeon declare to his M.A., "Her records have been falsified. She is a Renegade, wanted for spreading propaganda about William Halpert and his Board. Alert the police that we have her in custody."

No, Ali wanted to scream. But she could no longer move her lips.

Dear Reader,

Thank you so much for reading my work! I know there's a lot of options out there these days, and I am so honored that among them, you chose to spend your time reading mine. Would you please consider reviewing it on your favorite online retailer, and on Goodreads? As a self-published author, I depend on positive reviews from readers like you!

I'm really excited about where this series is going. If you'd like to get sneak previews and updates when the next books are available, please follow me on Amazon, or sign up for my newsletter at www.authorcagray.com. I look forward to connecting with you.

Thank you again for reading my work!

All the best,
C.A. Gray

Acknowledgements

To my editors, Cyndi Deville (my mom), Lindsay Schlegel, and Jim Strawn: I couldn't do this without you. Thank you so very much for your ongoing support and wonderful ideas!

To my husband, Frank Baden: thank you for sticking with me as we discussed OVER and OVER possible cover and title ideas, and for even sketching out your vision for the cover (which turned out great!)

To my sister-in-law, Keilee Deville: thanks for all the title brainstorming! I'd never heard the term "uncanny valley" before you sent it to me, and it conveys one of the main ideas of the book perfectly.

To my PA, Tiana Griffin: thank you so much for all your tireless social media posting and energetic support. It's great to have you in my corner!

And thank you Lord, for giving me the schedule and the flexibility to consistently write. I am so blessed that I get to do this.

Also by C.A. Gray:

Intangible: Piercing the Veil, Book 1
Invincible: Piercing the Veil, Book 2
Impossible: Piercing the Veil, Book 3

The Liberty Box
The Eden Conspiracy: The Liberty Box Trilogy, Book 2
The Phoenix Project: The Liberty Box Trilogy, Book 3

About the Author

C.A. Gray is a Naturopathic Medical Doctor (NMD), with a primary care practice in Tucson, Arizona. She has always been captivated by the power of a good story, fictional or otherwise, which is probably why she loves holistic medicine: a patient's physical health is invariably intertwined with his or her life story, and she believes that the one can only be understood in context with the other. She is blessed with exceptionally supportive family and friends, and thanks God for them every single day!

Made in the USA
San Bernardino, CA
17 March 2020